Blood Trail

C. J. BOX

BERKLEY PRIME CRIME, NEW YORK

THE BERKLEY PUBLISHING GROUP
Published by the Penguin Group
Penguin Group (USA) Inc.
375 Hudson Street, New York, New York 10014, USA
Penguin Group (Canada), 90 Eglinton Avenue East, Suite 700, Toronto, Ontario M4P 2Y3, Canada
(a division of Pearson Penguin Canada Inc.)
Penguin Books Ltd., 80 Strand, London WC2R 0RL, England
Penguin Group Ireland, 25 St. Stephen's Green, Dublin 2, Ireland (a division of Penguin Books Ltd.)
Penguin Group (Australia), 250 Camberwell Road, Camberwell, Victoria 3124, Australia
(a division of Pearson Australia Group Pty. Ltd.)
Penguin Books India Pvt. Ltd., 11 Community Centre, Panchsheel Park, New Delhi—110 017, India
Penguin Group (NZ), 67 Apollo Drive, Rosedale, North Shore 0632, New Zealand
(a division of Pearson New Zealand Ltd.)
Penguin Books (South Africa) (Pty.) Ltd., 24 Sturdee Avenue, Rosebank, Johannesburg 2196,
South Africa

Penguin Books Ltd., Registered Offices: 80 Strand, London WC2R 0RL, England

BLOOD TRAIL

A Berkley Prime Crime Book / published by arrangement with the author

PRINTING HISTORY
G. P. Putnam's Sons hardcover edition / May 2008
Berkley Prime Crime mass-market edition / May 2009

ISBN: 978-0-425-22808-1

BERKLEY® PRIME CRIME
Berkley Prime Crime Books are published by The Berkley Publishing Group,
a division of Penguin Group (USA) Inc.,
375 Hudson Street, New York, New York 10014.
BERKLEY® PRIME CRIME and the PRIME CRIME logo are trademarks of Penguin Group
(USA) Inc.

PRINTED IN THE UNITED STATES OF AMERICA

20   19   18   17   16   15   14   13

For Roxanne . . .
And Laurie, always

"When I came across the world of Joe Pickett, I was reminded of the time I discovered Tony Hillerman." —Michael Connelly

PRAISE FOR

Blood Trail

"C. J. Box knows the territory and exploits it skillfully in this riveting thriller. In addition to his wilderness savvy, Box creates credible characters, most particularly his all-too-human protagonist, and spins a story crammed with shock and suspense."   —*The San Diego Union-Tribune*

"Writing beautifully about the mountain West and its people, Box takes care to present both sides of the controversial issue of hunting. The narrative alternates between the searchers and the killer, whose identity will keep readers guessing up to the surprising climax."   —*Publishers Weekly* (starred review)

"Award-winning mystery writer Box ratchets up the suspense in this tightly plotted example of his writing genius . . . His sense of place and talent for character development are on a par with those of James Lee Burke. Highly recommended."
—*Library Journal*

"The people and scenes and enduring conflicts . . . will stick with you for a long time."   —*Kirkus Reviews*

"Box always addresses a New West issue, but there's something great about the way he's waited until the eighth installment to tackle the one that would seem most obvious given his hero's occupation."   —*Booklist* (starred review)

"C. J. Box brings back Wyoming game warden Joe Pickett . . . and in doing so, shows why he has pretty much sewn up the state as his own territory."   —*The Cleveland Plain Dealer*

continued . . .

Sleep!
There is hunting in heaven—
Sleep safe till tomorrow.

—WILLIAM CARLOS WILLIAMS

It's strange how often human beings
die without any kind of style.

—GUY SAJER, *The Forgotten Soldier*

1

I AM A HUNTER, a bestower of dignity.

I am on the hunt.

As the sun raises its eyebrows over the eastern mountains I can see the track through the still grass meadow. It happens in an instant, the daily rebirth of the sun, a stunning miracle every twenty-four hours, so rarely experienced these days by anyone except those who still live by the natural rhythm of the real world, where death is omnipresent and survival an unfair gift. This sudden blast of illumination won't last long, but it reveals the direction and strategy of my prey as obviously as a flashing neon OPEN sign. That is, if one knows where and how to see. Most people don't.

Let me tell you what I see:

The first shaft of buttery morning light pours through the timber and electrifies the light frost and dew on the grass. The track made less than an hour before announces itself not by prints or bent foliage but by the absence of dew. For less than twenty seconds, when the force and angle of the morning light is perfect, I can see how my prey hesitated for a few moments at the edge of the meadow to look and listen before proceeding. The track boldly enters the clearing before stopping and veering back to the right toward the guarded shadows of the dark wall of pine, then continues along the edge of the meadow until it exits between two lodgepole pines, heading southeast.

I am a hunter.

As a hunter I'm an important tool of nature. I complete the circle of life while never forgetting I'm a participant as well. Without me, there is needless suffering, and death is slow, brutal, and without glory. The glory of death depends on whether one is the hunter or the prey. It can be either, depending on the circumstances.

I KNOW FROM SCOUTING the area that for the past three mornings two dozen elk have been grazing on a sunlit hillside a mile from where I stand, and I know which way my prey is headed and therefore which way I will be going. The herd includes cows and calves mostly, and three young male spikes. I also saw a handsome five-by-five, a six-by-five, and a magnificent seven-point royal bull who lorded over the herd with cautious and stoic superiority. I followed the track through the meadow and the still-dark and dripping timber until it opened up on the rocky crest of a ridge that overlooks the grassy hillside.

I walk along the edge of the meadow, keeping the track of my prey to my right so I can read it with a simple downward glance like a driver checking a road map. But in this case, the route I am following—filled with rushes, pauses, and contemplation—takes me across the high wooded terrain of the eastern slope of the Bighorn Mountains of Wyoming. Like my prey, I stop often to listen, to look, to draw the pine and dust-scented air deep into my lungs and to taste it, savor it, let it enter me. I become a part of the whole, not a visitor.

In the timber I do my best to control my breathing to

keep it soft and rhythmic. I don't hike and climb too fast or too clumsily so I get out of breath. In the dawn October chill, my breath is ephemeral, condensing into a cloud from my nose and mouth and whipping away into nothingness. If my prey suspects I am on it—if it hears my labored breathing—it might stop in the thick forest to wait and observe. If I blunder into him I might never get the shot, or get a poor shot that results in a wound. I don't want that to happen.

I almost lose the track when the rising terrain turns rocky and becomes plates of granite. The sun has not yet entered this part of the forest, so the light is dull and diffuse. Morning mist hangs as if sleeping in the trees, making the rise of the terrain ahead of me seem as if I observe it through a smudged window. Although I know the general direction we are headed, I stop and observe, letting my breath return to a whisper, letting my senses drink in the scene and tell me things I can't just see.

Slowly, slowly, as I stand there and make myself not look at the hillside or the trees or anything in particular, make the scene in front of me all peripheral, the story is revealed as if the ground itself provides the narration.

My prey paused where I pause, when it was even darker. It looked for a better route to the top of the rise so as not to have to scramble up the surface of solid granite, not only because of the slickness of the rock but because the surface is covered with dry pockets of pine needles and untethered stones, each of which, if stepped on directly or dislodged, would signal the presence of an intruder.

But it couldn't see a better way, so it stepped up onto the ledge and continued on a few feet. I now see the disturbance caused by a tentative step in a pile of pine needles, where a quarter-sized spot of moisture has been revealed. The disturbed pine needles themselves, no more than a dozen of them, are scattered on the bare rock like a child's pick-up sticks. Ten feet to the right of the pocket of pine needles, a small egg-shaped stone lies upturned with clean white granite exposed to the sky. I know the stone has been dislodged, turned upside down by an errant step or stumble, because the exposed side is too clean to have been there long.

Which means my prey realized scrambling up the rock face was too loud, so he doubled back and returned to where it started. I guess he would skirt the exposed granite to find a better, softer place to climb. I find where my prey stopped to urinate, leaving a dark stain in the soil. I find it by the smell, which is salty and pungent. Pulling off a glove, I touch the moist ground with the tips of my fingers and it is a few degrees warmer than the dirt or air. It is close. And I can see a clear track where it turned back again toward the southeast, toward the ridge.

On the other side of the ridge will be the elk. I will likely smell them before I see them. Elk have a particular odor— earthy, like potting soil laced with musk, especially in the morning when the sun warms and dries out their damp hides.

Quietly, deliberately, I put my glove back on and work the bolt on my rifle. I catch a glimpse of the bright, clean brass of the cartridge as it seats in the chamber. I ease the safety on, so when I am ready it will take no more than a thumb flick to be prepared to fire.

As I climb the hill the morning lightens. The trees disperse and more morning light filters through them to the pine-needle forest floor. I keep the rifle muzzle out in front of me but pointed slightly down. I can see where my prey stepped, and follow the track. My heart beats faster, and my breath is shallow. I feel a thin sheen of sweat prick through the pores of my skin and slick my entire body like a light coating of machine oil. My senses peak, pushed forward, asserting themselves, as if ready to reach out to get a hold on whatever they can grasp and report back.

I slow as I approach the top of the ridge. A slight morning breeze—icy, bracing, clean as snow—flows over the ridge and mists my eyes for a moment. I find my sunglasses and put them on. I can't risk pulling up over the top of the hill and having tears in my eyes so I can't see clearly through the scope.

I drop to my knees and elbows and baby-crawl the rest of the way. Elk have a special ability to note movement of any kind on the horizon, and if they see me pop over the crest it will likely spook them. I make sure to have the crown of a pine from the slope I just climbed up behind me, so my silhouette is not framed against the blue-white sky. As I crawl, I smell the damp soil and the slight rotten odor of decomposing leaves and pine needles.

There are three park-like meadows below me on the saddle slope and the elk are there. The closest bunch, three cows, two calves, and a spike, are no more than 150 yards away. The sun lights their red-brown hides and tan rumps. They are close enough that I can see the highlights of their black eyes as they graze and hear the click of their hooves against stones as they move. To their right, in another park, is a group of eight including the five-by-five. He looks up and his antlers catch the sun, and for a moment I hold my breath for fear I've been detected. But the big bull lowers his head and continues to chew, stalks of grass bouncing up and down out of the sides of his mouth like cigarettes.

I let my breath out.

The big seven-point is at the edge of the third park, at least three hundred yards away. He is half in the sun and half in shadow from the pine trees that border the meadow. His rack of antlers is so big and wide I wonder, as I always do, how it is possible for him even to raise his head, much less run through tight, dark timber. The big bull seems aware of the rest of the herd without actually looking at them. When a calf moves too close to him he woofs without even stopping his meal and the little one wheels and runs back as if stung by a bee.

The breeze is in my face, so I doubt the elk can smell me. The stalk has been perfect. I revel in the hunt itself, *knowing this feeling of silent and pagan celebration is as ancient as man himself but simply not known to anyone who doesn't hunt. Is there any kind of feeling similar in the world of cities and streets? In movies or the Internet or video games? I don't think so, because this is* real.

Before pulling the stock of the rifle to my cheek and fitting my eye to the scope, I inch forward and look down the slope just below me that has been previously out of my field of vision. The sensation is like that of sliding the cover off a steaming pot to see what is inside. I can feel my insides clench and my heart beat faster.

There he is. I see the broad back of his coat clearly, as well as his blaze-orange hat. He is sighting the elk through his rifle scope. He is hidden behind a stand of thick red buckbrush so the elk can't see him. He's been tracking the big bull since an hour before dawn, through the meadow, up the slope, over the ridge. Those were his tracks I've been following. He is crouched behind the brush, a dark green nylon daypack near his feet. He is fifty yards away.

I settle to the ground, wriggling my legs and groin so I am in full contact. The coldness of the ground seeps through my clothes and I can feel it steady me, comfort me, cool me down. I thumb the safety off my rifle and pull the hard varnished stock against my cheek and lean into the scope with both eyes open.

The side of his face fills the scope, the crosshairs on his graying temple. He still has the remains of what were once mutton-chop sideburns. His face and hands are older than I recall, wrinkled some, mottled with age spots. The wedding band he once wore is no longer there, but I see where it has created a permanent trough in the skin around his finger. He is still big, tall, and wide. If he laughs I would see, once again, the oversized teeth with the glint of gold crowns in the back of his mouth and the way his eyes narrow into slits, as if he couldn't look and laugh at the same time.

I keep the crosshairs on his temple. He seems to sense

*that something is wrong. His face twitches, and for a mo-
ment he sits back and looks to his right and left to see if he
can see what, or who, is watching him. This has happened
before with the others. They seem to know but at the same
time they won't concede. When he sits back I lower the
crosshairs to his heart. He never looks directly at me, so I
don't have to fire.*

*I wait until he apparently concludes that it was just a
strange feeling, and leans forward into his scope again,
waiting for the seven-point bull to turn just right so he of-
fers a clean, full-body shot. My aim moves with him.*

*I raise the crosshairs from his heart to his neck just
below his jawbone and squeeze the trigger.*

*There is a moment when a shot is fired by a high-
powered hunting rifle when the view through the scope is
nothing more than a flash of deep orange and the barrel
kicks up. For that moment, you don't know if you hit what
you were aiming at or what you will see when you look
back down the rifle at your target. The gunpowder smell is
sharp and pungent and the boom of the shot itself rockets
through the timber and finally rolls back in echo form like
a clap of thunder. There is the woofing and startled grunts
of a herd of elk as they panic as one and run toward the
trees. The seven-by-seven is simply gone. From the blanket of trees, birds fly out like shooting sparks.*

Here's what I know:

I am a hunter, a bestower of dignity.

2

JOE PICKETT was stranded on the roof of his new home. It was the first Saturday in October, and he was up there to fix dozens of T-Lock shingles that had blown loose during a seventy-five-mile-per-hour windstorm that had also knocked down most of his back fence and sandblasted the paint off his shutters. The windstorm had come rocketing down the eastern slope of the mountains during the middle of the night and hit town like an airborne tsunami, snapping off the branches of hoary cottonwoods onto power lines and rolling cattle semitrucks off the highway and across the sagebrush flats like empty beer cans. For the past month since the night of the windstorm, the edges of loosened shingles flapped on the top of his house with a sound like a deck of playing cards being shuffled. Or that's how his wife, Marybeth, described it since Joe had rarely been home to hear it and hadn't had a day off to repair the damage since it happened. Until today.

He had awakened his sixteen-year-old daughter, Sheridan, a sophomore at Saddlestring High, and asked her to hold the rickety wooden ladder steady while he ascended to the roof. It had bent and shivered as he climbed, and he feared his trip down. Since it was just nine in the morning, Sheridan hadn't been fully awake and his last glimpse of her when he looked down was of her yawning with tangles of blond hair in her eyes. She stayed below while he went up and he couldn't see her. He assumed she'd gone back inside.

There had been a time when Sheridan was his constant companion, his assistant, his tool-pusher, when it came to chores and repairs. She was his little buddy, and she knew the difference between a socket and a crescent wrench. She kept up a constant patter of questions and observations while he worked, even though she sometimes distracted him. It was silent now. He'd foolishly thought she'd be eager to help him since he'd been gone so much, forgetting she was a teenager with her own interests and a priority list where "helping Dad" had dropped very low. That she'd come outside to hold the ladder was a conscious acknowledgment of those old days, and that she'd gone back into the house was a statement of how it was now. It made him feel sad, made him miss how it once had been.

It was a crisp, cool, windless fall day. A dusting of snow above the tree line on Bighorns in the distance made the mountains and the sky seem even bluer, and even as he tacked the galvanized nails through the battered shingles into the plywood sheeting, he kept stealing glances at the horizon as if sneaking looks at a lifeguard in her bikini at the municipal pool. He couldn't help himself—he wished he were up there.

Joe Pickett had once been the game warden of the Saddlestring District and the mountains and foothills had been his responsibility. That was before he was fired by the director of the state agency, a Machiavellian bureaucrat named Randy Pope.

From where he stood on the roof, he could look out and see most of the town of Saddlestring, Wyoming. It was quiet, he supposed, but not the kind of quiet he was used

to. Through the leafless cottonwoods he could see the re-
flective wink of cars as they coursed down the streets, and
he could hear shouts and commands from the coaches on
the high-school football field as the Twelve Sleep High
Wranglers held a scrimmage. Somewhere up on the hill a
chain saw coughed and started and roared to cut firewood.
Like a pocket of aspen in the fold of a mountain range,
the town of Saddlestring seemed packed into this deep
U-shaped bend of the Twelve Sleep River, and was laid out
along the contours of the river until the buildings finally
played out on the sagebrush flats but the river went on. He
could see other roofs, and the anemic downtown where the
tallest structure was the wrought-iron and neon bucking
horse on the top of the Stockman's Bar.

In the back pocket of his worn Wranglers was a long list
of to-do's that had accumulated over the past month. Marybeth had made most of the entries, but he had listed a
few himself. The first five entries were:

Fix roof
Clean gutters
Bring hoses in
Fix back fence
Winterize lawn

The list went on from there for the entire page and half of
the back. Joe knew if he worked the entire day and into the
night he wouldn't complete the list, even if Sheridan was
helping him, which she wasn't. Plus, experience told him
there would be a snag of some kind that would derail him
and frustrate his progress, something simple but unantici-
pated. The gutter would detach from the house while he
was scraping the leaves out of it, or the lumber store
wouldn't have the right fence slats and they'd need to order
them. Something. Like when the tree branches started to
shiver and shake as a gust of wind from the north rolled
through them with just enough muscle to catch the ladder

and send it clattering straight backward from the house to the lawn as if it had been shot. And there he was, stranded on the roof of a house he really didn't even want to live in, much less own.

The wind went away just as suddenly as it had appeared.

"Sheridan?"

No response. She was very likely back in bed.

"Sheridan? Lucy? Marybeth?" He paused. *"Anybody?"*

He thought of stomping on the roof with his boots or dangling a HELP! message over the eave so Marybeth might see it out the kitchen window. Jumping from the roof to the cottonwood tree in the front yard was a possibility, but the distance was daunting and he visualized missing the branch and thumping into the trunk and tumbling to the ground. Or, he thought sourly, he could just sit up there until the winter snows came and his body was eaten by ravens.

Instead, he went to work. He had a hammer and a pocketful of nails in the front of his hooded sweatshirt. And a spatula.

As he secured the loose shingles he could see his next-door neighbor, Ed Nedny, come out of his front door and stand on his porch looking pensive. Nedny was a retired town administrator who now spent his time working on his immaculate lawn, tending his large and productive garden, keeping up his perfectly well-appointed home, and washing, waxing, and servicing his three vehicles—a vintage Chevy pickup, a Jeep Cherokee, and the black Lincoln Town Car that rarely ventured out of the garage. Joe had seen Nedny when he came home the night before applying Armor All to the whitewall tires of the Town Car under a trouble light. Although his neighbor didn't stare outright at Joe, he was there to observe. To comment. To offer neighborly advice. Nedny wore a watch cap and a heavy sweater, and drew serenely on his pipe, letting a fragrant cloud of smoke waft upward toward Joe on the roof as if he sent it there.

Joe tapped a nail into a shingle to set it, then drove it home with two hard blows.

"Hey, Joe," Ed called.

"Ed."

"Fixing your roof?"

Joe paused a beat, discarded a sarcastic answer, and said, "Yup."

Which gave Ed pause as well, and made him look down at his feet for a few long, contemplative moments. Ed, Joe had discerned, liked to be observed while contemplating. Joe didn't comply.

"You know," Ed said finally, "a fellow can't actually *fix* T-Lock shingles. It's like trying to fix a car radio without taking it out of the dash. It just can't be done properly."

Joe took in a deep breath and waited. He dug another nail out of the pocket of his hooded sweatshirt.

"Now, I'm not saying you shouldn't try or that you're wasting your time. I'm not saying that at all," Ed said, chuckling in the way a master chuckles at a hapless apprentice, Joe thought. The way his mentor-gone-bad Vern Dunnegan used to chuckle at him years ago.

"Then what are you saying?" Joe asked.

"It's just that you can't really fix shingles in a little patch and expect them to hold," Ed said. "The shingles overlap like this." He held his hands out and placed one on top of the other. "You can't fix a shingle properly without taking the top one off first. And because they overlap, you need to take the one off *that*. What I'm saying, Joe, is that with T-Lock shingles you've got to lay a whole new set of shingles on top or strip the whole roof and start over so they seat properly. You can't just fix a section. You've got to fix it all. If I was you, I'd call your insurance man and have him come out and look at it. That way, you can get a whole new roof."

"What if I don't want a whole new roof?" Joe asked.

Ed shrugged affably. "That's your call, of course. It's *your* roof. I'm not trying to make you do anything. But if you look at the other roofs on the block—at my roof—you'll see we have a certain standard. None of us have patches where you can see a bunch of nail heads. Plus, it might leak. Then you've got ceiling damage. You don't want that, do you?"

"No," Joe said defensively.

"Nobody wants that," Ed said, nodding, puffing. Then, looking up at Joe and squinting through a cloud of smoke, "Are you aware your ladder fell down?"

"Yup," Joe answered quickly.

"Do you want me to prop it back up so you can come down?"

"That's not necessary," Joe said. "I need to clean the gutters first."

"I was wondering when you were going to get to that," Ed said.

Joe grunted.

"Are you going to get started on your fence then too?"

"*Ed* . . ."

"Just trying to help," Ed said, waving his pipe, "just being neighborly."

Joe said nothing.

"It isn't like where you used to live," Ed continued, "up the Bighorn Road or out there on your mother-in-law's ranch. In town, we all look out for each other and help each other out."

"Got it," Joe said, feeling his neck flush hot, wishing Ed Nedny would turn his attention to someone else on the street or go wax his car or go to breakfast with his old retired buddies at the Burg-O-Pardner downtown.

Joe kept his head down and started scraping several inches of dead leaves from his gutter with the spatula he'd borrowed from the kitchen drawer.

"I've got a tool for that," Ed offered.

"That's *okay*, Ed," Joe said through clenched teeth, "I'm doing just fine."

"Mind if I come over?" Nedny asked while crossing his lawn onto Joe's. It was easy to see the property line, Joe noted, since Ed's lawn was green and raked clean of leaves and Joe's was neither. Nedny grumbled about the shape of Joe's old ladder while raising it and propping it up against the eave. "Is this ladder going to collapse on me?" Ed asked while he climbed it.

"We'll see," Joe said, as Nedny's big fleshy face and pipe appeared just above the rim of the gutter. Ed rose another rung so he could fold his arms on the roof and watch Joe more comfortably. He was close enough that Joe could have reached out and patted the top of Nedny's watch cap with the spatula.

"Ah, the joys of being a homeowner, eh?" Ed said.

Joe nodded.

"Is it true this is the first house you've owned?"

"Yes."

"You've got a lovely family. Two daughters, right? Sheridan and Lucy?"

"Yes."

"I met your wife, Marybeth, a couple of weeks ago. She owns that business management company—MBP? I've heard good things about them."

"Good."

"She's quite a lovely woman as well. I've met her mother, Missy. The apple didn't fall far from that tree."

"Yes, it did," Joe said, wishing the ladder would collapse.

"I heard you used to live out on the ranch with her and Bud Longbrake. Why did you decide to move to town? That's a pretty nice place out there."

"Nosy neighbors," Joe said.

Nedny forged on. "What are you? Forty?"

"Yup."

"So you've always lived in state-owned houses, huh? Paid for by the state?"

Joe sighed and looked up. "I'm a game warden, Ed. The game and fish department provided housing."

"I remember you used to live out on the Bighorn Road," Nedny said. "Nice little place, if I remember. Phil Kiner lives there now. Since he's the new game warden for the county, what do you do?"

Joe wondered how long Nedny had been waiting to ask these questions since they'd bought the home and moved in. Probably from the first day. But until now, Nedny hadn't had the opportunity to corner Joe and ask.

"I still work for the department," Joe said. "I fill in wherever they need me."

"I heard," Nedny said, raising his eyebrows man-to-man, "that you work directly for the governor now. Like you're some kind of special agent or something."

"At times," Joe said.

"Interesting. Our governor is a fascinating man. What's he like in person? Is he really crazy like some people say?"

Joe was immensely grateful when he heard the front door of his house slam shut and saw Marybeth come out into the front yard and look up. She was wearing her weekend sweats and her blond hair was tied back in a ponytail. She took in the scene: Ed Nedny up on the ladder next to Joe.

"Joe, you've got a call from dispatch," she said. "They said it's an emergency."

"Tell them it's your day off," Nedny counseled. "Tell 'em you've got gutters to clean out and a fence to fix."

"You'd like that, wouldn't you, Ed?"

"We all would," Nedny answered. "The whole block."

"You'll have to climb down so I can take that call," Joe said. "I don't think that ladder will hold both of us."

Nedny sighed with frustration and started down. Joe followed.

"My spatula, Joe?" she asked, shaking her head at him.

"I told him I had a tool for that," Ed called over his shoulder as he trudged toward his house.

"I'M NOT used to people so close that they can watch and comment on everything we do," Joe said to Marybeth as he entered the house.

"Did you forget about my mother on the ranch?" she asked, smiling bitterly.

"Of course not," Joe said, taking the phone from her, "but what's that saying about keeping your friends close and your enemies closer?"

The house was larger than the state-owned home they'd lived in for six years, and nicer, but with less character than the log home they'd temporarily occupied on the Long-brake Ranch for a year. Big kitchen, nice backyard, three bedrooms, partially finished basement with a home office, a two-car garage filled with Joe's drift boat and snowmo-bile, and still-unpacked boxes stacked up to the rafters. It had been three months since they bought the house but they still weren't fully moved in.

Ten-year-old Lucy was sprawled in a blanket on the living room floor watching Saturday morning cartoons. She had quickly mastered the intricacies of the remote control and the satellite television setup and reveled in living, for the first time, as she put it, "in civilization." Sheridan was, Joe guessed, back in bed.

Marybeth looked on with concern as he said into the telephone, "Joe Pickett."

The dispatcher in Cheyenne said, "Please hold for the governor's office."

Joe felt a shiver race down his back at the words.

There was a click and a pop and he could hear Governor Spencer Rulon talking to someone in his office over the speakerphone, caught in midsentence: ". . . we've got to get ahead of this one and frame and define it before those bastards in the eastern press define it for us—"

"I've got Mr. Pickett on the line, sir," the dispatcher said.

"Joe!" the governor said. "How in the hell are you?"

"Fine, sir."

"And how is the lovely Mrs. Pickett?"

Joe looked up at his wife, who was pouring two cups of coffee.

"Still lovely," Joe said.

"Did you hear the news?"

"What news?"

"Another hunter got shot this morning," Rulon said.

"Oh, no."

"This one is in your neck of the woods. I just got the report ten minutes ago. The victim's hunting buddies found him and called it in. It sounds bad, Joe. It really sounds bad."

If the governor was correct, this was the third accidental shooting of a big-game hunter in Wyoming thus far this fall, Joe knew.

"I don't know all the details yet," Rulon said, "but I want you all over it for obvious reasons. You need to mount up and get up there and find out what happened. Call when you've got the full story."

"Who's in charge?" Joe asked, looking up as his day of homeowner chores went away in front of his eyes.

"Your sheriff there," Rulon said, "McLanahan."

"Oh," Joe said.

"I know, I know," the governor said, "he's a doofus. But he's your sheriff, not mine. Go with him and make sure he doesn't foul up the scene. I've ordered DCI and Randy Pope to get up there in the state plane by noon."

"Why Pope?" Joe asked.

"Isn't it obvious?" Rulon said. "If this is another accidental death we've got a full-blown news event on our hands. Not to mention another Klamath Moore press conference."

Klamath Moore was the leader and spokesman for a national anti-hunting organization who appeared regularly on cable news and was the first to be interviewed whenever a story about hunting and wildlife arose. He had recently turned his attention to the state of Wyoming, and particularly Governor Spencer Rulon, whom he called "Governor Bambi Killer." Rulon had responded by saying if Moore came to Wyoming he'd challenge him to a duel with pistols and knives. The statement was seized upon by commentators making "red state/blue state" arguments during the election year, even though Rulon was a Democrat. In Wyoming the controversy increased Rulon's popularity among certain sectors while fueling talk in others that the governor was becoming more unhinged.

"Why me?" Joe asked.

The governor snorted. Whoever was in the room with him—it sounded like a woman—laughed. Something about her laugh was familiar to Joe, and not in a good way. He shot a glance toward Marybeth, who looked back warily.

"Why you?" Rulon said. "What in the hell else do you have to do today?"

Joe reached back and patted the list in his pocket. "Chores," he said.

"I want fresh eyes on the crime scene," Rulon said. "You've got experience in this kind of thing. Maybe you can see something McLanahan or DCI can't see. These are your people, these hunter types. Right?"

Before Joe could answer, he heard the woman in the governor's office say, "Right."

Joe thought he recognized the voice, which sent a chill through him. "Stella?"

"Hi, Joe," she said.

At the name Stella, Marybeth locked on Joe's face in a death stare.

"I was going to introduce you to my new chief of staff," the governor said, "but I guess you two know each other."

"We do," Stella Ennis purred.

"Joe, are you there?" Rulon asked.

"Barely," Joe said.

WHILE JOE changed into his red uniform shirt with the pronghorn antelope game and fish department patch on the shoulder and clipped on his J. PICKETT, GAME WARDEN badge above the breast pocket, Marybeth entered the bedroom and said, "Stella Ennis?"

The name brought back a flood of memories. He'd met her in Jackson Hole on temporary assignment three years before. She was the wife of a prominent and homicidal developer. She'd "befriended" the previous Jackson game warden and complicated his life. She tried to do the same with Joe, and he'd been attracted to her. It was a time in their marriage when they seemed on the verge of separation. They persevered. Now they owned their first home.

"The governor introduced her as his new chief of staff," Joe said.

"How is that possible?" she asked. "Wasn't her husband convicted of trying to kill her?"

Joe shook his head. "He was never charged because Stella turned up alive and well. Marcus Hand was his lawyer. The Teton County DA plea-bargained the rest of the charges and Don Ennis paid some fines and moved to Florida."

"How did she wind up in the governor's office?"

"I have no idea," Joe said. "She's resourceful."

"This state is too small sometimes," she said.

"Yes it is."

Marybeth approached Joe and pulled him to her with her hands behind his neck, so their faces were inches apart. "Stay away from her, Joe. You know what happened last time."

"Nothing," Joe said, flushing.

"Yes, but," she said.

"Honey . . ."

"She's a very good-looking woman. I've seen pictures of her. She's beautiful, and very dangerous. But so am I."

He smiled. "You have nothing to worry about."

"I believe you."

"Besides, it sounds like I'll be too busy dealing with Sheriff McLanahan and Randy Pope. I'm not looking forward to *that*."

"I don't trust her," Marybeth said. "But I do trust you."

"You should."

"Plus, Sheridan and Lucy would kill you if you ever did anything untoward."

"That I'm sure of," Joe said.

"So what's going on? Another hunter?"

"Apparently," Joe said. "I don't know much yet, but the governor's worried."

"Any idea how long you'll be gone this time?"

"I should be back tonight."

"No," she said. "I mean on this case."

He buckled on his holster with the .40 Glock, pepper spray, and handcuffs and reached for his Stetson that was crown down on the dresser.

"I don't know," he said. "We don't know if it's another accident or foul play. Everyone's jumpy because of those other hunters who got shot. No one wants to imagine that someone is hunting hunters, but everyone is thinking that."

She nodded. She didn't need to tell him there were parent-teacher conferences later in the week at Lucy's junior high and Sheridan's high school. Or about the party they'd been invited to with members of their church. Or about the fact that she wanted him home while she battled with her mother and needed his support.

"I'll be home as soon as I can," he said.

She walked him to the door. Lucy was still watching television and didn't look at him. She simply said, "Gone again?"

Joe stopped, hurt. Marybeth pushed him gently out the door into the front yard.

"We'll be here when you get home," she said. Then: "It looks like there's someone who would like to go with you."

He turned, hoping Sheridan was on the porch pulling on her jacket. But it was Maxine, his old Labrador who had turned white four years before and was now half-blind, half-deaf, and fully flatulent.

"Come on, girl," Joe said.

Maxine clattered stiff-legged down the sidewalk, her

tail snapping side to side like her old self. Joe had to lift her back end into the cab.

"I *am* curious how she ended up on the governor's staff," Marybeth said. "I'll have to do a little snooping."

Joe kissed her. "You've made your point," he said. "There's nothing to worry about here. I need to go."

"I understand," she said, "but Ed Nedny is going to be real upset with you."

3

PHIL KINER, the new game warden of the Saddlestring
District, was waiting for Joe in his green Ford four-wheel-
drive pickup with the Wyoming Game and Fish logo on
the door in front of Joe's old home on Bighorn Road. Joe
drove an identical pickup. Joe tried not to let it get to him
that Phil now lived in his former state-owned home with
the view of Wolf Mountain, tried not to allow the nostalgia
he'd let in that morning eat further into him, but when he
saw the house he couldn't help it. The picket fence needed
painting and the corral needed repair. When he shot a
glance at the windows of the house he saw the images and
ghosts of his younger family looking out as they had once
posed—Marybeth, Sheridan, Lucy—and his foster daughter, April. He shook his head hard to rid himself of the
memory and stanched his longing for the innocence and
naivete of that time.

Kiner unrolled his window as Joe pulled up beside him
nose to tail, the quintessential cop maneuver so neither
would need to get out of his vehicle. "Have you been listening on your radio?"

"Not really," Joe said, a little ashamed he'd been so pre-occupied on the eight-mile drive out.

"McLanahan's up ahead, waiting for us," Kiner said. "He knows the general area but doesn't know where this elk camp is at. He needs for us to get there and show him."

"Whose camp?"

"Frank Urman from Cheyenne. He's the victim. You know him?"

"The name's familiar," Joe said. "I think I know the camp."

"Good, because I don't."

Kiner said it without bitterness, which Joe welcomed. Throughout the first year Kiner took over, he hadn't contacted Joe for advice or background on the district Joe had overseen for six years. Marybeth speculated that it was either misplaced pride or Kiner's fear of displeasing Randy Pope by creating the impression he was close to Joe. Either way, it hurt. Joe tried to put himself in Kiner's shoes, and when he did he understood the dilemma but still thought Kiner should have reached out. They had reconciled only after Sheridan slugged Kiner's son Jason in the lunchroom at school and both sets of parents were called in for a conference with the vice principal.

"How many are up there?" Joe asked.

"Three," Kiner said. "Related to the victim, from what I can tell so far. They sound really pissed off, so we need to get up there before they go after whoever shot the fourth guy."

"Is it possible it was an accident?" Joe asked.

"It sure as hell doesn't sound like one, but we won't know for sure until we get there," Kiner said, raising his eyebrows. "But from what I've heard, it sounds fucking horrible. In fact, I can't even believe what they're telling the dispatcher they found."

"What?"

"Turn on your radio," Kiner said while putting the pickup in gear and roaring off.

Joe sat for a moment, took a deep breath, and followed. He kept far enough back of Kiner's dust cloud to look up at the looming dark mountains as they framed the valley. Fingers of fall color probed down the slopes and folds. The sky had turned from brilliant blue to a light steel gray as a film of cloud cover moved from the north, bringing, no doubt, a drop in temperature and possibly snow flurries. He turned on his radio beneath the dash and clicked it to the mutual aid channel. It was crackling with voices.

The dispatcher said, "Mr. Urman, I understand. But please remain where you are and don't pursue anyone on your own. We've got units on the way."

"That's easy for you to say, lady," the man Joe assumed was Urman said with barely controlled fury, "you haven't seen what happened to my uncle this morning. And whoever did it is still out there."

"Mr. Urman—"

"Somebody shot him with a high-powered rifle," Urman said, "like a goddamned elk!"

Joe swallowed hard.

"Like a goddamned elk," Urman repeated in a near whisper, an auditory hitch in his voice.

As he followed Kiner, Joe did a quick inventory of his pickup. He'd been practically living in it for the past month and it showed. The carpeting on the floorboards showed mud from the clay draws and arroyos near Lusk, the Little Snake River bottomland of Baggs, the desert of Rawlins, the Wind River foothills out of Pinedale. There was a gritty covering of dust on his dashboard and over his instruments. The console was packed with maps, notes, citation books. The skinny space behind his seat was crammed with jackets and coats for every weather possibility, as well as his personal shotgun, his Remington WingMaster twelve-gauge, his third since he'd become a full-time game warden. An M-14 carbine with a peep sight was under the seat, a Winchester .270 rifle was secured in brackets behind his head. The large padlocked metal box in the bed of the vehicle held evidence kits, survival gear, necropsy kits, heavy winter clothing, tools, spare radios, a tent and sleeping bag. Single-cab pickups for game wardens with all this gear was proof that whoever it was in the department who purchased the vehicles had never been out in the field.

Since he'd lost his district and been assigned to work "without portfolio" for the governor, Joe filled in across the state whenever and wherever he was needed. Since there were only fifty-four game wardens covering the ninety-eight thousand square miles of the state, he was constantly in demand. If a warden was sick, injured, or had extended duty in court or on assignment, Joe was asked to substitute. Because he was moving around so much, agency biologists had asked him to gather samples from big-game animals across the state so they could monitor the spread of chronic wasting disease. CWD was a transmissible neurological disease that attacked the brains of deer and elk and was similar to mad cow disease. From a few isolated cases in the southwest of the state, the disease seemed to be moving north and was turning into a significant threat to the wild game population. Joe was concerned, as were many others. Too many animals were showing positive results for CWD, although not yet in crisis proportions.

He never knew what his schedule would be from week to week. The requests came via third party or from the wardens themselves. They never came straight from Director Pope, who had chosen not to communicate directly with Joe in any way. Joe liked it better that way as well, but he never forgot for a moment that Pope had fired him and would do so again in an instant if he could find justification. Joe's relationship with the governor was vague, and after the case in Yellowstone Joe wasn't sure he could trust him. But Rulon had not given Joe any reasons to doubt his sincerity since then, other than his generally erratic behavior, a sign of which was hiring Stella Ennis as his new chief of staff.

The two trucks raced up the state highway, wigwag lights flashing. A herd of pronghorn antelope raced them for a while before turning south in a flowing arc toward the breaklands. Cows looked up but didn't stop grazing.

They passed the entrance to Nate Romanowski's place. Nate was an outlaw falconer with a mysterious background who'd made a pledge to protect Joe and his family after Joe proved his innocence in a murder investigation. Currently, Nate was in federal custody involving the disappearance of two men—one being the former sheriff—two years before. He'd asked Joe to continue to feed his falcons, which Joe did every day he could. Sheridan filled in when Joe was out of town, getting a ride to Nate's old stone house from Marybeth. Nate's trial had been postponed twice already. Joe missed him.

Farther up the road, Joe saw Sheriff McLanahan's GMC Blazer and two additional county vehicles waiting for them. The sheriff and his men let them pass before joining in. Joe caught a glimpse of McLanahan as they rocketed by. McLanahan had completed his physical and mental transformation from a hotheaded deputy to a western character who spoke in semiliterate cornball folk-isms. The huge handlebar mustache he'd grown completed the metamorphosis.

"It looks like the posse is now complete," McLanahan said over the radio. "Carry on, buckaroos."

Joe rolled his eyes.

THE CARAVAN of law-enforcement vehicles was forced to ratchet down its collective speed as it entered the Big Horn National Forest. Kiner eased to the shoulder to let Joe overtake him and lead the way. The gravel road gave way to a rougher two-track that led through an empty campground and up the mountain in a series of switchbacks. Frank Urman's camp was located over the top of the mountain through a long meadow.

The dispatcher called out his number and asked for a location.

"This is GF-52," Joe said. "I'm with GF-36 and local law enforcement. We're headed up the mountain now to the subject's camp."

"Hold for Director Pope."

Joe grimaced.

"Joe?" It was Pope. Joe could hear the whine of the state airplane in the background.

"Yes, sir."

"Joe, we're about thirty minutes out. When we land we've got to get vehicles and get up there to the scene. About how long will it take for us to get there?"

"At least an hour, sir."

"Damn it."

After a beat, Pope said, "Do you know what happened yet? Is it as bad as we hear it might be?"

"We don't know," Joe said, "we're not yet on the scene."

"Who is the RP?"

"The reporting party is named Chris Urman," the dispatcher broke in. "He's the victim's nephew."

"How many people are involved?" Pope asked.

"Involved?" Joe asked. "As far as we know there is one victim."

"No, I mean how many people know about this? How many have heard what happened to him?"

"I don't know, sir," Joe said.

"I'm issuing a direct order," Pope said. "This is to you and Kiner. Don't give any statements to anybody until I get there. Don't talk with anyone or tell anybody what happened. Got that?"

As had happened many times before when Pope was on the radio, Joe held the mike away from him and looked at it for answers that never presented themselves.

"Affirmative," Kiner finally said, "no public statements until you're on the scene."

"You got that, Joe?" Pope asked.

"I got it," Joe said, "but we've got the sheriff behind us, and anybody listening to the scanner will know we've got a situation here."

"Look," Pope said, his voice rising, "I can only control my own people. I can't control anything else. All I ask is that you follow my direct goddamned order, Joe. Can you do that?"

"Of course, sir," Joe said, feeling his ears get hot.

"Good. I'll call when we land. In the meantime, you two keep off the radio. And I'll politely ask Sheriff McLanahan to do the same."

McLanahan broke in. "Shit, I heard you. Everybody did."

"Everybody?"

"We're on SALECS—the State Assisted Law Enforcement Communications System," McLanahan said. "If you want to go private you need to switch to another channel."

Pope didn't respond and Joe pictured him stammering and angrily hanging up. Joe waited awhile before cradling the mike. When he looked in his rearview mirror he could see Kiner signaling him with two fingers, meaning he wanted Joe to switch to the car-to-car band so no one could hear them. The frequency worked as long as the vehicles were in sight of each other, and not much farther than that.

"Joe," Kiner said, "do you have any idea what's going on with Pope? I've never heard him like this."

"I have," Joe said.

"So what's up? Why in the hell is the director flying up from Cheyenne for this? Since when does he get personally involved in a case? And especially since you two avoid each other like the plague?"

"I was wondering that myself," Joe said.

"There's something going on here we don't know about, that's for damned sure."

Joe nodded. "I agree."

"Me too," McLanahan said.

"What are you doing on our channel?" Kiner asked McLanahan. Joe held his tongue.

"Just remindin' you boys who's in charge of this investigation," McLanahan drawled.

JOE WAS struck immediately by the three hunters waiting for them at the camp. They looked young, hard, fit, and intense, and they started walking up the rough two-track to meet the convoy of law-enforcement vehicles as soon as Joe cleared the rim and saw them. Many of the hunters Joe encountered were older and softer. These three reminded him of an elite commando unit on patrol. All three had their rifles with them and carried them naturally. Joe and Kiner pulled over so Sheriff McLanahan could take the lead.

The sheriff stopped and got out of his Blazer to meet the hunters. They introduced themselves as Chris Urman, Craig Hysell, and Jake Dempster. Urman appeared to be in charge, and Joe stood with Kiner and listened as the hunters described what had happened.

"Uncle Frank wanted to scout elk on his own this morning," Urman, Frank's nephew, told McLanahan. Urman was tall, with a long face and steady eyes. While he spoke he slung his rifle from one shoulder to the other with a fluid, well-practiced movement and without pausing. Joe thought, *Military*. "He said he'd be back by breakfast unless he got his bull. I made him take a radio so he could call in either way. He was supposed to be back here by oh-eight-hundred hours at the latest, and when he didn't show up by oh-eight-thirty we tried to call him. Craig here said he heard a shot around oh-seven-thirty," Urman said, gesturing to one of the other hunters, who stepped forward.

The hunter held out his hand, said, "Craig Hysell. I heard just one shot. I waited to hear a second but it never came. I thought it was from the east, where Frank went, but I couldn't be sure because of the way sound echoes around up here."

Joe noted the times in his spiral.

The third hunter, Jake Dempster, was dark, with a stern expression. "I didn't hear it," he said.

"So when he didn't come in for breakfast you went looking for him," McLanahan said.

"Yes, sir," Urman said. "And we found him."

"You didn't see nobody else?"

"No, sir, we didn't see anyone and we didn't hear any vehicles. There's only one road into this camp and nobody came down it until you just now. But there sure as hell was somebody out there. And for all we know, he still is."

"Can we drive to the scene?" McLanahan asked.

"We've gotta walk. There's no road."

"Well," McLanahan said, "lead the way."

Urman turned crisply and started up a trail and his companions fell in behind him. Joe, Kiner, and McLanahan and his two deputies followed.

"WE JUST got back from Iraq," Jake Dempster told Joe over his shoulder. "Wyoming National Guard. Chris's uncle Frank invited us all to come here elk hunting when we got back. He was a good old guy. This is his camp. We've been looking forward to this trip for seven months. It's the only thing that got me through some days when it was a hundred and forty degrees and I was sick as hell of dealing with those Iraqi knuckleheads."

"Thanks for your service," Joe said.

Dempster nodded. "We all saw some pretty bad stuff over there where we were stationed, near Tikrit. You know the stories."

"Yup."

"But in two years over there in the world's armpit, I never seen anything like this," he said. "Shooting Uncle Frank was bad enough but what was done to his body afterwards is something else. If we catch who did it, you're gonna see Chris go medieval on his ass. And me and Craig are going to help him. So I hope you guys catch whoever did it fast, because you'll be doing them a favor."

Dempster's eyes were hard and clear. Joe said, "I believe you."

"I gotta tell you something else," Dempster said as they walked. "I realize it can't be used as evidence or anything, but my buddies and I were talking last night how we felt like someone was up here watching us. I thought it was just me, so I kind of hesitated saying anything. But when Urman brought it up, both me and Craig said we'd felt the same thing yesterday while we were hunting."

Joe knew the feeling. He'd had it. Sometimes it was a game animal watching him, sometimes a hunter in a blind. And sometimes he never learned what caused it.

"I got that same buzz once over in Iraq," Dempster said. "We were on patrol and parked at an intersection one night. It was pure black because the lights were out. I could feel it on my neck when I looked outside the Humvee. Then one of our guys who had night-vision goggles opened up on an insurgent sniper up on a roof and took him out. The sniper had been sighting in on us on the street. That's what it felt like yesterday, that someone was looking at me through a scope but I couldn't see him."

JOE ADMIRED hunters who hunted seriously and with respect not only for the animals they pursued but for the resource itself. Most of the hunters in Wyoming were like that, and they had passed their respect along to the next generation. While the numbers of hunters had declined over the years, it was still a vibrant local tradition. Good hunters considered hunting a solemn privilege and a means to reconnect with the natural world, to place themselves back on earth, into a place without supermarkets, processed foods, and commercial meat manufacturing industries.

Hunting was basic, primal, and humbling. He had less respect for trophy hunters and thought poachers who took the antlers and left the meat deserved a special place in hell, and he was happy to arrest them and send them there.

He valued those who shot well and took care of their game properly. This involved field dressing the downed animal quickly and cleanly, and cooling the meat by placing lengths of wood inside the body cavity to open it up to the crisp fall air. Back limbs were spread out and the game was then hung by the legs from a tree branch or game pole. The game carcass was then skinned to accelerate cooling, and washed down to clean it of hair and dirt. The head was often removed as well as the legs past their joints. It was respectful of the animal and the tradition of hunting to take care of the kill this way.

Over the years, Joe had seen hanging in trees hundreds of carcasses of deer, moose, elk, and pronghorn antelope that had been field-dressed, skinned, and beheaded.

This was the first time he'd ever seen a man hung in the same condition.

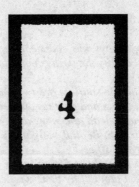

4

I watch them come over the ridge through my rifle scope. They come down the trail single file, like wild turkeys. I'm much too far away to hear their conversation but I find I don't need to since their actions and gestures tell me what they're thinking and saying to one another. I'm surprised there are so many of them so quickly, and I thank God I was finished and away from there before they showed up. I'm also grateful the soldiers decided to call law enforcement rather than to pursue me on their own. It could have gone either way, I know, when the three of them stood near the hanging body an hour ago and argued over what to do. Their leader, the tall one, wanted to come after me right then and there after discovering the body. It was obvious by the way he unslung his rifle and held it like the weapon it was, light in his hands and deadly. His friends calmed him down eventually and argued persuasively to call the authorities once they got back to their camp. I have nothing against the soldiers, and I fear their abilities and their young aggression. No doubt they've been well trained in tactics and strategy. Although it is my aim to elude them, there is always the chance that through sheer will and physical ability they will run me down and force a confrontation.

Behind the soldiers are two men wearing cowboy hats with red shirts and patches on their shoulders. Game wardens. One is lean and wary and the other big and already out of breath. Behind the game wardens are members of the sheriff's office.

They stop about fifteen yards from where the body is hanging. I can tell by their physical reactions to the body how the sight affects each of them. The soldiers/hunters gesture to confirm what they've described, where they were standing when they found the corpse. One of the deputies turns away and looks up at the tops of the trees, gazing at anything other than what is in front of him. The other stares morbidly at the body, as does the sheriff, who looks perplexed. The big game warden has lost all his color and seems frozen and ineffectual, as if the life has gone out of him, his face frozen into a white mask. The lean game warden steps aside into the trees and bends over with his hands on his knees, is violently sick. The sheriff points at him and nudges his deputy, and the two of them exchange glances and smirk.

I watch the game warden who threw up. When he's done, he rises and wipes his mouth with his sleeve. He's angry, but not at the sheriff for making fun of him. By the way he glares in my direction and at the forest and meadows he can see, I think he's angry with me. For the briefest moment, I can see his eyes lock with mine although he doesn't register the fact because he's not sure I'm here. The crosshairs of the scope linger on his red shirt over his heart. I could squeeze the trigger and make the shot—it's a long way but there is no wind and my angle is decent— but I won't because it would give my position away. There's something about the set of his jaw and his squint that tells me he is taking this personally.

Of all of them, I decide he's the one to worry about.

———

WHEN HE FINALLY rejoins the others, I rise to my knees and use the trunk of a tree to get to my feet. My legs are tired from walking most of the night and they shake from the dissipating adrenaline that still burns through my thigh and calf muscles. I feel for a moment like sleeping, but I know I can't.

I move slowly in the shadows of the timber. A quick movement could startle a lurking animal or a nesting bird and give me away. Although it is cold, I stay away from anywhere the sun is filtering through the trees to avoid a sun-caught glint from my rifle barrel or scope. I cap my scope and sling my rifle over my shoulder. The spent car-tridge is still in the chamber because I've learned not to eject it after firing and risk the possibility of it being found. I look around on the bed of pine needles where I lay to make sure I haven't dropped anything. Then I nose my boot through the shape that's still defined in the needles, erasing the impression of my body.

I pick up the daypack, which now sags with weight.

My bare hands, my clothes, even my face are sticky with blood. My concern isn't the blood that is on me. The clothes will be burned and the blood will be washed off my skin and scraped out from beneath my fingernails. What worries me, always, is leaving a track, leaving a trace of myself.

I know Edmond Locard's Principle, the central theory of modern forensic crime-scene investigation: something is always left behind.

And this time, like the other times, I have left something for them intentionally. What I don't want to leave is some-thing unintentional, something that can lead them to me.

Before I leave the area for my long hike back, I use my binoculars to take a last look at the investigators. As I do, I see the lean game warden studying the ground beneath the hanging body and squatting to retrieve what I placed in the grass.

AS A HUNTER I am looked down upon in Western society. I am portrayed as a brute. I am denigrated and spat upon, and thought of as a slow-witted anachronism, the dregs of a discredited culture. This happened quickly when one looks at human history. The skills I possess—the ability to track, hunt, kill, and dress out my prey so it can be served at a table to feed others—were prized for tens of thousands of years. Hunters fed those in the tribe and family who could not hunt well or did not hunt because they weren't physically able to. The success of the hunter produced not only healthy food and clothing, tools, medicine, and amenities, but a direct hot-blooded connection with God and the natural world. The hunter was the provider, and exalted as such.

I often think that in the world we live in today, where we are threatened by forces as violent and primitive as anything we have ever faced, that it would be wise to look back a little ourselves and embrace our heritage. We were once a nation of hunters. And not the effete, European-style hunters who did it for sport. We hunted for our food, our independence. It's what made us who we are. But, like so many other virtues that made us unique, we have, as a society, forgotten where we came from and how we got here. What was once both noble and essential has become perverted and indefensible.

Here's what I know:

Those who disparage me are ignorant.

Those who damage me will pay.

And:

A human head is pretty heavy.

5

THE TELECONFERENCE with Governor Spencer Rulon
was scheduled for 7 P.M. in the conference room in the
county building in Saddlestring. Joe sat waiting for it to
begin at a long table with his back to the wall. In front of
him on the table were three manila files brought by Randy
Pope, a spread of topo maps, and, in a plastic evidence bag,
the single red poker chip he had found in the grass near the
body. The poker chip had been dusted for prints. None
were found. Sheriff McLanahan had ordered food in from
the Burg-O-Pardner—burgers, fries, coffee, cookies—and
the room smelled of hot grease and dry-erase markers. Joe's
cheeseburger sat untouched on a white foam plate.

"You gonna eat that?" Kiner asked.

Joe shook his head.

"You mind?"

"Not at all."

"I can't believe I'm hungry," Kiner mumbled as he un-
wrapped Joe's cheeseburger.

Joe shrugged. He had had no appetite since that morning and could not get the image of Frank Urman's hanging

body out of his mind. The photo spread of the crime scene tacked on a bulletin board didn't help.

McLanahan and his deputies occupied the other end of the table, digging into the box of food like hyenas over a fresh kill. On the wall opposite Joe were three television monitors and two stationary cameras. The county technician fiddled with a control board out of view of the cameras and whispered to his counterpart in the governor's office in Cheyenne.

Robey Hersig, the county attorney and Joe's friend, read over the crime-scene report prepared by the sheriff. At one point he gulped, looked up, said, "Man oh man," before reading on. It was good to see Robey again, but Joe wished the circumstances were different, wished they were on Joe or Robey's drift boat fly-fishing for trout on the Twelve Sleep River.

"Five minutes before airtime, gentlemen," the technician said.

Director Randy Pope paced the room, head down, hands clasped behind his back. Pope was tall and thin with light blue eyes and sandy hair and a pallor that came from working indoors in an office. He had a slight brown mustache and a weak chin, and his lips were pinched together so tightly they looked like twin bands of white cord.

"Pope is making me nervous," Kiner whispered between bites. "I've never seen him like this before."

"Me either," Joe said.

"He's not just passing through either," Kiner said. "He got a room at the Holiday Inn. He'll be here awhile."

"Terrific," Joe said sourly.

"I wish he'd sit down," Kiner said. "He's making me jumpy."

"Two minutes," the technician called out.

Pope stopped pacing and stood and closed his eyes tightly and took a deep breath. All eyes in the room were on him, but he seemed too preoccupied with his own thoughts to know or care, Joe thought. Joe found it difficult to work up the anger he once felt toward Pope now that his nemesis was in the room instead of barking orders or making innuendos over the phone. Since his arrival, Pope had surprised Joe with his lack of animosity at the crime scene, and Joe was equally pleased, puzzled, and suspicious.

The director took his seat next to Kiner and gathered the files in front of him, then stacked them one on top of the other. Joe read the tabs on the files. The bottom one read J. GARRETT, the middle one W. TUCKER, the top one F. URMAN. He looked to Pope for some kind of explanation of the files but the director avoided meeting Joe's eyes.

"What's with the three files?" Joe asked.

"Not now, Joe," Pope said out of the side of his mouth.

"Why are you and the governor so directly involved in this case?"

Pope shot Joe a look of admonition tinged with panic, and repeated, "Not now, Joe."

The middle monitor flickered, revealing the top of a desk and the State of Wyoming seal on the wall behind the desk. The technician brought the audio up as Wyoming Governor Spencer Rulon filled the screen and sat down. Rulon was a big man with a wide, expressive face, a big gut, a shock of silver-flecked brown hair, a quick sloppy smile, and eyes that rarely stayed on anything or anyone very long. Joe thought the governor had gained some weight since he'd seen him last, and his upper cheeks seemed rounder and ruddier. He wondered if Stella was there in the room, if she would appear on the screen.

"Are we live?" Rulon asked. His voice was gravelly.

"Yes, sir," Pope answered.

"Sheriff, we'd like to thank you for the use of your facilities."

McLanahan nodded, still chewing. "You paid for 'em," he said.

"There are benefits to being flush with cash," Rulon said

with a slight smile, referring to the hundreds of millions of dollars of energy severance taxes flowing into the state. "This is one of 'em."

Rulon's eyes left the camera and shifted to his monitor. "I see we've got everyone here. Director Pope, Sheriff McLanahan, Robey, Joe Pickett. How you doing, Joe?"

"Fine, Governor," Joe said, shifting in his chair for being singled out. "Considering."

"Game Warden Phil Kiner is present as well," Pope said quickly.

"Okay," Rulon said without enthusiasm. Joe could feel Kiner deflate next to him at the governor's cool reaction to the mention of his name. Then: "What have we got here, gentlemen?"

Pope cleared his throat, indicating to everyone in the room that he planned to take the lead. Joe wasn't surprised.

"Mr. Frank Urman's body was found this morning about three miles from his elk camp. Urman was sixty-two. He owned a hotel and gas station in Sheridan. What we heard over the radio turned out to be true. He was killed and mutilated in a manner that suggests he was left to resemble a game animal."

Rulon winced, and Joe's eyes wandered to the photos on the bulletin board.

"The crime scene has been taped off and contained," Pope said. "State and local forensics spent the afternoon there and they're still up there working under lights. The body is being airlifted to our lab in Laramie for an autopsy. The scene itself was pretty trampled by the time we got there, I'm afraid. Mr. Urman's nephew and his friends were all over the scene."

"Is it possible they had something to do with it?" Rulon asked. Before becoming governor, Rulon had been the federal district prosecutor for Wyoming, and Joe thought he easily slipped back into the role.

"We haven't ruled it out," Pope said at the same time

McLanahan said, "They didn't do it." The two exchanged glances.

"Which is it?" Rulon asked.

"They've been separated and questioned," Pope said. "We're comparing their stories and we will re-interview them later tonight to see if their recollection has changed any. But I've got to say we'd be real surprised if any of them had anything to do with the shooting. They're all cooperating. They're vets just back from Iraq, and they seem too angry with what happened to have had anything at all to do with the crime."

Rulon seemed to mull this over. "So you've got nothing?"

Pope sighed and nodded. "Correct."

McLanahan said, "No footprints, no DNA, no fibers, no casing, no weapon, no motivation. Squat is what we've got. Squat. Not a goddamned thing."

"Do we know if the murder victim was targeted or random?" Rulon asked.

"I'd say random," Pope said quickly. "I think he was murdered because he was a hunter. The way his body was mutilated suggests the killer was sending us a pretty strong message."

"You've got a good grasp on the obvious, Director Pope," Rulon said, letting an edge of impatience into his tone. "What else can you tell me? What steps are being taken to find the shooter?"

Joe watched the blood drain from Pope's face as the director seemed to shrink in size.

"Governor," Pope said, "you've got to believe me that we're doing everything we can. The scene is being analyzed and we'll start a grid search of the entire mountain tomorrow. We've got every single law-enforcement body in the county questioning everybody they locate in a fifty-mile radius from the scene up there to see if anybody saw anything like a lone hunter or a vehicle leaving the area.

I'm bringing all of our agency crime-scene investigators up here to comb the Bighorns. APBs are out. We'll find something, I'm sure. A footprint, a spent cartridge, something."

Rulon sat back, looking away from the camera at something or somebody in the room. Joe thought, *Stella?*

"What about this?" Joe asked Pope, holding up the small evidence bag with the poker chip he'd found in the grass near the body. Joe had been examining it through the plastic. The chip was old, red, and had a faded stamp of a flower of some kind on one side. It was blank on the other. A residue of dark powder clung to the chip and the inside of the bag, but no print was found on it besides Joe's.

"Urman probably dropped it," Pope said dismissively. "Poker games and elk camps go together like shoes and socks."

McLanahan snorted.

The governor asked the sheriff, "Do you have something to say about this, Mr. McLanahan?"

The sheriff sat back in his chair and slowly stroked his new mustache. "Well, you know Joe," McLanahan said, "I don't mean to beat the devil around the stump or nothin', but ole Joe kinda likes to play to the gallery in situations like this. A poker chip is just a damned poker chip, is what I think."

The governor paused a few beats, as did Pope.

"Get out," Rulon said, waving his hand at the camera as if shooing away a fly. "Get out of the room, Sheriff McLanahan. And take your minions with you. I don't have the time or patience to learn a foreign language."

McLanahan was taken aback, stammered, "This is my building. This is my case!"

"This is my state," Rulon countered. "If you expect any more favors from me, you'll gather up and leave the room. I need to have a talk with my men."

McLanahan unwisely looked to Joe for help, then Pope.

"This ain't wise," the sheriff grumbled, pulling himself to his feet. His deputies followed suit, with Deputy Mike

Reed struggling to keep from laughing. "This ain't wise at all."

Robey asked Rulon, "Do you mind if I stay?"

"Joe, what do you think?" Rulon asked. Joe could feel Pope's eyes on him. The director was miffed he hadn't been asked that question.

"Robey's integral to this case," Joe said.

"He stays then," Rulon commanded.

"And I ain't?" McLanahan said.

"I'll stay and report back," Robey said under his breath to Deputy Reed, who winked.

The governor sat back and waited until he heard the door slam shut.

"Are they gone?" he asked.

"Yes, sir," Pope said.

"What the hell is wrong with him? What's this 'beat the devil around the stump' crap?"

Joe said, "He thinks he's a western character."

"I have no patience with those types," Rulon said, "none at all. There's room for only one character in this state, and that's me."

Joe grinned, despite himself. And he thought he heard Stella giggle off-camera. *Okay, then*, he thought.

"Since they're gone, let's get to it," Rulon said into the camera. "We received word about an hour ago that Klamath Moore is in the state. He plans to come up to Saddlestring with his entourage in tow. Apparently, he already knows about our victim and how he died."

Randy Pope went white.

Joe had seen footage of Klamath Moore being arrested at anti-hunting and animal-rights rallies and being interviewed on cable-television news programs for several years. He was a bear of a man, Joe thought, who came across as passionate and charismatic as he thundered against barbarians and savages who slaughtered animals for fun. There was a documentary film on his exploits that had won prizes in England.

Randy Pope said, "That guy is a nutcase. He's my worst nightmare. How'd he find out about Frank Urman so fast?"

"We'd all like to know that," the governor said. "My guess is one of his followers has a police scanner and heard the whole thing today and tipped off the big man. But we can't spend much time and energy finding out who tipped him off, because in the end it doesn't matter. What does matter is how fast we can find the shooter and put him away so Klamath has to go home. The longer that guy stays here, the more trouble he'll cause."

"Hold it," Robey said, realization forming. "Klamath Moore is the guy who—"

"He's the guy who thinks hunters should be treated the same way he thinks animals are treated by hunters," Rulon said. "He's the main force behind most of the protests you hear about where hunters get harassed in the field or game animals get herded away from lawful hunting types. He sends his people into the hills in Pennsylvania on the opening day of deer season tooting kazoos and playing boom boxes. The media loves him because he's so fucking colorful and politically correct, I guess."

"Why is he coming here?" Robey asked.

Rulon said, "Think about it for a second. The only reason he'd come to Wyoming is to give aid and comfort to whoever shot Frank Urman and the two other hunters we know about."

With that, Joe sat up. Now he knew what was in the two other files Pope had brought with him.

Pope sighed.

"Two we know about," Rulon said. "There may be more for all we know. I've got DCI going over every 'hunting accident' that's occurred in the last ten years. One to four people a year are killed during hunting season, and sometimes none at all."

That was true, Joe knew. Most of the fatalities were the result of carelessness within a group of hunters, and often involved family members—hunters who mistook other hunters for game, hunters who didn't unload their guns, or, the biggest killer of all, hunters climbing fences or crawling through timber when their gun went off and killed a companion or themselves. Rarely were there hunting accidents where the shooter wasn't quickly identified, and most of the time the assailant confessed in tears.

"How long have you suspected this?" Joe asked Pope.

Pope shrugged. "We couldn't be sure. We still aren't, but today . . ."

"Whoever did that to Frank Urman wants us to know it," Rulon said. "In fact, he wants the whole country to know it."

Kiner said, "Jesus," and sat back in his chair. Robey moaned and put his head in his hands.

"And it's not only that," Pope said. "This could kill us as an agency. It could just kill us. Hunting and fishing brings in over four hundred million dollars to the state. Licenses pay our salaries, gentlemen. If word gets out that hunters are being hunted in the state of Wyoming, we'll all be looking for work. We'll be ruined.

"Think about it," Pope continued, as Joe and Robey exchanged looks of disgust. "Using our economic multiplier, we know that every elk is worth six thousand dollars to us. Every bear, five thousand. Bighorn sheep are twenty-five thousand, every deer is worth four thousand, and every antelope is three thousand. The list goes on. If hunters aren't hunting, our cash flow dries up."

"Try not to use that argument with any reporters, Randy," Rulon said with undisguised contempt.

"So that's what this is about," Joe said. "That's why you're up here personally."

"Of course," Pope said. "Why else?"

"Well, an innocent man got killed and butchered, to start," Joe said.

"Save me your sanctimony," Pope spat, "unless . . ." Pope stopped himself. Joe had been braced and ready for Pope to light into him, to accuse him of insubordination, destruction of government property, playing cowboy—all the reasons he'd used to fire him in the first place two years ago. Joe wouldn't have been surprised if Pope brought up the disappearance of J. W. Keeley, the Mississippi ex-con and hunting guide who'd come to Twelve Sleep County to get revenge and had never been heard from again—the darkest period of Joe's life. But for reasons Joe couldn't fathom given their acrimonious history, Pope bit his tongue.

"Unless what?" Joe asked.

"Nothing," Pope said, his face red, his nose flared from internalizing his emotions. "This case is too serious to expose those old wounds. We need to work together on this. We need to put our past aside and find the shooter."

Robey, who had been ready for an explosion and had placed his hands on the edge of the table so he could push away quickly and restrain Joe, looked as perplexed to Joe as Joe felt.

Pope took a deep breath and extended his hand. "I need you on this one. I don't know what it is, but you seem to have a knack for getting in the middle of trouble like this. Plus, you know the area and the people because this is your old district. We need you here on the ground."

Joe shook Pope's hand, which was clammy and stiff, his long, thin fingers like a package of refrigerated wieners.

The governor said, "That's what I love to see. A little love and cooperation among my employees."

"HOW TRAMPLED is the crime scene?" Rulon asked.

"Trampled," Pope said. "We've all been all over it, not to mention Urman's nephew and his friends."

"What about the immediate area? Did you determine where the shot was fired?"

"Not yet," Pope said. "We ordered the forensics team to stay at the immediate crime scene. I was thinking we'd go up there tomorrow when it's light and see what we can find."

Rulon made a face. "Do you think it's possible the shooter is still up there somewhere?"

"Possible," Pope said, "but unlikely. Why would he hang around?"

"Maybe he's waiting for you to all go home," Rulon said. "Look, I have an idea. Before I was governor, I prosecuted a case on the reservation where this poor old woman was raped and murdered in her mountain cabin. There was no known motive and no obvious suspects, but my assistant hired this guy named Buck Lothar to go to the crime scene. You ever heard of him? Buck Lothar is a master tracker; it says it right on his card. He's some kind of mercenary who contracts with law enforcement and the military all over the world to hunt people down. He can look at the ground and tell you how many people walked across it, what they look like, and how big they are. Scary guy, but damned good. Anyway, we hired Lothar to go to the res, and within three days he'd tracked down the loser who did the crime and got away on foot. Lothar produced enough evidence— plaster footprints, fiber from the bad guy's clothes he found caught in a thornbush, a cigarette butt tossed aside we could pull DNA from. We put the bad guy away. I'm thinking we should hire Buck Lothar. I think he lives somewhere in Utah when he's not in Bosnia or the jungles of the Philippines or the Iraqi desert tracking down insurgents. If he's home, I'll send him up there as soon as we can. I'll fly him up on the state plane."

Pope nodded his head the whole time the governor was speaking, warming to the idea.

"Form a ready-response team," Rulon said. "I want you all on it except for Kiner. Work with Lothar, give him whatever he needs and wants. Maybe he can find our shooter."

"That's a great idea," Pope said. "We can use some help."

"And if he can't find anything," Rulon said, "we'll keep him on retainer and you keep your team together until the next hunter goes down."

"The next hunter?" Robey said.

"I'm sure there will be another," Rulon said sourly, "that is, if there are any hunters left in Wyoming after Klamath Moore's press conference tomorrow."

This time, Pope moaned.

"Lothar's expensive," Rulon said, "but you can afford his fee."

"This is coming out of my budget?" Pope said, his voice rising.

"Yes, it is. The legislature is auditing my discretionary fund and I don't want this on it. Think of it as an investment in the future health and welfare of your agency."

"But—"

"No buts. Now, I've got to be going, gentlemen. My chief of staff is signaling me. We've got some Chinese delegation in the next room wanting to buy wheat or oil or something. I've got to go. So get this done and send Klamath Moore back home as soon as you can."

Rulon started to push away from his desk.

"Governor?" Joe said.

"Yes, Joe."

"Sir, I have no doubt that what you say about Buck Lothar is true. I've heard about him. But there's someone else who is as good or better, and who knows this country."

Rulon quickly said, "Joe, we can't go there."

"Nate Romanowski is in federal custody," Joe said. "You could work a deal to get him out. We could use him."

Pope blanched, and Robey said, "Joe . . ."

"Not an option," Rulon said. "Forget it."

"We might need him," Joe said.

"If Lothar can't get it done," Rulon said, "we'll talk. But for now the other option is off the table. Good night, gentlemen."

With that, the screen went black. Before it did, Joe saw Stella's hand with dark-red-painted nails gesture to the governor to follow her. Follow her where? Joe thought.

IN THE HALLWAY, Joe asked Pope if he could take the files home with him to read that night.

"I'd like a copy too," Robey said.

Reluctantly, Pope handed them over. "I'll wait here while you make copies," he said. "But I don't need to tell you how important it is we don't say anything about the fact that we may have a serial killer going after hunters. We aren't sure yet it's the case, and that kind of speculation would kill us as an agency."

"Got it," Joe said, "although with Klamath Moore's press conference tomorrow, it won't be a secret anymore."

Pope winced as if he had a painful tooth.

JOE LEANED against the wall while Robey ran the pages through the machine and the light from the copier strobed the walls.

Kiner had left the meeting with his head down and refused to acknowledge Joe's good-bye.

"What did Kiner do to piss off the governor?" Robey asked.

"He supported the governor's opponent in the last election," Joe said.

"Rulon holds a grudge," Robey said, nodding. "Did you come out for Rulon at the time?"

"No. But I didn't make a point of it, like Phil did."

"Interesting," Robey said. "And what in the hell is going on with Pope? He's had a complete change of heart when it comes to you. I know for a fact for the last two years he's had it in for you, even calling my office to see if he could get any dirt on you."

Joe shrugged.

"Maybe he really does need you this time."

"Maybe."

"But you're not sure."

"There's always something going on with that guy. He's the best and meanest bureaucrat I've ever been around. He should give seminars."

Robey smiled.

Joe fingered the poker chip in the plastic bag. "I don't remember anyone saying they were playing poker. Besides, Frank Urman's clothes were up on the hill in a pile. They were cut off him before he was hung and skinned. I don't see how the poker chip could have just been there, do you?"

Robey shrugged. "Pope shut you down pretty fast."

"I wonder why," Joe said.

"Are you thinking the killer left it as a calling card?"

"Maybe," Joe said.

Robey handed Joe his set of files. "Call me when you've read these and let's see if we can figure anything out."

"I might be up late," Joe said. "I'm having trouble getting the image of Frank Urman's body out of my head."

"Don't worry, I'll be up," Robey said.

OUT OF HABIT, Joe started home in the direction of Bighorn Road before turning around, remembering he now lived in town.

6

SIXTEEN-YEAR-OLD SHERIDAN PICKETT was at her desk in her upstairs room under the pretense of doing homework, which she'd actually completed an hour before. The door was shut, meaning she didn't want to be disturbed. Which, of course, meant nothing to her younger sister, Lucy, who opened it and stuck her head in. "I need to use the computer."

Sheridan quickly hid what she was doing. "Can't you see I'm busy?"

Unfortunately, Lucy could see the computer screen from the doorway and the three IM conversations Sheridan had going.

"I've got homework too," Lucy said. "You've been in here for two hours and I need the computer. Do you want me to tell Mom you won't let me use it? What are you doing, anyway?"

"I said I was busy. Do I need to start locking my door?"

"You do that and Mom and Dad will move the computer to the living room."

Sheridan mumbled a curse under her breath because her sister was right.

"Give me ten minutes," Sheridan said.

"Five."

"Ten!"

"I'll be back."

Sheridan sighed and uncovered her project. She was writing a letter. A letter! Until recently, she'd never written one and rarely received them. With text messaging, IM, and e-mail, letters, she thought, actual letters that were folded and placed in envelopes with a stamp on them were a thing of the past, like phones with dials. She didn't even know where to buy stamps until a few months ago. The little booklet of stamps she purchased was hidden in her purse, and the envelopes and stationery were folded into her dictionary, a gift from Grandmother Missy that she never used because she had SpellCheck. But she'd found out the only way to communicate with her mentor was by sending a letter.

THE LAST few months had been tumultuous. In addition to starting her sophomore year at Saddlestring High, her family had moved from her grandmother's ranch into town. Since Sheridan had grown up isolated from neighbors and traffic, she found the new situation both liberating—her friends were a bike ride away and after all these years she no longer needed to ride the bus to and from school—and stifling. Everyone was so close to everybody else. She no longer saw the mule deer as they floated in the half-dark to the river to drink, or the elk that fed in the shorn hay meadows. It took a month to get used to the sounds outside the house at night—cars racing up the street, dogs barking, sirens. She wasn't sure she liked it.

Her mother's company, MBP Management, continued to do well, even though her mom rarely talked about it like she used to. Since her mom had decided to trim back her hours and turn over more of the workload to her employees, she was able to be home more. Which was good, since her dad was gone so much on special assignments around the state. He called every night, though, except when he was in remote areas without telephones or cell service. Several of her mom's new client businesses were start-ups on the reservation that bordered Twelve Sleep County and was occupied by Northern Arapaho and Eastern Shoshone. The proximity of the new businesses made it easier for her mom to stay close to home. In fact, Sheridan thought, after so many years out on Bighorn Road or on the ranch, their lives were achingly, numbingly dull. When she mentioned this to her mother, Marybeth smiled and said, "Dull is good, sweetie. Dull is good."

Dull was certainly better than the last few months on the ranch, with her parents and her grandmother battling. Grandmother Missy, who didn't look or act like a grandmother at all, wanted them to stay so she could keep some control over them. She was into control. She was also into what she had heard her mother refer to as "trading up." Grandmother Missy, who was still beautiful and petite and looked like a porcelain doll, was on her fourth marriage, this time to rancher and good guy Bud Longbrake. Sheridan liked Bud, who was jovial, hardworking, and kind to her and Lucy. But Missy wanted more, and the rumors of her spending time with a multimillionaire named Earl Alden who had bought a ranch in the area turned out to be true. Everybody in Saddlestring knew about the affair except Bud Longbrake, it seemed. Not that Sheridan was involved in any discussions between her parents on the subject—they weren't like that. Her mother was THE MOM, not a gossipy friend like some of her friends' moms. Sheridan's mom kept a parental distance that used to infuriate her before she realized, slowly, that it was an indication of trust, love, and maturity, and not proof of unreasonable shrewishness after all. For Sheridan, this was a revelation, and she was beginning to respect her mother for being a parent and not her best girlfriend. It was the same with her father, although he was easier to manipulate because her moods and tears turned him into the male equivalent of a Labrador.

What she knew she had learned by overhearing, or what she could intuit from looks or gestures her parents gave each other, or the way they behaved after interacting with Missy on the ranch. Sheridan had overheard her parents agonizing over whether or not to tell Bud and finally deciding it was best to leave, to buy their first-ever house and move out, which they did during the summer. Bud helped them by loaning them a ranch truck and an empty stock trailer. Missy spent the moving days in her bedroom with the shades drawn and didn't say good-bye.

Grandmother Missy had not been to their new house, and Sheridan's only contact with her was a birthday card on her sixteenth birthday. Sheridan put it in a drawer. The situation was different with Lucy, though, who received not only a card but a dozen presents—including an iPod Nano and designer clothing. Sheridan considered her sister her grandmother's in-house spy, her way of infiltrating the new Pickett household. Lucy denied the charge, saying she didn't know why she'd been showered with gifts but at the same time saying she had no intention of sending them back.

"Why should I?" Lucy had said. "A girl needs clothes." To prove her loyalty, she offered to give Sheridan the iPod. Instead, they decided to share it.

"WHAT WERE you doing in here?" Lucy asked again when she came back ten minutes later, her eyes darting from the computer to the desk to the drawer Sheridan had just hidden her half-written letter in.

"Working," Sheridan said. "None of your business."

"Dad's home," Lucy said. "Maybe you can ask him about a car now."

Since Sheridan had turned sixteen, she was legal to drive, and she'd already passed the driving test and had a permit, but the idea of driving herself around was intimidating. She liked to be taken places. So did Lucy, who was unabashed in her desire for Sheridan to get a car so she could get rides with her sister. Lucy loved living in town.

"How's the mood?" Sheridan asked.

"Intense."

"What's going on?"

Lucy said conspiratorially, "Some hunter got shot. But it's much worse than that."

"What?"

"That's what Dad said," Lucy said, then paused for effect before whispering, "And whoever did it cut off his head and took it."

"Oh my God."

Sheridan scrambled out of her chair and both girls huddled near the partially open door to listen. Sheridan heard her dad say, "The governor formed a team to go after whoever did it. He's also bringing in an expert in tracking."

Mom asked a question they couldn't hear, but they heard Dad say, "You've heard of Klamath Moore? He's giving some kind of press conference tomorrow. This thing might turn out to be real big." Sheridan noted the name.

"Honey," Dad said, "it was probably the worst thing I've ever seen."

"I can't imagine," Mom said. "Actually, I can. It makes me sick."

Lucy whispered to Sheridan, *"He said the man was gutted out and hung from a tree."*

Sheridan felt a wave of nausea wash over her.

They listened for a few more minutes until they could hear dishes clanking and their parents sitting down for a very late dinner.

"That's horrible," Sheridan said.

"It is," Lucy said. "You probably shouldn't ask about a car tonight."

"WHAT'S THIS, a letter?" Lucy asked, sitting down at the desk and opening the drawer.

Sheridan quickly snatched it from her sister and put it behind her back.

"Who are you writing to? Who writes letters?"

"That's none of your business."

"Does Mom know?"

Sheridan hesitated. "I don't think so."

"Does Dad?"

"Maybe."

"Oooooh," Lucy said, smiling wickedly. "Let me guess."

"Lucy . . ."

"I think I know."

"Just do whatever you have to on the computer and leave me alone."

Lucy turned with a smirk.

"Before you get going, do one thing for me," Sheridan said. "Google the name Klamath Moore. I'll spell it."

The search produced dozens of entries. Lucy clicked on the top one, which turned out to be Moore's organizational website. There was a photo of him—he was tall, fat, with a flowing head of hair like a rock star—surrounded by Hollywood celebrities on a stage. Behind the stars was a big banner reading STOP THE CRUELTY—LIVE AND LOVE LIFE ITSELF.

"Bookmark it," Sheridan said. "I'll read it later."

SHERIDAN PUT her pajamas on and got ready for bed while Lucy did her homework, a paper on global warming assigned by her fifth-grade science teacher. As she printed it out, Lucy asked her sister, "So, does Nate Romanowski write back?"

Sheridan considered lying, but Lucy could read her face. "Yes, he does." She knew her face was burning red.

"What does he say?"

"He's schooling me in falconry. He's the master falconer and I'm his apprentice."

"Hmmm," Lucy said smugly, tapping the edges of her report on the desk to align the pages. "That's interesting."

"What do you mean?"

"Nothing, it's just interesting."

"Knock it off."

"And knowing this probably means a lot of rides when you get your car."

"I'd rather have a falcon than a car, if I had to choose," Sheridan said. "I think I'd like to start with a prairie falcon, maybe a Cooper's hawk."

That set Lucy back. "God, you're weird."

Sheridan shrugged.

"Sherry, you're in high school. The boys like you—you're a hottie on everyone's list. If you start walking around with a stupid bird on your arm . . ." Lucy was pleading now, her hands out in front of her, palms up. "People will think you're some kind of nature girl. A geek. A freak. And they'll think of me as Bird Girl's little sister."

"Could be worse," Sheridan said.

"How?"

"I could, like, I don't know, like *goats* or something. Or emus. You don't understand. Falconry is a beautiful art. It is known as the sport of kings. Think of that: *the sport of kings.* It's ancient and mysterious. And it's not like the birds are your pets. You don't just walk around with them on your arm like a pirate with a parrot on his shoulder. God, you can be so juvenile sometimes."

Lucy took a deep breath to reload when there was a knock on the door. "You girls all right in there?" said their dad.

"Sure," Sheridan said, "come in."

He stuck his head in but didn't enter, his eyes moving from Lucy to Sheridan and back, knowing he'd inter- rupted something. Sheridan noted the sparkle of gray in his sideburns she'd recently noticed for the first time. He was excited about something, motivated. There was a glint in his eye and a half-smile he couldn't contain, the look he got when he had a purpose or a cause. "Better get going," he told Lucy, who was notorious for extending her bedtime. "No stalling tonight."

After he'd left, Lucy picked up her report in her most haughty manner. "There may not be any more falcons left if the earth keeps heating up," she said, "so you might as well get that car."

"Do you realize that what you just said makes no sense at all?"

Lucy rolled her eyes.

"Good night, Lucy."

"Good night, Sheridan." And over her shoulder as she skipped out of the room, *"Nature Geek. Bird Girl."*

7

THE PROBLEM with my route back at night through the forest is an elk camp that has sprung up on the trail. Three canvas wall tents, four cursed four-wheel ATVs, the detritus of hunters in a campsite: chairs, clotheslines, a firepit ringed with pots and pans. I am grateful they don't have horses who could whinny or spook at my presence and give me away. Because of the canyon walls on both sides, the only way to proceed is through the sleeping camp. Inside the tents are at least four armed hunters, maybe as many as eight or nine. I can hear snoring and the occasional deep cough.

I think: what's wrong with these people? Don't they know hunters are being hunted? Why do they not stay home? What makes them come out here while their fellow mouth-breathing Bubbas are being killed and gutted? Of course, these men have nothing to fear from me, but they don't know that.

I lower the daypack to my feet and my shoulders relax from the strain of the last few hours. The moon is almost full and the stars are crisp and white, pulsing, throwing off enough light that there are shadows. For the past week, I've been preparing for this midnight trek. I've been loading up on foods high in vitamin A, which enhances night vision. Beef liver, chicken liver, milk, cheese, carrots and carrot juice, spinach. I can tell that eating these foods has helped greatly since I've only had to use my flashlight (fitted with a red lens) twice. Another tactic for walking in complete darkness outdoors is called "off-center vision," and I'm good at it. The trick is not to look directly at objects—in my case, landmarks like dead trees or odd-shaped boulders I noted on my trek in—or they'll seem to disappear. Looking at objects full-on directly utilizes the cone area of the retina, which is not active during times of darkness. Instead, I look to the left, right, above, or below the object I'm observing in order to use the area of the retina containing the rod cells, which are sensitive in darkness. If I keep moving my eyes around the object of interest, I can "see" what I'm looking at better than if I shine my headlamp on it. Plus, I'm not blinded afterward by the light. I've done my best to stay near the trail in but not to literally retrace my steps. As on the way in, I avoid soft ground where I may leave footprints as well as brush where I may break twigs in passing through. I stay as much as I can to hard-packed game trails or rock, disturbing as little as possible.

Earlier in the night, after I left my place of hiding where I observed the forensics team do their work, I methodically discarded evidence that could implicate me. I used the geology of the area to my advantage, especially the huge granite boulders piled up on top of each other and the scree on the denuded faces of two mountains I passed. The cache of clean clothing I'd left behind was easy to find in the dark and I changed from top to bottom, from boots to hat. I cleaned the barrel and chamber of my rifle with a field cleaning kit so thoroughly it would be difficult to tell it has been fired recently. I scrubbed exposed skin—the bands of skin between my gloves and coat cuffs, my face and neck—clean of gunpowder residue with wet *wipes I brought in a ziplock bag. My old bloody clothing I wadded up tight and slipped into a crack in the boulder field where it dropped away deep. So deep, I barely heard when it landed. The depth beneath these boulder fields always astonishes me, and I wonder what lives in the dark within them. I imagine that whatever is down there scuttling in the absolute blackness will feast on the blood-drenched clothing and eventually reduce it to scat. The single spent cartridge and rifle cleaning patches I dropped in separate slits in the boulder scree. I washed my skinning knife in a spring-fed creek with biodegradable soap, and buried the washcloth under a log so heavy it strained me to turn it over.*

I am now probably the cleanest hunter in the Rocky Mountains, and the thought makes me smile. It may be silly to take such precautions, I know that. After all, a hunter who has discharged a weapon is not an unusual circumstance. But if caught, I'd rather err on the side of caution. I'd rather be ruled out immediately by the fact that I haven't fired a shot all day. Nevertheless, my hunting license, habitat stamp, and maps of the area are in my backpack and they are proof of my legitimacy. If stopped and questioned, it's the reason I'm out here. The only thing that can possibly link me to the crime if I were stopped is the human head, which is triple wrapped in plastic inside the daypack. As I walk along, I practice hurling it away from me until I become quite good at it. I think I can do it unobtrusively by swinging it behind my back and throwing it off to the side. The trick, I think, is not to turn and watch where it lands, which might draw attention to it. And hope it lands on soft pine needles and doesn't thump against a hollow tree trunk or crash through branches. Luck so far has been on my side. Still, though, I don't want to take any risks.

And I fear that one of the elk hunters will awaken and step outside his tent and see me as I pass through. I don't want to have to use my knife again.

I WAIT outside the elk camp for most of an hour. My hearing is acute. I've identified five breathers in the tents. Two in two tents, one in one. The two in the tent on the left, farthest from the fire pit, are sleeping the hardest. They make lots of noise, and occasionally one of them snorts and coughs. I guess they had the most to drink, or they're heavy smokers, or they're the oldest. Maybe all three. The two in the right-side tent sleep in almost whispers, and they concern me. Men who lie awake at night often breathe rhythmically, as if they are sleeping. Since this is their first night in the camp and the first night elk hunting, one or both could be awake, nervously anticipating the dawn. Or just not comfortable in cots and sleeping bags. But the single breather in the single tent worries me the most. Since he is by himself, I guess he is either the leader if they are friends or more likely a hired hunting guide. Some guides are maternal, and look out for their clients' every comfort. Some are jerks, the kind of men who want to show off their ability and manhood to clients in the hope they'll be talked about and admired. Either way, if the single is a guide and feeling proprietary about the camp and responsible for the other hunters, he could present problems for me.

Experienced tent campers know that animals pass through their camps all night long, especially if they've camped near water or on a trail, which is the case here. The sound of footfalls will not likely produce an automatic confrontation. I'm more worried about someone coming outside to urinate or simply because he can't sleep and seeing me. I work my skinning knife out from beneath my jacket so the handle is within easy reach. And I know, if necessary, I can arm my weapon and fire within two seconds.

From what I can see, they're experienced campers. Their food is hung high in mesh bags far from the camp-

site so as not to attract bears. There are pots and skillets on rocks around the fire pit but they look clean and are placed upside down. Nevertheless, it would be easy to accidentally kick one and make a racket. Another hazard are the thin tent lines attached to stakes in the ground. They're easy to trip over or walk into because they blend so well with the night.

The layout of the campsite is now burned into my consciousness after studying it for so long. When I close my eyes I can see it, and I prefer this picture to the real one, which is confused by shafts of starlight. Eyes closed, I walk through the camp like a shadow, every sense tingling, reaching out, reporting back. I sense a tent line and veer left to avoid it. When my boot tip touches the head of an ax left in deep grass, my foot slides smoothly around it like a fish in a stream confronted with a river rock.

In seconds I'm through the camp. I go a little farther down the trail until I'm once again back in the shadows of the trees before I open my eyes and look back. The camp is still, the hunters sleeping. I think how what I've just done could be dramatized and told around a campfire:

With a human head in a pack, the hunter of hunters walked right through the sleeping elk camp without making a sound. . . .

8

THE MORNING FLIGHT from Denver with master tracker
Buck Lothar on board was late arriving at Saddlestring
Regional Airport, and Joe spent the time reviewing the
files Robey had copied the night before, noting the ever-
growing crowd assembling in the lobby, and wondering
when exactly it had happened that white-clad federal TSA
employees had come to outnumber passengers and airline
personnel in the little airport. Or at least it seemed that
way.

The airport was humble, with two counters for regional
commuter airlines, a single luggage carousel, a fast-food
restaurant that was always closed, and several rows of orange plastic chairs bolted to the floor facing the tarmac
through plate-glass windows. The painted cinder-block wall
across from the airline counters was covered with crooked
and yellowing black-and-white photos of passengers in the
fifties and sixties boarding subsidized jets that used to
serve the area. In the photos, the men were in suits and the
women in hats. Local economic development types had
created a display case to showcase local products, which

consisted of . . . a package of jerky. Outside, a resident herd of six pronghorn antelope grazed between runways, the morning sun on their backs. When Joe was district game warden, he received calls from the county airport authorities every few weeks to come and try to scare the antelope away because the herd tended to spook and scatter when airplanes landed, and at least one private aircraft had hit one. Despite the use of cracker shells and rubber bullets fired into their haunches that dispersed the animals for a few days, they always returned.

Robey sat a few seats down from Joe, reading his copies of the same files. He was dressed in full-regalia Cabela's and Eddie Bauer outdoor clothing for his first day on the crime team, and Joe had stifled a smile when he picked him up that morning. Robey's boots were so new they squeaked when he got up to get another cup of coffee so weak the only taste was of aluminum from the pot itself. Randy Pope paced through the airport, working his cell phone. From snippets Joe could hear whenever Pope neared, his boss was dealing with personnel and legislative issues back in Cheyenne. Pope was a bureaucratic marvel, firing orders, interrupting calls he was on to take more important ones, keeping several people on hold at once, and jockeying between them as he paced.

As the arrival time came and went and an announcement was made by a spike-haired blonde with a tongue stud that the United Express flight from Denver would be at least twenty minutes late, Joe tried to discern the makeup of the people in and around the airport waiting for the aircraft to arrive. It was difficult to count them because they didn't gather in one place so much as flow through the airport and back to their cars—many of which were campers and vans—in the parking lot. He didn't recognize any of them, which was unusual in itself. They didn't fit the profile of those usually found in the Saddlestring Regional Aiport: ranchers waiting for a new employee, usually one who spoke Spanish; a coal bed methane company executive greeting a contractor; or various local families picking up loved ones who had ventured out. Instead, the people waiting had an earthy, outdoor look. There was a wide-eyed, anxious, purposeful attitude about them Joe—at first—couldn't quite put his finger on. A very attractive olive-skinned, black-haired woman struck him in particular. She seemed to be removed from the throng but with them at the same time, caring for her baby in a stroller and thanking those who approached her and complimented her on the child. Joe noted her dark eyes, high cheekbones, and pegged her for Shoshone. She had a dazzling smile and seemed to exist in a kind of bubble of serenity that he found mesmerizing.

"I wonder who she is?" Joe asked aloud.

Robey shook his head, distracted. "We heard from the sheriff of Sheridan County this morning," he said to Joe, sitting back down with his coffee, "following up on Frank Urman. They're trying to determine if he had any known enemies, business problems, wife problems, threats, the usual."

Joe tore his eyes away from the woman and child and looked at Robey.

"They've found nothing to go on so far. Urman was fairly active in city and county government, belonged to a couple of groups—Elks and the American Legion—but kept a pretty low profile. He was well liked and respected, from what they say. He spent a lot of his time hunting and fishing, but that describes just about everybody in Wyoming."

Joe nodded, and tapped the files on his lap. "It describes John Garrett and Warren Tucker too," he said. "I was hoping when I read the files something would jump out at me. Or better yet, that there would be some kind of connection between the victims. Tucker and Garrett were around the same age, fifty-four and fifty-two, I think. That got me going for a few minutes until I saw that Urman was sixty-two."

Robey said, "What, you thought they might be members of the same group?"

"Just thinking."

"The only similarity I could find is that all three are white, middle-aged or older, hunters—and dead," Robey said.

Joe grunted, and looked back at his files.

JOHN GARRETT was a CPA from Lander, Wyoming. Three weeks before, his body was found with a single gunshot wound to the head in the back of his pickup on a side road in the Wind River Mountains a few miles out of Ethete. He'd told his wife he was going deer hunting by himself after work, like he did every year since they'd been married, but this time he didn't come home. She reported his disappearance that night, saying she was worried because he was not answering his cell phone. The sheriff's deputy who found Garrett's vehicle said Garrett's body was laid out next to a four-point buck deer in the bed of his pickup. The buck had apparently been shot and dragged to the truck. Garrett's rifle was found on the open tailgate. Ballistics confirmed it had recently been fired. Judging by the way Garrett's body was found with his head near the cab of the truck, the deputy and others soon on the scene speculated that the accountant had somehow accidentally shot himself with his own rifle in the act of pulling the body of the deer into the back. Imagining a scenario where the accountant accidentally discharged his loaded rifle—which he may have leaned against the tailgate while he struggled to pull a two-hundred-pound carcass into his vehicle—was *not* that crazy. Although forensic technicians couldn't determine the exact sequence of events that led to the accident, enough disparate factors— his discharged rifle, the dead deer, the fact that his body was found in his own pickup—led to the conclusion that it was a bizarre hunting accident with no witnesses. Death had been instant. The slit across Garrett's throat was attributed to him falling on the point of the buck's antler after he'd been shot.

WARREN TUCKER, the second victim, was a former Wyoming resident who owned a construction company in Windsor, Colorado, but still hunted every year in his former state with his son, Warren Junior, a high-school football coach in Laramie. Tucker Senior's body was found the week before in the Snowy Range Mountains near Centennial. According to Tucker Junior's affidavit, father and son were hunting elk from a camp they'd used for twenty years when the incident occurred. Senior took the top of a ridge while Junior positioned himself at the bottom, a thick forest between them. This was a strategy they'd used for years, and it had proved to be very successful. Elk in the area tended to stay in the black timber on the mountainside during the daytime but ventured out in the evening to graze and drink. Therefore, the herd would exit either over the top of the treeless bare ridge where Senior would get a shot at them or down through the bottom meadow where Junior was set up. Which was why he thought it was so strange, Junior testified, when he heard a single shot in the distance near the top of the ridge in the midafternoon because usually there was no action going on that time of day. He'd tried to contact his father by radio for several hours after he heard the shot, but there was no response. That in itself wasn't cause for alarm, Junior said, because if Senior was stalking a big bull he might have turned his radio off to maintain silence. Senior was also getting more forgetful as he aged, and sometimes didn't turn his radio on at all, which drove Junior crazy. But Senior had always shown up before, often with blood on his hands from harvesting his elk for the year. This time, though, when dusk came and went and he'd not heard anything from his father, Junior became alarmed. Junior was an experienced outdoorsman and knew not to set off into the timber in the dark to try to find his father. Instead, he wisely went the short distance back to camp and built a huge fire he hoped his father would see or smell, and kept trying to raise him on his radio. After a few hours, Junior started firing rifle shots in the air, three at a time, and waiting in vain for the sound of answering shots in the distance. None came. It was a very long night.

Junior contacted Albany County Search and Rescue. The county responded with a team at dawn, and with Junior they fanned out and scoured the black timber and the ridge. Unfortunately, it was Warren Tucker Jr. who found his father's battered, naked, upside-down, eviscerated body on the bottom of an old rockslide.

According to the report written by the head of the search-and-rescue team, it was assumed at first that Warren Tucker Sr. had lost his footing at the top of the ridge, perhaps firing his rifle as he lost his balance, and cartwheeled 350 feet down the length of the old slide to his death. The sharp and abrasive nature of the scree on the slide had not only stripped the victim's clothes away, but sliced through his soft belly. Somehow, a broken branch had been thrust into the victim's body in the fall as well, exposing his body cavity.

It was only when the Albany County coroner determined that Warren Tucker had a bullet hole from a high-powered rifle beneath his left nipple that the incident changed from a horrifying accident to a possible murder.

Joe had now read the files, including the burgeoning Frank Urman file, three times. He could see how both the Garrett incident and the Tucker death could initially be classified as accidents. Only when the two were considered together was there a linkage, and it was still not a definitive one.

Joe felt an uneasy rumble in his stomach and looked up at the ceiling of the airport.

"Are you okay?" Robey asked.

"Yup."

"What are you thinking?"

"Nothing good," Joe said. He slid closer to Robey so they could talk without anyone hearing them. "So, let's assume it's the same killer."

"We don't know that yet," Robey said.

"No, we don't. But let's assume. With Garrett, the killer places the body next to a dead deer in the back of a pickup. He also slits Garrett's throat—just like the deer—to send a message that wasn't noticed. With Tucker, the killer ramps up his sociology lesson by gutting the victim the same way a hunter field-dresses a game animal. Again, the message doesn't get through because nobody is thinking of the deaths as murders, or linked in any way at this point."

Robey nodded. "Go on."

"Which must have frustrated the hell out of the killer, to spend all that time and energy making statements nobody gets. With Frank Urman, he doesn't want to leave any doubt at all what he's doing, what he's trying to say. He not only shoots the poor guy, he guts him and hangs him from a tree like a deer or an elk."

"So you're saying we've got a socially conscious serial killer on our hands," Robey whispered, looking over his shoulder to make sure none of the people wandering through the airport were directly behind him. "A guy who is so anti-hunting he's killing hunters and treating their bodies the way a hunter treats big game."

"Maybe," Joe said.

"Which is why Klamath Moore is coming to Wyoming. Not just to protest hunting in general, but to support whoever is doing this."

"Look around you," Joe said. "Who do you suppose these people are here to greet?"

The blood drained from Robey's face. "Oh no," he said weakly.

"HAVE YOU ever fantasized about being hunted?" Joe asked Robey as the two of them stood outside so Robey could smoke a cigar. The United Express flight was minutes from landing, according to the last announcement. Joe could hear the faint buzzing of an airplane in the big cloudless sky, but he couldn't yet see it.

"Say again?" Robey had taken up cigar smoking after going on a fly-fishing excursion to Patagonia, a fiftieth-birthday gift from his wife. Apparently, all the well-heeled fishermen down there ended the day with a cigar and Robey had followed suit. Now, he smoked not only after a day of fishing but whenever he was nervous.

"I think every hunter thinks about it," Joe said. "I have. I don't think there's any way you can be out in the field with a gun or a bow and not at some point let your mind wander and fantasize about somebody hunting you the way you're hunting the animal. I think it's natural, just not something anyone really talks about."

Robey took a short draw, then removed the cigar from his mouth and studied it.

"And I don't think the fantasy is restricted to hunters," Joe said. "I think every fisherman, hiker, camper, and bird-watcher has it at some time or other. Don't tell me you've never had it."

"Okay, I've had it," Robey said reluctantly. "I remember getting that feeling recently in Patagonia. Sort of a chill that went all the way through me for no good reason. I looked all around and couldn't see anyone except a couple of fishermen who'd become my friends. But I couldn't shake it for hours."

Joe said, "Maybe it's come to pass."

Robey made a sour expression. "Pope and the governor may really have something to worry about after all. If what we're talking about turns out to be true, it'll destroy the hunting and fishing economy in Wyoming and maybe all up and down the Rockies. Hunters will just stay home."

Joe nodded. "To be honest with you, Robey, it's not the

hunters who stay home I'm worried about. It's the hunters who don't."

Robey looked up.

"I'm worried about the guys who want to take this killer on. And believe me, there will be some."

"I never thought of that."

"You've never driven up to a hunting camp and looked into the eyes of some of these men," Joe said. "They live for it, and they'll die for it too. And don't assume we're talking about roughnecks and outlaws. There is a certain percentage of men in the world who would feel neutered if they couldn't hunt. The way they see it, it's all they have these days to prove to themselves they're still men. It's a one- or two-week validation of who they really are, or who they think they are. They'll look on this situation as a personal challenge."

Robey shook his head. "Joe, we don't even have proof that the killings are related yet."

"We will," Joe said.

"How?"

"Let's start by finding out if the three of them were killed with the same weapon. I'll ask the head necropsy guy at the game and fish lab in Laramie to take a look at all three autopsies."

"The game and fish guy? Why not state forensics?"

"Our guys are better," Joe said. "We have a lot more game violations than the state has murders."

"Oh."

"Another thing—the poker chip we found by Frank Urman."

"What about it?"

"I didn't read anything about poker chips in the files on Tucker or Garrett. But those cases were investigated as accidents at the time, not murders. There are no listings of items found around the victims, the contents of pockets, or personal possessions gathered up or impounded. The possessions and clothing of the victims could have been returned to the families or they might be in a box at the county sheriff's or coroner's because no one's dealt with them yet."

Robey made a note. "I can ask my staff to follow up on the poker chips, or lack thereof," he said, his cigar bobbing as he talked.

"The more we know about the Garrett and Tucker killings, the more we can help out Lothar the Master Tracker," Joe said. "Those crime scenes are cold as ice, and he won't have any interest in them. So we should try and learn as much as we can."

Robey chuckled as he repeated, *"Lothar the Master Tracker . . ."*

WHEN AN aircraft emerged from the sky, the restless crowd in the airport murmured and began to knot together near the cordoned-off passenger ramp, and the dozen TSA employees grouped near the metal detector eyed them and raised their walkie-talkies to their mouths in alarm.

Pope approached Joe and Robey. He closed his phone for the first time that morning and fixed it in a phone holster on his belt.

"Finally, eh?" Pope said.

"Lothar the Master Tracker," Robey growled melodramatically. Pope glared at him. Joe looked away to hide his smile.

A collective groan came from the crowd as the spiky-haired airline agent announced that the approaching plane was a private jet, not United Express, but that United Express would be landing within five minutes.

"A private jet?" Pope asked, raising his eyebrows. "Saddlestring has private jets?"

"We have a lot of 'em," Robey said. "The Eagle Mountain Club up on the hill has lots of wealthy folks."

As he spoke, the jet touched down on the farthest runway, scattering the herd of antelope. Joe watched it brake and taxi to the far end of the tarmac to the private fixed base operator, FBO—which was larger and better appointed than the public airport—and turn with an ice skater's dramatic flair and stop.

"Who is it?" Pope asked.

"His name is Earl Alden," Joe said, observing as a black Suburban with smoked windows drove out onto the tarmac to greet the jet. A petite and attractive older woman got out of the Suburban and walked up to the unfolding airplane stairs to greet the lone passenger, a tall man with silver hair and a pencil-thin mustache.

"I've heard of him, who hasn't?" Pope said. "Who's the woman?"

Joe sighed. "Her official name is Missy Vankueren-Longbrake."

"She's a babe."

"She's my mother-in-law," Joe said.

He looked at Robey and shook his head with disgust. "Why can't people just get old and sweet anymore?" Joe said, thinking not only about Missy but about his own father, who was suffering from dementia brought on by years of alcoholism. His father was in a facility in Billings. The last time he'd gone to see his father he had to introduce himself as his son. His father had said, "Joe? Joe Schmoe? Go get me a flask, Joe Schmoe."

THE UNITED EXPRESS flight landed five minutes later. Joe stood well back from the crowd, watching as the passengers descended the stairs and walked the short distance across the pavement to the airport. He heard a woman in the crowd gasp, "There he is!"

Klamath Moore wore an oversized white smock that accentuated his tanned and weathered face. His long blond hair blew around his face in the breeze, and he brushed it back and tucked it behind his ears as he gazed at the airport, knowing instinctively how important it was to make a powerful first impression, Joe thought.

Robey said to Joe, "Did we find out how Klamath Moore knew about the circumstances of Frank Urman's death almost before we did?"

"Nope," Joe said. "I've got a couple of other questions as well. One is if I've been underestimating my boss for the last few years. He seems to have picked up on the fact that these hunting accidents weren't accidents mighty quick."

"Self-preservation may be the answer to that one," Robey said. "Guys like Pope can sniff out a threat to their jobs before anyone even knows there's a threat."

"Maybe so," Joe said, not buying the answer.

When Moore stepped inside the terminal, the crowd cheered. Moore raised both of his arms in celebration, and boomed, *"Save the wildlife!"*

"Jesus," Pope said, joining Joe and Robey, his expression sour as if he were sucking on something bitter.

Joe watched Moore shake hands and roughly hug his followers, pulling their bodies into his with a primitive force just shy of assault. But when he got to the dark-eyed woman and her baby, Moore visibly softened and took them into his arms. They left the airport together, Moore carrying the infant, holding hands.

BUCK LOTHAR, perhaps miffed that his arrival had been upstaged, made no effort to make a powerful first impression. Joe approached a tall, angular man at the luggage carousel, said, "Mr. Lothar?" The man shook his head, said, "You're lookin' for someone else."

"That would be me," said a short, overeager fireplug of a man with a close-cropped beard, a lantern jaw, aviator glasses, and eyes that went in two different directions. "I'm Buck Lothar. Can you help me with my gear and my dogs?"

"Sure," Joe said, shaken by his mistake. While Robey and Pope introduced themselves, Joe watched in his peripheral vision as Moore and his contingent loudly filtered out of the airport into waiting cars, trucks, and vans. Lothar's gear consisted of four huge duffel bags made of camo cloth. It was obvious from the military patches on the bags Lothar was well traveled. Two large animal carriers—each with a bloodhound in it—slid down the aluminum leaves of the carousel. "Butch and Sundance," Lothar said.

Joe carried two of the bags, Robey one, and Pope the last, albeit reluctantly. Lothar let the dogs out of their carriers and leashed them.

"Sorry I can't help," Lothar said. "My back. My foot too. I'm still recovering from jungle rot inside my boot and I can't put any added pressure on it."

"Jungle rot?" Pope asked.

"From tracking insurgents in Indonesia," Lothar said, guiding the dogs to a patch of grass so they could defecate. "We got 'em, if you were wondering."

Outside, Joe tossed the bags into the back of his pickup. Pope put his bag into the back of his state Escalade. Lothar stood on the curb and supervised.

"Let's get to the crime scene while it's still warm, gentlemen," Lothar said, rubbing his hands together and chortling.

"I'll meet you up there," Pope said to them. "I've got a buddy to pick up."

With that, Pope roared away from the curb, leaving the three of them with the two dogs.

"I guess we'll all fit into the pickup," Joe said.

"I don't think we have a choice," Robey said.

"I've been in much worse situations than this," Lothar said jauntily, making it sound vaguely to Joe like something the deceased Crocodile Hunter would say.

"A BUDDY?" Robey grumbled as he climbed into the middle seat of Joe's pickup, pushing aside coats and gear, followed by Lothar, who took the passenger seat. "Pope's got a buddy?"

YELLOW CRIME-SCENE tape had been stretched around tree trunks and stapled to pieces of hammer-driven lath in a hundred-foot perimeter around where Frank Urman's body was found. Two state DCI employees had been left to guard the scene, and they scrambled to their feet from where they had been sitting on the tailgate of a pickup chewing tobacco when Joe's vehicle and Pope's Escalade nosed over the ridge near them and parked.

Pope climbed out of his car with his cell phone pressed to his ear, and motioned to the DCI men that they could go. His gesture to them was a backhanded flicking of his fingers as he walked, as if shooing away a street vendor. Joe noticed that the two exchanged dark looks and one mouthed, "Asshole," before they left.

"He makes friends everywhere he goes," Joe said to Lothar, who pretended not to hear.

Since Pope didn't take the time to introduce his friend, Joe offered his hand.

"Joe Pickett."

"Wally Conway," the man said, smiling warmly. Conway

was in his midfifties, with longish, thinning brown hair, bulldog jowls, and an avuncular nature. Joe got the impression Conway was good at putting people at ease, making them smile. He wore a huge down coat that was reversible: camo on the outside and blaze orange on the inside. A hunter. Joe had seen him around town but didn't know him.

"You're an architect, right?" Joe said.

"Yes, and you are—were—the local game warden," Conway said. "I've been following your exploits for years."

Since Conway was Pope's friend he'd no doubt heard, from Pope, that Joe held the record for the most damaged vehicles and equipment in departmental history—and was insubordinate as well. It was hard to gauge how close the two men were since Pope had shown no deference to Conway since they'd arrived.

"I hope you don't mind me crashing the party," Conway said, looking to Pope to explain his presence but Pope was busy on the phone. "Randy and I go back a long way. Since he was in the area, he asked me to come along. I hope you don't mind. I promise to stay out of the way."

"Nice to meet you," Joe said. He liked Conway's pleasantness, and wondered how he and Pope could be friends. But given Pope's sudden change of attitude toward him, Joe thought he might have been too rough on his boss. Maybe, just maybe, there was a human being in there somewhere, he thought.

Pope snapped his phone shut and stepped between Wally Conway and Joe. "You met already," he said.

Joe nodded.

Robey and Lothar stepped forward and Pope introduced his friend to them. Conway asked if there was anything he could do to help out, and Lothar suggested they unload his gear from Pope's Escalade. Which left Joe and Pope standing together.

"What?" Pope asked defensively.

"I didn't say anything."

"You were giving me that look, like, *why are you bringing*

a civilian up here? Like, *why didn't you clear this with the governor?"*

Joe said, "I was?"

Pope stepped forward and shook his finger in Joe's face. "The reason is, Joe, I need people around me I can trust. And I trust Wally Conway."

"And you don't trust me," Joe said.

Pope started to say something but stopped. Instead, he smiled a triumphant smile.

Joe shook his head and turned away.

THE ONLY THINGS Buck Lothar retrieved from his duffel bags for the hike down the hill were a square-shaped camo daypack and a telescoping rod of some kind. He also buckled on a holster. Joe recognized the weapon as similar to his.

"Sig Sauer P229," Lothar said. "I prefer it to the Glock .40 you're wearing."

"I prefer a shotgun," Joe said. "I can't really hit anything with a handgun, anyway." Thinking, *Except from three inches away,* a dark reminder of an episode from two years prior that still gave Joe night sweats and filled him with guilt.

"Tracking stick," Lothar said, answering Joe's unasked question about the rod in his hand. "I'll show you how it works a little later."

"What about your dogs?"

"We'll leave them up here for now," Lothar said. "My understanding is that there have been dozens of you people down there trampling all over the crime scene, right?"

"Right."

Lothar said, "All those scents will just confuse them. If we can figure out where the shooter was and isolate a scent, I might bring them down later. But not until."

Joe shrugged, and reached in the carriers to pet the dogs. They lapped at his fingers.

"Dogs are helpful," Lothar said, "but nothing beats human observation and brain power. We might not even need them."

Robey said, "Wouldn't we need a piece of clothing or something from the shooter to offer to the dogs? Don't they need to have the scent beforehand so they know who they're after?"

Lothar smiled paternalistically. Joe had the impression he did a lot of that.

"It would help if we had an article of the shooter's clothes, of course," Lothar said, "but it rarely happens that we're that lucky. No, these are great dogs. *Great* dogs. With a great handler—me—they can track blind. You see, humans always leave something behind. Even in the worst-case scenario, when they haven't left something obvious like a cigarette butt or a clothing fiber caught in a thornbush, the shooter will have shed dead skin cells. Tens of thousands of them. They fall off the body like rain." Lothar gestured to Robey. "They're falling off *you* as we speak, and settling to the ground all around you." Which made Robey look in vain at the grass around his boots, as if he could see a pile of his dead skin cells.

Lothar continued, "Each dead skin cell is unique to the individual, with a unique scent. If we can find where the shooter stopped for a period of time—and there hasn't been too much deterioration of the ground due to weather or trampling—we should be able to get a scent on him. But first, we need to rule out dozens of things."

Lothar patted the top of one of the carriers. "Butch and Sundance are like my samurai swords. I don't pull them out of their scabbards unless I plan to use them to track down a man."

"Not even for a drink of water?" Joe asked.

Pope snapped, "Joe, they're *his* dogs."

Before Joe could reply, Pope's cell phone burred and Pope snatched it out of his breast pocket and turned away. Conway was visibly uncomfortable, not knowing whether to stand with Joe, Robey, and Lothar or stick close to his friend, who was walking up the hill gesturing as he talked. Joe felt sorry for him.

"What's the deal with those two?" Lothar whispered.

Joe shrugged.

"This isn't one of those *Brokeback Mountain* kinds of deals, is it? I mean, this *is* Wyoming." He grinned to show he was kidding.

Robey sighed and looked heavenward. "You know," Robey said, "I think I've heard just about enough *Brokeback Mountain* jokes to last me a lifetime."

"Yup," Joe said.

"Think about it," Robey said heatedly, "men can't even go fishing together anymore without someone making a *Brokeback Mountain* joke. And now a man can't go hunting without getting butchered! What are we supposed to do, fucking *knit*?"

"Man," Lothar said, still grinning, "you guys are a little sensitive . . ."

LOTHAR AND POPE led the way down the hill with Joe, Conway, and Robey following. Lothar kept up a nonstop chatter. Pope nodded and prodded. He seemed pleased, Joe thought, proud of having Buck Lothar next to him, on his team. While Lothar told the story of tracking down an escaped inmate from the SuperMax prison in Cañon City, Colorado, who had gotten out by shrink-wrapping himself in plastic and hiding among rolls of clean linens, Pope looked over his shoulder at Joe and Robey and beamed at them, as if to say, "He's on *our* side."

"What kind of weapon was used, do we know that?" Lothar asked. Pope looked to Robey.

"No bullet was found," Robey said. "The best guess of our forensics guys based on the entrance and exit holes is a thirty-caliber."

Lothar snorted.

"What?" Pope asked.

Again the paternalistic smile. "A .30 bullet is used in at least eleven configurations that I know of, from a .308 carbine to a .30-06 to a 300 Weatherby Magnum. Plus, if you don't actually have the lead and you're basing the finding on the hole size, it could have just as easily been a 7mm with seven configurations or a .311 with three more configurations! Your shooter could not have used a more common caliber, so this tells us exactly nothing. *Nothing!*"

Robey leaned into Joe and whispered, "TMI." *Too much information.*

THEY DUCKED under the crime-scene tape. Lothar asked Joe to show him where the body was hung and how. The master tracker stared at the space where Urman had been hung as if studying the body that was no longer there. Finally, he grunted as if coming to a conclusion of some kind and began walking the perimeter with his chin cupped in his right hand. Joe started to follow but Pope reached out and stopped him.

"Let him do his job," Pope said softly. "This is what we hired him for."

For fifteen minutes, Lothar studied the ground, the trees, the tape, the horizon, the opposite hillside, before pronouncing the crime scene "as useless as tits on a boar" because of the way it had been trampled by Urman's nephew and friends as well as law enforcement for two days.

"We can just forget this as being any help at all," Lothar said. "We've got to shift focus to where the shot was fired from and where the victim was hit. If we can pinpoint those two locations, we might have something to work with."

"Makes sense to me!" Pope said with enthusiasm.

LOTHAR SAID to Joe, "When starting a search, there are three methods to choose from: the Grid Method, which consists of seven ninety-degree turns followed by seven intersecting ninety-degree turns; the Fan Method, where we start here at the center point where Urman's body was hung and walk away in a straight line fifty yards or so, complete a one-hundred-and-seventy-degree turn and walk back to the center point, then do it again a few feet over from the first trek until a pattern like a fan emerges; or the Coil Method, which is to start at the incident area and circle it, coiling back to it with three-meter spacing. I think this scene calls for the Coil Method."

Joe nodded, studying the folds and contours of the landscape. Behind him was black timber. In front was the saddle slope they had walked down from the vehicles, and on the other side of the slope the timber cleared and rose to a ridge, topped by granite outcroppings that had punched through the grass.

"Any questions?" Lothar asked.

"One," Joe said. "What happened to the prisoner who escaped from the SuperMax in Colorado?"

"I meant about search methods," Lothar said impatiently.

"We can coil around," Joe said, pointing across the meadow toward the rising slope, "but it makes sense to me that Frank was probably shot up there. That's where an elk hunter would be so he could look down on the meadows to the south."

Pope said, "Joe, would you please let the man do his work?"

"Actually," Lothar said, looking where Joe had gestured, "he makes a lot of sense. Joe knows more about animal hunting than I do, so he's probably right. We should start up there. My area of expertise is man hunting, not elk hunting."

Pope huffed and crossed his arms across his chest, chastened.

"So what about the escaped prisoner?" Joe asked.

"Butch and Sundance treed him near Colorado Springs." Lothar sighed, as if the conclusion of the story was so boring and inevitable that it was a waste of his time. "And a guard killed him with an AR-15. He fell out of the tree like a sack of potatoes."

JOE BEGAN to admire Lothar's skill as they crossed the saddle slope. It was like hunting or stalking in super-slo-mo, Joe thought. Lothar moved a foot or two, then squatted to study the ground in front of him for bent grass stalks, footprints, depressions, anything left behind. Robey had stayed back at the crime scene to call his office, and Pope was still there, once again working his cell phone. Wally Conway was with him. As Joe and Lothar distanced them-selves from Robey and Pope, the quiet took over. Whether it was Lothar's caution and study affecting him or the fact that just the day before a man had been hunted down and mur-dered at this very location, Joe's senses seemed to tingle.

The afternoon was cooling down quickly as a long gray sheet of cloud cover was pulled across the sun. Joe felt the temperature drop into the midforties. It dropped quickly at this elevation, and he zipped his jacket up to his chin. A slight breeze kicked up, enough to make the tops of the trees sound like they were sighing. Whirls of wind touched down in the far-off meadows, making dead leaves dance in upward spirals.

He nearly stumbled into Lothar, who had dropped to his hands and knees and lowered his head to ground level until his jaw was nearly in the dirt, looking toward the opposite slope.

"All right," Lothar said, "the story is starting to tell itself to us."

"What story?"

"Come down here and see for yourself."

Joe bent to his hands and knees, mimicking Lothar's perspective.

"What am I looking at?" Joe asked.

"Get your head low," Lothar said, "so low the grass

touches your cheek, and look toward the mountainside over there."

Despite feeling a little silly, Joe all but pressed his face against the ground. When he did, from his new angle, he could clearly see two lines, like dry-land ski tracks, through the grass on the far slope.

"Those are heel marks," Lothar said, "where our shooter dragged Urman from where he shot him to where he hung him in the trees. They're hard to see because the grass is so short and the sun is straight over our heads. But when you get down at grass-stop level, you can see where Urman's boot heels or boot toes bent the top of the grass and made furrows."

Joe grunted, impressed. He assumed Urman's body had been moved to where it was hung up, but surprised it had been moved such a long way.

"It makes sense now when you think of it," Joe said, standing up and brushing bits of grass and dirt from his clothing. "The shooter wanted to hang him from a tree like a deer or elk, and the nearest trees are back where we started. So he had to drag the body across here."

"Which means," Lothar said, "we have a good chance of finding a footprint. If the shooter was dragging the body, he was setting his feet hard into the ground to pull. Urman wasn't a small man, so it would have been hard work. Even though the ground is hard and dry, he might have made a footprint we can find because he was stepping down with so much effort in order to drag the body along."

Joe nodded.

"I've got a question for you," Lothar said. "You mentioned that far hillside would be a good place to hunt because one can see so well from there."

"Yup."

"If it were you, where would you set up to look for elk? Where specifically?"

Joe studied the slope, fixing on the granite outcroppings. Several were too low down to provide a good field of vision into the valley. But there was one outcropping toward the top of the slope that not only offered a hunter enough cover to hide behind, but was high enough up the slope to see well into the valley below. Joe pointed at it. "There."

THE SPLASH of blood on the granite was dark, almost black. It was puncture-wound blood, entry-wound blood. A few feet away on the rock was a spray of bright red arterial blood where the bullet exited Frank Urman's body and tumbled somewhere down the saddle slope. From where Joe stood above the outcropping, he could visualize a herd of elk grazing in the meadows below, downslope.

"From the angle of the entry and the exit," Lothar said, "we can assume without doing any definitive ballistics or testing that the shooter"—he turned and pointed over Joe's head to the top of the ridge behind them—"was there."

Joe followed Lothar's finger. On the horizon was a bump of a knoll—perfect to hide behind.

"Will we be lucky enough to find a shell casing?" Lothar asked aloud but rhetorically as they climbed toward the knoll. "A cigarette? Anything? It's a shame Americans don't smoke anymore. In Europe, Asia, and the Middle East I can always count on finding butts."

Joe labored up the slope directly toward the knoll.

"No!" Lothar said. "Stop. Do not go up there."

Joe stopped, confused.

"Look," Lothar said, and Joe turned. In a depression in the granite, filled with fine sand deposited by the wind over the years, was a definitive boot print.

"It's perfect," Lothar said, as if examining a diamond. "I'd guess size eleven, Vibram soles but worn enough so the track is distinctive, one eighty, two hundred pounds based on the impression. Perfect!"

"It looks fresh," Joe said. "The wind or weather didn't get to it overnight."

"Even better than that," Lothar said, "is I doubt it was

made yesterday. I think it's today's track, last night's at the very worst. Our man is still around."

Joe felt a chill wash over him.

While Lothar slipped his daypack off to prepare to make a composite cast, Joe looked back at the knoll.

"Don't you want to see what's up there?" Joe asked.

"Not now."

"What do you mean? When, then?"

"Not until dark," Lothar said. "We come back at dark."

"Why wait?"

Lothar looked up. "Joe, do you remember how when you got down on the ground down there you could see clearly where the victim was dragged? But that when we were just walking along we couldn't discern a thing?"

"Yes."

"That's why we track at night. It all comes out at night. You'll see what I mean. Trust me."

"But won't he get away?"

Lothar nodded. "He might. But if he took the chance of coming back here, for whatever purpose, he might have reason to stick around."

BACK AT the crime scene, Lothar briefed Pope on what they'd found and how he intended to take action. When Lothar mentioned the possibility of the shooter still being in the area, Joe saw Pope's face drain of color.

"Maybe we should retreat to the vehicles," Pope said. "You know, so we can rest up."

"You mean get out of the line of fire," Lothar said. "Good idea."

As they hiked back to the trucks, Pope said, "The governor is prepared to issue a warning urging hunters to pack up their camps and go home. He's preparing to close all state lands and alert the Forest Service, Bureau of Land Management, and private landowners of what's going on."

"My God," Joe said.

"That's right," Pope said. "I begged him to hold off, to give us a few days. But he's worried as hell that Klamath Moore will spill the beans anytime now. If Moore tells the world that hunters are being systematically hunted down and executed and it looks like the governor has been withholding that information, he'll look worse than incompetent. He'll be liable, and so will we."

Joe grunted.

As THEY walked up the hill toward the trucks, Joe felt vulnerable and exposed in more ways than one. Literally, they were in the open on the slope, and if the shooter was still out there it would be an easy shot with a scoped, high-powered rifle. He looked over his shoulder at the mountainside he and Lothar had just scoured. It wasn't inconceivable that the shooter could drop back over the rim into the knoll he'd used to kill Frank Urman and train his rifle on the four of them.

"AND THE hits just keep on coming," Robey said to Joe and Pope as they approached the vehicles. "I talked with the sheriff's departments in Albany and Fremont counties. One guess what was among the items found in John Garrett's pocket when his body was brought in, and what was found inside the mouth of Warren Tucker but wasn't included in the reports for some unknown goddamned reason?"

"Red poker chips," Joe said.

"Yes," Robey said. "Red poker chips."

"Maybe the governor should close things down," Joe said. "It's looking like what we hoped it wasn't."

"That's what Rulon's new chief of staff is advising him," Pope spat. "She's telling him he should have done it yesterday."

Joe thought, *She's a smart woman.*

Pope reached out and grasped Lothar's arm. "We've got to find this shooter. Do you understand? We've got to find him *tonight*."

Lothar pulled away, annoyed. "I can't promise anything," he said.

"But you need to," Pope said, his eyes bulging with the kind of intensity Joe had seen directed at him several times. "That's why we brought you here. That's why we're paying you. This guy out there is about to destroy my agency."

Lothar looked away from Pope to Joe and Robey and mouthed, *Asshole*.

Wally Conway, who'd seen the interaction, looked away passively, not taking sides.

10

THE AFTERNOON got colder as they waited for darkness. Joe sat in his pickup next to Robey and glassed the timber and meadows through his spotting scope, looking for movement of any kind. He got the strange feeling that the birds and wildlife had subtly withdrawn from the area, clearing the stage for whatever was going to happen later. Robey nervously ate pieces of jerky from a cellophane bag he'd brought along. Piece after piece, chewing slowly. The cab of the truck smelled of teriyaki and anticipation.

Pope appeared at Joe's window, blocking his view through the scope.

"I'm heading back into town," Pope said, not meeting Joe's eye. "I can't run the agency with a cell phone that keeps going in and out of signal range. Let me know how things go tonight. Wally has agreed to stay here with you. Lothar's getting all of his stuff out of my Escalade. He'll have to wait with you."

"You're *leaving*?" Joe said.

"Do I have to repeat myself? You heard me." With that, he patted the hood of Joe's pickup and walked away.

"Bastard," Robey said through a mouthful of beef jerky.

"Would you rather have him here with us?" Joe said.

"No, but . . ."

"Let him go," Joe said. "Wacey Hedeman once said of Sheriff McLanahan—before he was sheriff—'Having him on the payroll is like having two good men gone.' That's how I feel about Pope being here."

"He's scared," Robey said.

"So am I," Joe said, getting out to help Lothar retrieve his gear from Pope's vehicle.

AS DUSK approached, the wind died down and the forest went silent, as if shushed. Joe used his tailgate as a workbench and checked the loads in his Glock and shoved an extra twelve-shot magazine into the pocket on the front of his holster. He loaded his shotgun with double-ought buckshot and filled a coat pocket with extra shells. Because of the cold stillness, the metal-on-metal sounds of his work seemed to snap ominously through the air. He'd strapped on his body armor vest and pulled on his jacket over it, and filled a daypack with what he thought he might need: flashlight, radio, first-aid kit, bear spray, GPS unit, rope, evidence kit, Flex-Cuffs, a Nalgene bottle of water.

Lothar approached him. "I think it should just be the two of us," he said.

Joe looked up at the back of Robey's head in his pickup. He could see his friend's jaw working as he ate more jerky. "I hate to leave Robey alone," Joe said. "He's not used to this kind of thing."

Lothar said, "Man tracking isn't a group sport. The more people we have, the more likely we'll blow our advantage. You have the experience and the equipment and he doesn't. Simple as that. Besides, we need someone here in camp with a radio in case we need to relay information. If all of us are deep in the timber without a way to call for help if we need it, we're screwed."

Joe started to object when Robey swung out of the pickup. "I overheard," he said, "I'll be fine, Joe. I'm a big boy."

Wally Conway, who'd stood by silently watching Joe prepare his weapons, said, "I'll be here with him."

Joe felt bad about overlooking Conway, said, "You're right, I'm sorry. But at least call the sheriff's office so he can send up a couple of deputies. Or get those DCI boys back that Pope sent home. You may need help and we may need reinforcements."

"I said I'm fine," Robey said, adding some heat to his voice. Joe didn't want to press it at the risk of further alienating his friend. Robey had rodeoed in college until he broke both his pelvis and sternum in Deadwood, which is when he decided to get serious about law school. Although he'd gotten plump and soft over the years, he didn't want to acknowledge the fact.

"Robey—"

"Really," Robey said to Joe with force. "Just get me set up with a weapon and a radio and I'll be here when you guys get back."

"I can shoot," Conway said weakly. "I've hunted all my life. I can help out any way you want me to."

Lothar looked away as if he had nothing to do with the quarrel.

"I'm just wondering about our strategy here," Joe said to Lothar. "There's just four of us. I was thinking we might want, you know, an overwhelming show of force."

Lothar shook his head. "That's old school. We're going for a small, deadly force here. Matching wits with the bad guy and taking him down with as little fuss as possible. Isn't the idea here to get this guy before he makes the news? Isn't that what Pope and your governor want most of all?"

Joe grimaced. "Yup."

"Then let's do it this way," Lothar said. "We can always apply overwhelming force later if we need to. Your governor can fill the trees with the National Guard and the sky with helicopters. But in my experience, and we're talking fifteen years of it on just about every continent, it's better to go light and smart instead of dumb and big. If we can find this guy before he knows we're on him, we lessen the chance of unnecessary casualties. Plus, if we get him, we'll look damned good and maybe you can send this Klamath Moore guy home."

Joe looked at Robey and Conway. "You sure you don't want to call for backup?"

"I'm sure," Robey said.

Conway nodded, deferring to Robey.

Against his instincts, Joe let it lay.

FAR ENOUGH AWAY from the vehicles not to be overheard, Joe pulled out his cell phone. Despite what Pope had said about signals fading in and out, he had all bars. *"Pope . . ."* Joe hissed, as if it were a swear word. He punched the speed dial for home. While he waited for someone to answer, he saw Lothar showing Robey and Conway how to arm and fire an AR-15. Robey was sighting down the open sights as Lothar talked him through it.

Sheridan answered.

"Hi, Sherry," Joe said. "Is your mom around?"

I DON'T WANT to come out again, but I have no choice. When I saw him in the airport and found out why he's here and what he's doing, I knew I had an opportunity I may never get again. He has forced my hand. The question is whether or not he's doing it deliberately as part of his plan or it's something that just happened. But when I saw his face, heard his voice, saw that his attitude hadn't changed, I knew at that second that I would be out again, despite the fact that I'm physically tired and my absence may be noted.

I'm out of my vehicle and into the forest as the sun

drops behind the mountains. I move much more quickly than before, more recklessly than I am comfortable with. I skirt the path I blazed but once again I have no choice but to walk right through the middle of the elk hunters' camp on the trail. Luck is with me because the hunters aren't back yet and the camp is empty. Luck is also with them.

My objective is to get to the saddle slope where I made my statement yesterday and isolate my target and kill him before he knows I'm back.

I know the terrain so well now. It seems to flow under my feet. I feel like I'm gliding. . . .

11

IN THE opaque blue light of the full moon, Joe saw what Lothar meant when he said it all comes out at night. Joe stayed back, giving Lothar room to work, nervously rubbing the stock of his shotgun with his thumb, watching the master tracker work while keeping his ears pricked to sound and peering into the shadows of the forest for errant movement.

Lothar started at the single good boot print they'd found earlier. As the moonlight fell on the short grass it created shadows and indentures that couldn't be seen in the day. Using a slim flashlight held inches above and parallel to the ground, they could detect more now-visible footprints going up the hill toward the knoll. Lothar placed the tip of the tracking stick on the depression where the ball of the shooter's foot had pressed into the grass, and telescoped out the instrument to the ball of the second. With a twist of his wrist, he locked the tracking stick into the exact length of the shooter's stride.

"Thirty inches," Lothar whispered to Joe. "He has a

normal stride for a man in good shape. At that rate, even weighted down with a weapon and a light pack, we can expect him to travel at a normal pace of a hundred and six steps per minute, four to eight miles a day. A healthy and well-fed man can sustain this pace for four days."

Joe nodded.

"We'll use moonlight as long as we can," Lothar said, twisting the flashlight off. "We can see his footprints in the moonlight—"

"Which amazes me," Joe said.

Lothar grinned. "It's all about the ambient light. It strikes at a different angle and in a different way and it brings the shadows and depressions of a footprint out of the ground. It gives the ground a whole different texture. And now that we know the shooter's stride length, if we lose the track—like if he was walking on solid rock or something—we can estimate where he should have stepped and maybe find a dislodged stick or a mud transfer or something."

"Since we've got his track, why aren't we using the dogs?" Joe asked.

"Too loud," Lothar said, shaking his head. "Dogs might run him down, but of course he'd know we were behind them. This way, if we're able to find him purely on our own, we might catch him totally by surprise."

THERE WAS nothing left behind in the knoll they could see with the red flashlight lenses, no spent rifle cartridges, candy wrappers, cigarette butts, or definitive markings to reveal the shooter's height or weight. But Lothar had no doubt this was where the shot was fired by the way the grass was still pressed down in places and the clear view it afforded of the granite outcropping where Frank Urman was hit. They picked up the track as they cleared the top of the ridge, and in the moonlight it was so obvious even Joe could see it with his naked eye. Only once did Lothar need to use the flashlight and his tracking stick to find it again.

They followed the boot prints for half an hour as the moon rose. Because they were not using artificial light, Joe's eyes adjusted and he found himself able to see well by moon and starlight.

"There's something I don't get," Lothar whispered to Joe. "I get the feeling he came here the first time taking every possible precaution because I simply don't see his tracks on the way in or out, but that when he came back the second time he was sloppy and careless, just trucking along. What made him drop his guard?"

Joe shrugged. He was wondering the same thing.

"I like it," Lothar said, patting his weapon. "If he's become sloppy, we have a better chance of taking him down."

"That's what you want to do?" Joe asked. "Take him down? How about we try to arrest him first?"

Lothar snorted. "Do you think he'll let us?"

"I say we try."

Lothar grinned wolfishly. "I say we light him up and smoke his ass."

IT WAS difficult to walk without making any sound, Joe found. There was too much downed, dried timber and finger-thick branches that snapped when stepped on. Joe felt remarkably uncoordinated, and it seemed like he made twice as much noise as Lothar, who had a way of walking deliberately and silently by leading heel first and shifting his weight forward into each step. Joe tried to mimic the technique, stepped on an errant twig, whispered, *"Sorry!"*

Lothar stopped in the shadows, and Joe could tell by the angle of the tracker's head and the set of his shoulders he was about to receive another lesson in the art of man tracking.

"You've got to be quieter," Lothar said in an urgent whisper.

"I'm trying," Joe said.

"If he hears us he could set up an ambush."

"I *know* that."

"If we can maintain silence we might hear him first."

"You don't need to tell me that," Joe hissed back.

"Sound travels at a speed of seven hundred and twenty miles per hour, or about eleven hundred feet per second. The forest will slow that down a little, but if we hear something we can estimate distance. And if we see a flash of light like from a headlamp or flashlight, we can use sound and light to determine how to close in on him."

"So we can light him up and smoke his ass," Joe said with sarcasm.

"That would be correct. So step lightly."

WHILE THEY moved through the dark timber, Joe recalled his call to Marybeth. When he told her about seeing Earl Alden's jet land at the airport and Alden being greeted by her mother, there was a long silence until Marybeth sighed and said, "Here we go again."

When Marybeth asked when he'd be back, Joe said, "Early tomorrow," with a kind of heavy sigh he hoped would mislead her into thinking his assignment was benign. As usual, it didn't work. Under sharp questioning, he told her what had gone on, from seeing Klamath Moore and his throng at the airport to Randy Pope going back to town, leaving Joe up there with Conway, Robey, and Lothar the Master Tracker.

"There are so many things wrong in what you just told me," she said, "I don't know where to start."

"I know," he said sourly.

"What is Randy Pope up to?"

"I don't know."

"I wish you could just come home."

"Me too," Joe said. "I operate best on the margins, not in the middle of a team."

"Having Nate around hasn't hurt either," she said.

"True."

"Joe, be careful. Something about this doesn't sound right."

Joe agreed, and asked her to contact Sheriff McLanahan's office or Phil Kiner and request backup, whether Robey said he needed it or not.

NOW, AS HE shadowed Lothar through the shafts of moonlight in the trees, he wondered whether the shooter was just as aware of them as they were of him. Given the skill and experience the killer had shown (at least on his initial stalk and kill of Frank Urman), Joe didn't doubt the shooter was fully capable of making a stand and possibly even leading his pursuers into a trap. Maybe, Joe thought, the shooter's sloppiness was deliberate in order to make his tracks easy to follow. To lure them in. And despite Lothar's bold talk, Joe had no idea how the tracker would really react in a situation, whether he'd stand and fight or panic.

Joe wished he'd spent more time with Sheridan and Lucy that morning, wished he'd made love to Marybeth rather than inventorying his gear for the fourth time. Wished he wasn't on a dark mountainside with a man he didn't trust tracking a killer he couldn't fathom.

"WANT A piece of jerky?" Robey asked Wally Conway in Joe's pickup.

"No thanks," Conway said. "I don't think I could eat anything right now."

"I'm just the opposite," Robey said. "I can't stop."

"I guess people react to fear in different ways," Conway said.

The moon had risen over the treetops and was bathing the top of the pines and the mountain meadows in a ghostly blue-white. Although it was getting colder, Robey hadn't yet turned on the engine. He kept his window a quarter open as well, so he could hear shouts or shots if there were any. The truck radio was set to a channel Joe fixed for the handheld he had taken with him two hours before. There hadn't been a report from Joe and Lothar since they walked down the saddle slope. Lothar had told Robey not to expect one until they decided to head back. Lothar also asked him to try not to call them and break radio silence unless it was an emergency.

The longer it went, the more excruciating the wait became for Robey. He wanted to be home in his leather recliner watching television with a fire in the fireplace. He did not want to be in a freezing pickup in the dark with a friend of Randy Pope's whom he didn't know.

Finally, Robey said, "Wally, since it looks like we'll be here awhile, can I ask you a question?"

He could see Conway smile in the dark, see the flash of teeth. "Sure."

"Why are you here?"

Conway chuckled. "I was wondering that myself. I kind of feel like I've been thrust upon you guys, and it's an uncomfortable place to be, let me tell you."

Robey appreciated Conway's candor. He wondered how far it would go. "How long have you known Randy Pope, then?"

"It seems like forever," Conway said. "Jeez . . . thirty years, I guess, although that's hard to believe. Growing up, I never thought I'd know anybody thirty years. I met Randy at the University of Wyoming in Laramie. Heck, we were in the same fraternity and then we hunted together for years after that. I'd like to say we kept in touch but you know how guys are. I wouldn't hear from him for five years but I'd see him at a Cowboys game or something and we'd pick up the conversation we were having the last time we talked. That sort of thing drives my wife crazy, you know. She thinks men don't know how to be friends properly, and I think we do it exactly right. Why talk when you have nothing to say? I suspect it drives most women crazy, the way men do that."

Robey said, "So you haven't talked to him for a few years?"

Conway shook his head. "Nope, but like I say, that isn't all that unusual."

"What did he do—just give you a call this morning and say, 'I'm in the area, let's go on a manhunt'?"

Conway chuckled again. "That's not too far from what happened."

"I can't believe you came."

"I guess I didn't know all the circumstances," Conway said. "I thought it might be a chance to catch up with Randy, you know? But he's a busy man now that he's the director of the game and fish department. Today, he spent almost the whole time on his phone. But I'd like to do my part to catch the bad guy as much as anyone else. We can't have someone like that around."

"Nope."

"So you've known Joe Pickett for a while, eh?"

Robey nodded. "Yes. We fish together. There's no greater friendship."

"Did you know the game warden before Joe? Vern Dunnegan?" Conway asked. "He was quite a character."

"I knew him," Robey said without enthusiasm.

"He was a throwback. He kind of made his own law, if you know what I mean."

"That's one way to put it," Robey said. "That's why he's still in the Wyoming state pen."

Years before, Vern Dunnegan had retired as a game warden for the state and came back to Twelve Sleep County as the landman for a natural gas pipeline company. He used his relationship with local landowners and politicians to secure a right-of-way through the mountains but involved others—including some of Joe's friends—to eliminate a population of endangered species in the way. The crime spiraled out of control and resulted in murder and the attempted murder of Marybeth. Dunnegan was convicted and sent to prison. Joe shot him in the butt with a shotgun, and word was Dunnegan still had a pronounced limp.

"I know about that," Conway said. "But the man did right by me, and I'll always owe him for that."

Robey turned in his seat, confused.

Conway said, "We live here for the quality of life—to be able to go into the mountains to hunt and fish or just think restful thoughts. To think there's somebody up here assassinating innocent men—especially friends of mine—angers me to my core. Vern did us all a good turn once that allowed us to get on with our lives. I'm happy to do what I can to help."

Robey looked out over the darkened mountain landscape, noted the moon had risen a few more inches, then turned to Conway.

"What do you mean, friends of yours?"

Conway looked quizzically at Robey. "You mean Randy didn't tell you?"

I AM UPSET that my target is not at the crime scene and feel that I may have not only wasted my time but exposed myself unnecessarily. Aren't they supposed to be up here? Aren't they supposed to be investigating the killing?

I've chosen not to use the knoll again. It would be too obvious and risky because they're probably watching it. So I settle in farther up the ridge, behind some weathered rocks that provide both shelter and a place to take aim. When my breathing calms down from the long trek I let my eyes get used to the dark and peer through the scope of my rifle. Like all good-quality scopes, it gathers more light than the naked eye and I can see down the slope to where I hung Frank Urman in the trees. The band of light-colored material is crime-scene tape, I realize, and for a moment I

*expect to see my target within the perimeter. But he isn't
there. No one is there. I fight the building rage that has
formed in my chest and pushed upward into my throat.
I've taken a chance I shouldn't have taken. For nothing.*

*But I think I hear talking. It is low, more of a muffled
murmur than actual words. Sound carries up here, and
the distance of origin can be deceptive. I lean down hard
on the scope, sweeping it slowly through the trees, trying
to find the source. The wind shifts almost imperceptibly
and I realize the voices are coming not from the trees or
meadow but from above them.*

*I slowly climb the hillside with my scope until I can
make out the outline of a pickup truck. I can't see it so
much as make out its blocky outline against the star-
splashed horizon. Only one vehicle, which seems odd since
there were at least four men at the airport. Where has the
other vehicle gone?*

*Despite training the crosshairs of my scope on the
windshield for what seems like half an hour, I can make
out nothing, and no one, inside. If they are in there, and
I'm sure they are because I hear voices, they are talking in
the dark. I consider a blind shot but decide against it. I
don't do things blind. I strategize, I plan, then I act. I don't
just fire away if I don't know who I'm shooting at. It's the
first ethos of hunting: know what you're aiming at.*

*Sooner or later, someone from inside the pickup will
open a door and trigger the dome light and I will see who
is inside. Or turn on a light to look at a map.*

*But I can't wait all night. I'll be missed. This has to be
done soon or I'll have to abort and go back. But after taking this risk and having this opportunity, I don't want to
simply leave. I can't just leave.*

*Ayman al-Zawahiri of al-Qaeda, whom I've studied,
perfected a strategy he used for maximum casualties. In
Nairobi, Kenya, he set off two bombs timed a minute or so
apart in front of the American Embassy. The first bomb*

*created minimal damage but the surprise and impact of it
outside on the street made scores of people inside the embassy building rush to the windows to see what had just
happened. When the second bomb went off, hundreds were
killed or severely wounded by the shattered windows they
had just exposed themselves to. He justified the action by
saying that although he was sacrificing civilians and fellow Muslims, it was still for the greater good because it
effectively unleashed more terror on the infidels.*

It was a lesson learned.

And one to be applied.

THE FOREST had closed in and darkened around Joe and
Lothar and they moved silently under the narrow canopy.
They were on a game trail through the heavy brush.
Lothar kept nodding, as if saying, *yes, yes, yes, we're getting closer.* Ahead of them, through the dark timber, Joe
could both see and sense an opening lit by moonlight. Before breaking through the brush into the meadow, Lothar
stopped and looked over his shoulder at Joe, his eyes wide
and excited.

"What?" Joe mouthed.

Without speaking, Lothar pointed just ahead of him at a
space between two branches that opened into the meadow.
At first, Joe couldn't tell what Lothar was trying to show
him.

Not until Joe crouched a bit and saw how the moon lit
up the broken thread-thin strands of a spider's web did he
understand what Lothar was telling him. The strands un-
dulated in the near-perfect stillness like algae in a stream.
Which meant that there had been a web across the game
trail that had been broken through just moments before.
Joe felt the hairs on the back of his neck stand up, and an
involuntary chill swept through him that threatened to
make his teeth chatter.

In the timber on the other side of the small meadow a twig snapped.

They were on him.

Lothar nodded his head and gestured toward the black stand of pine trees on the other side of the meadow while unslinging his automatic rifle. Lothar used the barrel of his weapon to indicate to Joe that he should move to the left. Using Lothar's heel-first technique in the soft loam, Joe managed to distance himself about twenty feet without stepping on a branch or knocking his hat off in the heavy brush. As he moved he thumbed the safety off his shotgun and peered into the dark wall of trees, willing himself to see better.

The sharp voice came so suddenly he nearly dropped his shotgun.

"Drop your weapon! Drop it! Throw it out where I can see it!"

The man giving the command did so with authority that masked his exact position. Joe thought he heard a note of familiarity in the voice but couldn't place it.

"Throw it out. *Now!*"

"Okay," Lothar said. "Calm down, calm down."

"Is there anyone with you?" the voice asked.

Joe thought, *He doesn't know I'm here.* Would Lothar give him away?

"I'm coming out," Lothar said, stepping from the brush into the meadow, the moon bathing him in shadowed blue. He held his AR-15 loosely at his side. Joe could see Lothar's face in the moonlight. He was grinning.

What was Lothar doing? Why didn't he identify himself as an officer of the law? *Should I,* Joe asked himself, *and give away my position?*

"I said drop it!" the voice bellowed, and Joe detected a note of panic. He also realized where he'd heard the voice before.

Joe shouted, *"Lothar, no . . ."*

But before Joe could finish, Lothar howled a piercing rebel yell and leaned back and swung his weapon up, pulling the trigger as he did so, the automatic fire ripping the fabric of the night wide open, the muzzle flashes strobing the trunks of the trees.

"No!" Joe screamed, his voice drowned out by Lothar's AR-15 and by the single, deep-throated bark of a hunting rifle from the trees. Lothar's head snapped forward from a single high-powered bullet that hit him in the throat above his body armor, and he was thrown back, his weapon firing straight up into the night sky until it jumped out of his dead hand.

Joe kicked his legs back and let himself drop heavily to the ground, his shotgun out in front of him. The muzzle flashes of Lothar's weapon were seared blue-green into his vision in a pyrotechnic afterimage and he could see nothing, and the racketing automatic fire had made his ears ring. For good measure, he rolled to his left, hoping there would be no more shots.

"It's Joe Pickett!" he yelled out. "Hold your fire!"

From the shadows, Chris Urman, Frank's nephew, said, "Oh my God."

"I'm putting down my weapon," Joe called, peering down the barrel.

"Oh no," Urman said. "Oh no. *Who did I just hit? What have I done?"*

Urman's hunting rifle sailed out of the wall of pines, catching a glint of moonlight. Urman followed, holding his face in his hands.

A FULL AUTOMATIC WEAPON, at least a mile behind me, deep in the forest. What can that possibly be about? All I know is that some kind of mistake has been made, some kind of foul-up. And not by me. This is why they should never be allowed to leave the cities, where they belong, and come up here.

But in chaos, there is opportunity for the one who keeps his head.

Now I know why there are only two in the pickup truck on the horizon; it's because the others have been tracking me. I wonder if the men in the truck heard the gunshots as well? If so, I prepare myself and ease the safety off my rifle with my thumb. . . .

"Did you hear that?" Robey said, sitting up straight. He'd spent the last ten minutes trying to reconcile and process what Conway had told him about Randy Pope, about the other victims. Everything he had thought about the crimes had turned out to be potentially wrong, as if the foundation he'd relied upon was not only crumbling away but had been blown to bits. The information was explosive, so much so that Robey had briefly considered calling Joe with it, urging him to come back to the truck so he could tell him the world as they both knew it had suddenly changed. The only reason he didn't was concern for Joe's safety if Robey broke radio silence at the wrong time.

"I heard something," Conway said.

Robey said, "It sounded like automatic fire. Lothar has an AR-15, so it was probably him."

"Maybe they found our man," Conway said with gravity.

"God, I hope so," Robey said. "I hope they call in to tell us what's going on."

There was a pause as both men stared at the radio under the dash, at the softly glowing light of the channel.

"Talk to me, Joe," Robey whispered.

"Should we call him?" Conway asked.

"We'll give it a couple of minutes. I'd rather they call us so we know whatever happened is over."

"What if they don't?"

"I don't know," Robey said, feeling a line of sweat break across his upper lip like an unwanted mustache.

"JESUS, WHO IS THIS GUY?" Urman said to Joe. "Why didn't he identify himself? He scared the shit out of me, and then he started blasting—"

"His name is Buck Lothar," Joe said, pulling himself to his feet as the realization of what had just happened hit him. He ran to where Lothar was splayed out in the grass. No pulse, just involuntary twitching of his arms and legs. Blood flowed through the dry grass under his body, smelling hot and sharp.

"He was hired by the governor to track the man who shot your uncle," Joe said.

"Ah, man," Urman cried, dropping to his knees before Lothar's body. "I'm so sorry. Is there anything we can do? CPR or something?"

"I don't know," Joe said.

Urman bent over and struck Lothar's chest with his fist. The body bounced. "Anything?" he asked.

Joe shook his head.

Urman hit Lothar again and again, so hard Joe thought he heard the dull snap of a rib.

"That's enough," Joe said. "He's gone."

Urman sat back, his face so pale it was the same blue-white shade of the moon and stars. "I killed a man," Urman said.

"It was self-defense," Joe said. "I'll back you up on that one all the way."

"Jesus," Urman said, his eyes glinting with tears. "All that time in Iraq and I never killed anyone. . . ."

"And all this time," Joe said, his stomach turning sour, "we were following *you.*"

THE FRONT of the pickup Robey and Conway were in bucked slightly and a sharp crack snapped through the night. Robey reacted instinctively by grabbing the steering wheel with both hands.

"What was *that*?" Conway asked, his voice high. "A stray bullet?"

"I don't know," Robey said. "Listen . . ."

He could hear a hissing sound outside and felt the truck begin to list to the side. "I'm going to see what happened," he said, reaching for the door handle.

I SEE the dome light come on inside the pickup, illuminating the two men inside. I'm confused momentarily. I don't recognize them at first. Then I do. The one on the driver's side was in the airport today with the game warden and Randy Pope waiting for a passenger on the plane. The other at first confounds me because I didn't expect him here, never saw it coming.

I can't believe my good fortune. It's as if he was delivered to me, presented as a gift. He was the least guilty of them, but guilty all the same.

I quickly work the bolt action and chamber another round. The acrid but sweet smell of gunpowder haloes my head from the first shot. I make a mental note to retrieve the spent brass before I leave.

The pickup door opens and the man I don't know gets out. He walks to the front of the truck, squats down to look at the tire I shot as it flattens. As I thought, the action drew him out.

I clearly hear the man squatting by the tire say, "Come look at this," and see my prey reach for his door handle and I thank my good fortune once again and know my plan has worked. I put the crosshairs in the center of the target's chest and squeeze the trigger. An instant before the shot bucks the rifle upward, I see the other man unexpectedly stand up in the line of fire, but it's too late to stop . . .

CHRIS URMAN was explaining to Joe that he'd returned to the crime scene to track the killer on his own, that he'd been "less than impressed" with the sheriff and his ability to pursue his uncle's killer in a timely fashion, that he'd participated in enough night patrols in the Anbar Province to follow a track and keep his cool, when they heard the shot.

"What was that?" Urman asked.

"It came from back at the truck," Joe said, fighting a feeling of cold dread. He knew it wasn't Robey trying to signal him because he would have used the radio. It was someone else. It was Frank Urman's killer.

Joe snatched the radio from his belt as two more quick shots rolled through the mountains.

I'M OUT of breath from running down the saddle slope and up the other side to the pickup. The night is cold and still. The only sound I hear is from my hard breathing.

As I jam the poker chip into my prey's gaping mouth I hear the radio inside the truck come to life.

"Robey? This is Joe. Is everything all right?"

No, Joe, it isn't.

I have a decision to make. I had much more planned for my target but this may have to do for now.

"Robey, can you hear me?"

I have the urge to pick up the mike and tell him Robey can't hear him, but I don't.

And I hear the sound of a motor, another vehicle grinding up the road from the direction of town. I see a splash of headlights in the trees less than a mile away, hear an engine downshift.

As I step over the other body, apparently a man named Robey who had the bad luck to step in front of my first shot, I hear the radio again, the voice on the other end more urgent.

"Robey, this is Joe. Talk to me, Robey. Please talk to me. . . ."

I bend down and place my gloved hand on Robey's face and gently push his eyelids closed. I ask God to forgive me. This man did nothing to deserve this, and I truly am sorry.

12

AT THE SAME TIME, Wyoming Game and Fish Director Randy Pope pulled his departmental SUV into the lighted parking lot of the Saddlestring Holiday Inn. He was both tired and anxious, and a little surprised he'd heard nothing from Buck Lothar over the radio. He checked his wristwatch: 10:15 P.M. It just seemed later. The wait was killing him.

He'd had an unsatisfying dinner by himself in that Burg-O-Pardner restaurant on Main, finishing only half his steak, drinking only half his beer. The conversations at the tables around him among the locals were all about the murders of hunters in the mountains, how Governor Rulon may declare a state of emergency and lock all of them out of their own land, deny them their heritage and their rights. The word was out and it would spread like wildfire. There was no way to contain it, despite their best efforts. The news would be statewide quickly. Would it go national? These people, he thought. They had no idea what kind of pressure he was under. He'd kept his head down but was recognized nevertheless. When a fiftyish man who looked more like a bear than a human approached his table and asked him what the Game and Fish was doing to solve the crime, Pope said, "Everything we can."

"Then why in the hell are you sitting here eating a damn *steak*?" the local asked.

ALTHOUGH HE could have used a side door and gone straight to his room, Pope used the main entrance so he could pass the front desk. He'd clipped the handheld to his belt in case Lothar or Pickett called him. The hotel had been built in the early 1980s when it must have made some kind of sense to put a huge fake waterfall in the cavernous lobby to simulate something tropical. The sound of stale rushing water struck him as incongruous. Rooms rose on three sides of the lobby for three floors. Most were empty.

"Any messages?" he asked the night clerk, an attractive, slim blonde with a mesmerizing New Zealand accent. She was the reason he came in through the front doors.

"Why, yes," she said, handing him a message. "You're to call the governor." Her eyes widened as she said it, which he liked. She was impressed with his importance, finally. The night before, when he had explained to her who he was, she didn't get it. After going over how many employees he had under him, how big his agency was and therefore how prominent *he* was, she told him how the pop star Prince had once been in the hotel and said she wished she'd had a chance to meet him.

"In fact," she said, "he stayed in the same suite you're staying in—the Hunting Lodge."

Which was the best room in the place: two bedrooms, a kitchen, a bar, a living room decorated with deer, antelope, and mule deer trophies courtesy of the owner of the establishment. The walls displayed photos of the owner on safari, in the mountains, smiling over dead animals. Pope approved of the decor since hunting meant revenue for his agency, and wondered what Prince had thought of it, whoever he was.

"The governor, huh." Pope took the message, saying, "I see he left his private number for me to call him back," and glanced up to gauge her reaction, hoping she'd be impressed.

"When Prince was here he left the housekeeper a one-hundred-dollar tip," she said.

He detected an amused sneer at the corners of her pretty mouth.

THE CARPET in the hallways, like the rooms themselves and the stinking waterfall in the lobby, was tired, of another era, but this place was the best he could do in the sleepy little backwater town of Saddlestring. Pope dug his key card out of the back pocket of his jeans as he walked the length of the long hall, past the humming ice maker and vending machines, debating whether he should call the governor immediately or wait until he had something to report. He decided on the latter. The last thing he wanted was the governor to focus on and bring up the question of why he was back in town in his room instead of with his team at the crime scene.

He placed his left hand on the door while he bent to fit the key card into the lock with his right, and was surprised when the door swung open a few inches. Stepping back, he cursed housekeeping for being so careless. The last thing they would get from him, he thought, was a hundred-dollar tip.

Then he thought, *What if it isn't housekeeping?*

For the first time in his twenty-five-year career, Randy Pope drew his weapon from its holster somewhere other than the shooting range in Cheyenne. He'd fired the .40 Glock because of the departmental requirement to recertify, but it felt heavy and unfamiliar in his hand. He tried to remember where the safety switch was, and only then recalled it didn't have one. He simply needed to rack the slide and it was armed. He did so, loudly, signaling to whoever was inside his room that he meant business. He braced himself, and fought an involuntary quiver in his lower lip.

There was no sound, no reaction, from inside. Should he call the sheriff? Why should he, the head of an important state agency, a man whose hourly and daily decisions steered a multimillion-dollar department through the storm-tossed waters of state bureaucracy, risk his own life when he had dozens of less-valuable employees and local law enforcement available to do so on his behalf?

But what if it was nothing? Could he risk the embarrassment of calling the local sheriff if the housekeeper had simply forgotten to lock the stupid door to his suite? The gossip afterward would be vicious.

Damn it, he thought, and gently kneed the door open, both hands cradling his weapon in front of him.

The room looked to be in order. Nothing out of place. The garbage near the door had been emptied. A quick glance into his bedroom revealed the bed had been made, which meant the housekeeping staff had been there.

But had he left the light on in the sitting room? He couldn't remember leaving it on that morning.

He rounded the bar, his weapon out in front of him. There was a smell. Definitely an odor, he thought. Like something had died.

Then he saw it. The mounted elk head that had been over the fake fireplace was lying on the floor. The black glass eyes of the mount reflected the light from the hallway. Its mouth was pursed into a permanent, silent bugle. But why would·it smell?

His eyes shot up the wall to where the mount had been, and Randy Pope screamed, dropped his gun, and backpedaled across the carpet until he tripped and fell backward onto the faux-leather couch.

Frank Urman's severed head was spiked into the wall where the elk head mount had been that morning.

13

IN HER third-hour social studies class at Saddlestring
High School, Sheridan Pickett idly drew sketches of smiling
faces, flowers, and falcons in the margin of her notebook
while waiting for class to begin. Her teacher, Mrs. Whaling, an attractive, doe-eyed blonde from the Northeast
who, to Sheridan, infused the mountain West where she
now lived with too much Disneyfied romance, had announced earlier with breathless glee that there would be a
"very special guest speaker" that morning. When she did,
several boys including Jason Kiner and Sheridan's on-
again-off-again boyfriend Jarrod Haynes (a dream to look
at but a nightmare to have a conversation with) moaned
with audible disdain and their reaction was met with an
icy glare from their teacher. Sheridan kept her head
down.

Mrs. Whaling was fond of guest speakers. She was also
fond of showing movies during classtime that stretched
over several days, silent reading, and hour-long forays into
topics that had nothing to do with the curriculum. Sheridan

found the class a waste of time, but couldn't transfer out because she needed the requirement. She did her best to feign interest, read the textbook even though she wasn't sure Mrs. Whaling had looked at it in years, and try not to laugh at Jarrod's mumbled stupid jokes. He could be funny in an irreverent, sophomoric way, she had to admit.

Today was worse than most days already, though, because of what had happened at home the night before and that morning. A sense of dread had enveloped her before she entered the building that morning and she had trouble shedding it or pushing it aside. She'd not been able to concentrate on anything at school because her head and heart were at home, with her mom, with her dad.

She almost didn't notice when Mrs. Whaling opened the door to the hallway. A big man with flowing blond hair and a barrel chest and a thousand-megawatt smile came in trailing a dark, pretty woman pushing a stroller.

"Kids," Mrs. Whaling said beaming, grasping her hands together in thrall in front of her bosom, "this is Klamath Moore."

"Save the wildlife!" Klamath Moore boomed, thrusting his arms into the air as if signaling a touchdown.

SHERIDAN HAD been awakened by the telephone ringing at five-thirty that morning, a sound she normally would have slept right through. But it was the way her mother answered it out in the hall and talked—with such emotional earnestness and gravity—that connected with Sheridan's semiconsciousness in a primal mother-daughter way and jerked her awake. She lay there for a few moments in the darkness, hearing snatches of conversation as her mother paced up and down the hall the way she did when a situation was serious:

"Not Robey? Oh my God, Joe . . ."

". . . hospital . . ."

"Three people shot and the other two dead . . ."

"Are you sure you're okay? . . ."

"How could this happen?"

"Why did this Lothar guy start shooting? Why didn't he identify himself? He put both of you in danger . . ."

"Another poker chip?"

"This is awful, Joe, just awful . . ."

Sheridan wrapped herself in her robe and found her mother sitting at the kitchen table looking pale, her eyes hollow and staring at nothing at all, her hands and the cordless phone on her lap as the coffeemaker percolated on the counter.

"Mom?"

Her mother jumped at the greeting, and quickly tried to assume her usual confident look of parental authority. Sheridan appreciated the attempt although it was a failure.

"Are you okay? Is Dad okay?"

"Okay is not the word for it," her mom said. "I just talked to him. He's at the hospital. Our friend Robey Hersig is in critical condition and not expected to last the morning." Her mom took a deep breath, fighting back tears of frustration, and when she did so Sheridan felt a sympathetic welling in her own eyes even though she didn't yet know what the situation was, only that it was affecting her mother so deeply that she was talking to her adult-to-adult, which was both thrilling and frightening at the same time.

"Robey was shot last night up in the mountains where your dad was. Two other men were killed, one by accident, one not by accident—"

Sheridan interrupted, "But Dad's all right?"

Her mom nodded and her face softened. "He's not hurt. But he's hurting, and I feel for him. He said the man who shot the hunter came back and shot Robey and another man I don't know. It's complicated. He says he feels guilty he's the only one who made it through unscathed, that it was pure luck."

"Thank God he's okay," Sheridan said.

"Yes, thank God for that. But poor Nancy Hersig and their two children. I can't even imagine . . ."

Sheridan pictured the Hersig kids. A boy who was a junior in high school and somewhat of a derelict, and a girl in junior high she'd last seen clutching a lunch sack and backpack on the school bus.

"Will Mr. Hersig make it, do you think?"

"Joe said the doctors doubt it. But we can pray for him."

Sheridan shook her head. She didn't want all the horrible details but she was confused as to what had happened. She wasn't sure her mom even knew everything.

"Come here," her mom said, extending her arms.

Sheridan did, and let her mother pull her close and squeeze her the way she hadn't, it seemed, in years. Sheridan squeezed back.

"Your poor father," her mom said. "He's sick about this."

"I'm just glad he's not hurt."

"Me too, darling," her mom said. "Me too. But like him, I feel a little guilty for being so happy he is the only one who made it through unharmed."

"What's going on?" Lucy asked from the doorway.

Sheridan and her mother quickly released each other, her mom becoming a mother again. Sheridan morphed into the role of older sister.

As her mom sat Lucy down to tell her everything was all right, that there'd been an accident but her dad was okay, the telephone rang. Sheridan answered, hoping it would be her father.

"Hello, little lady," the voice said. "May I please speak with Joe?"

"Who is calling?"

"My name's Spencer Rulon. I'm the governor of Wyoming."

At the name, Sheridan narrowed her eyes, pursed her lips, said, "Quit trying to get my dad killed."

"Honey . . . I . . ." he stammered.

Her mom wrenched the phone away from her before she could say more.

KLAMATH MOORE paced the front of the classroom like a big cat in a cage, his shoulders thrust forward, his hands grasped behind his back, moving as if propelled by internal demons that would not let him rest.

Mrs. Whaling said, "By point of introduction, I've been following Mr. Moore and his cause for quite some time, long before I moved here from Vermont. I read his blog daily and I've seen him talk and debate on CNN and other networks. He's very controversial but very interesting, and he has some important things to say. When I heard he was here in our little community, I just had to invite him to school. Please welcome Mr. Klamath Moore. . . ." She stepped back and clapped, which at first was a dry, hollow sound in the room until the class got the message and joined in.

He said, "When your teacher called me this morning to ask if I could come talk to you before my press conference this afternoon, I jumped at the chance. Because any opportunity I have to address our nation's youth is vitally important. I appreciate it very much, and I thank you, Mrs. Whaling." He nodded to her as he said her name, and she blushed.

"Life without hunting is not only possible, it's important," Moore boomed. "Think about it. There was a time when it was a matter of life or death for human beings to hunt animals in order for people to survive. If the caveman didn't go out and kill a mastodon, his babies didn't eat. And even a hundred years ago there were still places in these United States where people hunted for subsistence because they had no choice."

Klamath Moore suddenly stopped and swept his eyes across the room, pausing for great effect, before whispering, "That time has passed."

He made it a point to find and hold sets of eyes until the viewer had no quarter and was forced to look away, conceding Moore's superior focus and passion. His voice was deep and raspy, his words dramatic, if well rehearsed, Sheridan thought. She recognized much of the exact wording from his website.

"I'm not saying there aren't still a few places on this earth where hunting is necessary, for remote tribes in remote places. But in this day and age, where technology has made it possible to feed us all without our having to go out and get our hands bloody, hunting is an anachronism. Can anyone in this room tell me why there are men in the richest country on the face of the earth who find it necessary to take a gun they shouldn't be allowed to have in the first place and go out into our nature—that's right, it belongs to all of us—and kill an innocent animal with a high-powered rifle simply for the twisted *fun* of it? How would you like it if somebody killed your pet dogs and cats, or your little sisters or brothers . . . simply because they loved doing it? It's the same thing, believe me."

Sheridan stopped sketching, realizing she had been idly working on a scene of a falcon dropping from the sky to hit a rabbit. Trying not to draw attention to herself, she moved her arm over the drawing so no one could see it.

As Klamath Moore went on, Sheridan found herself looking at the woman with him, who she assumed was his wife. The woman sat on a chair next to Mrs. Whaling's desk with her hands in her lap, her eyes on Moore. She was beautiful, with high cheekbones, obsidian eyes, and long dark hair parted in the middle. She wore jeans and a loose chambray shirt over a white top and little makeup because it wasn't necessary. Sheridan guessed she was Native, and

she had a kind of calm serenity about her that was sooth-
ing to behold. She'd not said a word, but her presence
seemed to bolster Moore's message in a way that was hard
to explain. As her man spoke, she would occasionally look
down into the stroller next to her and brush her sleeping
baby's apple-red cheeks with the back of her fingers. Sheridan resented Klamath more—and her teacher—for not in-
troducing the woman and baby as well.

"Hunting is a dying activity in the United States, I'm
happy to say," Moore said, "but it isn't dying fast enough.
Most studies say less than five percent of Americans hunt.
That's around fifteen million hunters. Around here, I'd
guess the percentage is much higher, maybe thirty percent? Fifty percent? Too damned many, that's for sure. But
whatever the number, these so-called sportsmen kill over
two hundred million birds and animals every year. *Two
hundred million!* That includes four million deer, two hundred thousand elk, twenty *million* pheasants, and over
twenty-five thousand bears. Think about this kind of
slaughter on a mass scale—it's horrendous! My mission in
this life is to hasten the overdue death of blood sports and
to raise awareness about what it really is, what it really
does. I firmly believe that every time a rich man pulls the
trigger and an animal dies, we as human beings die just a
little bit as well. In nature, predators kill only the sick and
weak. But hunters kill the biggest, healthiest, and strongest
in the herd, which plays hell with the balance of nature.
We will never achieve moral greatness until this practice is
abolished."

From behind Sheridan, a male voice mumbled, "What
bullshit." It was Jason Kiner. Jason's father, like Sheridan's,
was a game warden. Sheridan had fought with Jason the
year before but they'd mended fences, just like their fathers
had. Sheridan still wasn't sure she liked him, but she felt a
growing kinship with him as Moore went on because he,
like her, felt their fathers were being attacked here in their
classroom.

"Ah," Moore said, stopping and raising a stubby finger in the air. "I hear some dissent. That's okay, that's okay. I encourage it. It's the American way and I'm all for the American way. And I expect it, here in the heart of what I like to call the Barbaric States. Do you know what a barbarian is?"

No one raised a hand.

"The definition I like is thus: lacking refinement, learning, or artistic culture. That pretty much describes a hunter, I'd say. Think of him out there," he said, gesturing out the windows toward the Bighorns, "swilling beer, farting, trying to keep his pants up because he's so fat, using high-tech weapons to kill Bambi and Thumper so he can cut their heads off and stick them on his wall. Do you know how the word *barbarian* came to be?"

Again, no hands.

"The ancient Romans came up with it to describe the hordes of slimeballs who were trying to take them down. They spoke a different language which, to the Roman ear, sounded like '*Bar-bar-bar-bar.*'" He said it in a stupid, drooling way that made several kids laugh. "That's what I hear when so-called hunters tell me why they do it. They get all high and mighty and say they're *honoring* the animal they killed, or they're *getting right* with nature, or some other kind of nonsense. But when they go on and on all I can hear is—" He stopped, made his face slack and his eyes vacant, opened his mouth to appear like an idiot, and said, "*Bar-bar-bar-bar-bar.*"

Sheridan noticed how his wife did a well-practiced smile, and how several kids laughed, getting into it. Mrs. Whaling seemed a little uncomfortable with the way things were going, Sheridan thought. Her teacher's eyes darted around the room more than usual.

"Do you know what hunters actually do?" he asked. "Do you know what takes place? I've got no doubt some of your relatives probably hunt, this being the Barbaric States. But how many of you have actually been there?"

He paused. The silence started to roar.

Finally, Jason Kiner raised his hand. Moore nodded at him, as if approving. "Any more?" he asked.

Two boys in the back cautiously raised their hands as well. One was Trent Millions, a Native who split his time between his father's house on the reservation and his mother's house in town. Trent appeared puzzled by the question, since hunting on the reservation was done without controversy and was a matter of course.

Taking a deep breath, Sheridan raised her hand.

"Four of you?" Moore said. "Just four? I would have thought more. I guess hunting is dying out even in the bloody heart of the Barbaric States."

Then he looked at the kids one by one with their hands up and said, "You're all murderers."

Which startled Mrs. Whaling and made her turn white. "Mr. Moore, maybe—"

He ignored her.

"If you kill an animal for the joy of killing, you're a murderer," he said. Sheridan felt the eyes of most of the room on her now, but she kept her hand up. She felt her face begin to burn with anger and, surprisingly, a little shame. "Okay," he said, "you can put your hands down now if you want."

He shook his head sadly, said, "Blessed are the young for they know not what they do."

Sheridan kept her hand up.

"Right now as I speak to you," Moore said, pointing out the window, "there is a man up there in those mountains who is killing hunters. Unlike the innocent animals hunters kill, this man seeks and destroys other men who are armed and capable of fighting back. But this man who does to hunters what hunters do to innocent wild animals is considered a sicko, a mad dog, and that's why I'm here. I'm here to support him in his noble quest to raise awareness of what is happening over two hundred million times a year in this country. If we condemn him and say his methods are brutal and deviant, how can we turn around and say what hunters do is not? This man, whoever he is, should be celebrated as a hero! He's fighting for the animals who can't fight back themselves, and I, for one, hope he's just getting started."

Sheridan shot a look at Mrs. Whaling, who was now as white as a porcelain bowl.

"Not that I condone murder, of course," Moore said, quickly backtracking. "I condemn it when it's done to animals, and I condemn it when it happens to human beings, who are just animals themselves—but animals who should know better.

"For those of you who haven't murdered an animal, let me tell you how it's done," Moore said. "And those of you proud murderers feel free to correct me if I get any part of this wrong.

"Once the animal is down, after it's been shot, the first thing you do is take your knife out and slit its throat, right? So it will bleed out into the ground. Many times, the animal isn't even dead yet. Then you turn it on its back and slit it up the middle, right? So you can reach inside and *pull its guts out* into a pile, right?"

There were several gasps, and at least one girl put her face in her hands. Another plugged her ears with her fingers. Sheridan kept her hand up, glaring back at Moore.

"When that's all done and you're covered with blood and your hands stink of guts, you cut the head off the innocent animal and take it to a taxidermist. Then you proudly put it up on the wall as your trophy, as proof of what a big man you are."

He turned his eyes directly on Sheridan. "Or in your case, what a big girl you are. So tell me, how did it make you feel?"

"You're asking me?" Sheridan said. She noticed that the woman was looking at her as well, with a surprising nod of sympathy. In fact, the woman turned from Sheridan and glared at her husband.

"I'm asking you," Moore said. "Did you like it? Did you like taking the life of an innocent animal? Did it please you in some way?"

Sheridan's face was burning, and her throat ached.

"Klamath," the woman whispered, "leave her alone."

"Did you like the warm blood on your hands?" he goaded.

"I've never killed anything," Sheridan said.

Moore was perplexed. "Then why did you raise your hand?"

"I just wanted to show I oppose you," she said, her voice firm. "I'm an apprentice falconer. I've watched falcons hunt. They don't just kill the sick and weak, so I know you're lying. Plus, I see a big difference between hunting animals and killing a man. And I think you're an asshole and you should stop trying to intimidate us."

"Sheridan!" Mrs. Whaling gasped.

Sheridan thought she detected a slight smile in the woman's eyes.

The bell rang, saving the day.

Jason Kiner whooped. Jarrod Haynes said, "This is why I love that girl."

Klamath Moore stepped back to let the classroom empty, but Sheridan could feel his eyes burning through her. She kept her head down and clutched her books to her chest. She could hear Mrs. Whaling apologizing to Klamath Moore's back about Sheridan's language.

As she passed the woman, Sheridan felt a hand on her arm. She looked over to see the woman's large dark eyes on her. Then the woman reached up and stroked Sheridan's cheek with the back of her fingers, the same way she'd stroked her sleeping baby.

Sheridan didn't jerk back, but was shocked by the intimacy of the gesture.

"You're the daughter of the game warden, aren't you?"

Sheridan nodded her head.

"You're terribly misguided, but I hope your father knows what a brave daughter he has," she said, and looked at Sheridan with a sudden sadness that, for some reason, made Sheridan want to cry for the second time that morning.

14

JOE SAT ALONE in the middle of a row of red molded plastic chairs in the hallway of the Saddlestring Hospital near the secure doorway to ICU. On the other side of the doors, surgeons worked to save Robey Hersig's life. Joe rubbed at the stubble on his chin and covered his eyes with his hand and tried to get a few minutes of sleep. When he drifted off, though, violent recollections of the night before came rushing back as if his mind had just been waiting for the opportunity to try to expel them from his memory by force. Like the thought of Chris Urman and him carrying Buck Lothar's dead body through the dark forest, while Urman moaned with shame and guilt. Then Lothar's body slipping at times through their hands to crumple into a pile on the forest floor until they fashioned a travois of two stout lodgepoles and secured the body so they could drag and carry it through the brush. Or Joe's growing comprehension as they struggled through the black, unforgiving timber that he and Lothar had been tracking not the killer but Urman the entire night while the killer slipped around them and returned to the original crime scene. Remembering his guilt for not immediately identifying himself when Lothar stepped out into the meadow cradling his automatic weapon, and wondering if his choice to remain silent was tactical—as he thought at the time—or cowardly resulting in Lothar's death. Thinking of Robey's lack of response on the radio and failure to respond to Joe's periodic three-shot signaling, the first indication that something tragic had happened to his friend. Then finding Wally Conway's dead body and Robey bleeding out next to his slumping pickup at the same time Phil Kiner and Deputy Reed arrived twenty minutes too late to provide backup. Picturing the garish image of Wally Conway's face in the beam of a flashlight, his mouth open, the bright red poker chip next to his extended purple tongue. And the shocking realization that of the four of them who'd been on the mountain just two hours before, he was the only one still alive and unhurt, and that everything they'd done was misguided and stupid and epically wrong; that Robey, his friend and colleague and fishing partner since he'd been in Saddlestring and one of the most honest and good-hearted men Joe had ever known, in all likelihood wouldn't survive the morning.

"YOU SHOULD get yourself cleaned up, Joe." County coroner Will Speer stood before Joe and looked down through a pair of wire-rimmed glasses with pained sympathy in his eyes. Speer had a light brown thatch of hair and a graying mustache, and wore an open white lab coat.

Joe sat up, blinking, momentarily confused. He hadn't heard Speer walk down the hall and didn't know how long he'd been half-sleeping, suffering through the nightmares. Joe could smell himself: dried sweat and mud, with flowery bloodstains on his Wranglers and the sleeves of his red uniform shirt, half-moons of black blood under his fingernails that wouldn't wash out. "Maybe so," Joe said, nodding toward the ICU entrance, "but I think I'll wait until I hear about Robey."

Speer nodded. That he didn't volunteer words of encouragement was not lost on either of them.

"Does Nancy know?" Speer asked.

"She was in Casper at a meeting," Joe said. "She's on her way here."

"I bet that wasn't an easy conversation."

Joe shook his head. "Nope."

"Let's hope things calm down out there," Speer said, gesturing vaguely with his chin in the direction of the mountains. "I only have three drawers down in the morgue and they're all full. I don't think that's ever happened before."

It took Joe a moment to figure out what Speer meant. "Frank Urman, Lothar, and Wally Conway," Joe said. Meaning if Robey didn't pull through, Speer wouldn't know where to put his body.

"At least we were able to reunite Mr. Urman's head with his body," Speer said with bitter humor.

Joe winced. He'd forgotten about the hysterical cell phone call he'd received from Randy Pope as he, Kiner, and Reed drove down the mountain with all the victims. At the time, Joe cradled Robey in his arms, hoping the makeshift compresses they'd fashioned would stanch the flow of blood from the entrance and exit wounds in Robey's chest and back. Pope had screamed about finding the head mounted in his room, saying, "Now this is *personal!*" like the tagline to an action movie. Joe had said, "I'm busy right now," and closed his phone.

It was clear now to Joe what the killer had been doing between the time he shot Frank Urman and when he returned to the crime scene—mounting Urman's head on a plaque in Pope's hotel room. The savagery of the act was incomprehensible, and Joe did his best to shove it aside for later when he could better process the information.

"I suppose you heard," Speer said, "the governor closed

all hunting and access to state lands and he's asking the Feds to do the same."

Joe hadn't heard, but he wasn't surprised. Pope and the governor's worst-case scenario had materialized. Joe was numb and completely unmoved by the news, although he knew what kind of uproar was likely to erupt statewide. All he cared about now was what was happening on the other side of the ICU doors. He had several messages on his cell phone from the governor, but hadn't the will nor the energy to return them. He had four from Randy Pope. They'd been left while he was giving his statement to Deputy Reed earlier. Sheriff McLanahan had stood off to the side, a disdainful look on his face. Disdainful but triumphant, a look that said, *You froze me out of the investigation, and just look what happened. . . .*

Chris Urman was in custody in the sheriff's department, but Joe expected him to be released quickly. Joe told Deputy Reed that Urman had simply defended himself, firing only after being surprised by Lothar and being fired upon. Joe knew Urman felt horrible about what had happened, and had dismissed any suspicion he may have had of him on their trek back to the pickup to find Robey and Conway. Joe's pickup was still on the mountain, shot up and blood-stained. He'd need to send a tow truck for it. Another year, another damaged truck.

Speer leaned over and put his hand on Joe's shoulder. "Go home, Joe. Get cleaned up. Get some rest. There's nothing you can do here."

Joe shook his head. "I need to be here when Nancy comes. I need to apologize to her for putting Robey in that situation."

Speer shook his head sadly, gave Joe's shoulder a squeeze, and went back in the direction of his little morgue.

NANCY HERSIG looked frantic when she pushed through the hallway doors. Nancy had always been meticulous in her look and dress, always composed and calm, comfortable with herself. Given to jeans, sweaters, blazers, and pearls, Nancy Hersig was the queen of volunteer causes in Twelve Sleep County, heading up the United Way, the hospital foundation, the homeless shelter. But Joe saw a different Nancy coming down the hall. Her eyes were red-rimmed and looked like angry red headlights. Her makeup was smeared and the right side of her hair was wild, the result of raking it back with her fingers on the drive from Casper to Saddlestring.

Joe stood up and she came to him, letting him hold her. She began to weep in hard, racking sobs that had to hurt, he thought.

"I thought I was cried out," she said, her teeth chattering as she took a breath, "but I guess I'm not."

"It's okay," he said.

"What have you heard, Joe?"

"He's in surgery," he said, hoping a doctor would burst through the doors at exactly that moment with good news.

"What did the doctors say?"

Joe sighed. "That he's hurt real bad, Nancy."

"He's tough," she said, "he's always been tough. He used to rodeo, you know."

"I know."

"I wish I could see him and talk him through this."

Joe didn't know what to say, and simply held her. She regained her composure and gently pushed herself away, dabbing at her face with her sleeve. "God, I'm a mess," she said, her eyes sweeping across his face and lingering on the splotches of dried blood on his Wranglers.

"Is that Robey's?" she asked, pointing.

"We did all we could to stop the bleeding," Joe said, "but . . ."

She nodded and held up a hand, as if to say, *Don't tell me*.

"Nancy," Joe said, struggling to find the right words, "I'm just so damned sorry this happened. It didn't have to.

I never should have left him last night. I called for backup but it didn't get there in time."

Again, she shook her head. *Don't tell me.*

"I hate not being able to do something," he said, fighting back a surprising urge to cry.

"Oh, you can do something," she said, suddenly defiant. "You can find the man who did this and *put him down like a dog.*"

The vehemence in her words took him aback.

He said, "I will, Nancy. I'll find him."

"And put him down," she repeated.

"And put him down," he said.

She turned on her heel away from Joe and wrapped her arms around herself. "I don't know what I'm supposed to do now, Joe. I don't know whether to go get our kids and bring them here, or pray, or what. Maybe I should bust through those doors so I can see him.

"Joe," she said, looking over her shoulder, "there's no manual for this."

They both jumped when the ICU doors clicked open.

And they knew instantly from the look on the surgeon's face what had happened inside.

"I'm so sorry," he said, shaking his head.

Nancy didn't shriek, didn't wail. She stood immobile, stunned, as if she'd been slapped. Joe took a step toward her and she shook her head.

"I'll contact our grief counselor," the surgeon said in a mumble, his eyes fixed on the top of his shoes. "We did all we—"

"I'm sure you did," she said, cutting him off. "And there's no need for a counselor. I just want to see him. Let me see him."

The surgeon said, "Mrs. Hersig, I don't think—"

"I said, let me see him," she said with force.

The surgeon sighed and stepped aside, holding the ICU door open for her. As she passed, she reached out and squeezed Joe's hand.

"Maybe Marybeth could give me a call later," she said with a wan smile, "if she doesn't mind. I might need some help with the kids and arrangements. I'm not even sure what I'll need help with."

"She'll be there," Joe said.

"And remember what you promised me," she said.

"I do," he said, struck by the words—the same words and solemn tone he'd used for his wedding vow.

Nancy Hersig paused at the open door, took a deep breath, threw back her shoulders, patted her hair down, and strode purposefully into the ICU.

The surgeon looked at Joe, said, "Tough lady."

Joe nodded his agreement and dumbly withdrew his phone to call Marybeth.

"I FIGURED I'd find you here," Randy Pope said hotly, appearing at the other end of the hallway at the same time the ICU doors closed. "Finally checking your messages, I see. I've been calling you all morning, and so has the governor."

Joe held up a hand. "Give me a minute. I have a call to make."

"Joe, damn you, have you heard what's happened?"

"I said I need to make a call."

Pope quickly closed the distance between them.

"The governor's got his plane in the air to pick us up as we speak," Pope said. "He wants us in his office right away, and he means *right away*. He's furious about what happened out there last night, and so am I. We look like a bunch of incompetents."

Joe took a deep breath and leaned back from Pope, who was standing toe-to-toe, his face a mask of indignation.

"Give me a minute—"

"We don't have a minute."

"Randy," Joe said, speaking as calmly as possible, "Robey Hersig didn't make it. My friend is dead. I need to get in touch with Marybeth so she can come here and help out Nancy."

"Joe . . ." Pope said, reaching for Joe's phone to take it away from him. As Joe turned his head, Pope's knuckles grazed Joe's cheek.

Something red and hot popped in the back of Joe's head and he tossed the phone aside and backed Pope against the wall, squeezing his throat. The director's eyes bulged and his nose flared and he clawed at Joe's hands. Joe realized he was snarling.

Pope made a gargling sound and tried to pry Joe's hands away. Then his boss kicked Joe in the shin, so hard electric shocks shot through his body, and Joe realized what he was doing and let go and stepped back, as surprised at his behavior as Pope was.

"Don't touch me," Joe said.

Pope made the gargling sound again while doubling over, one hand at his throat, the other held up as if to ward off another attack.

"My God," Pope barked, "you tried to kill me! My own subordinate tried to kill me!"

"Your subordinate has a call to make," Joe said, retrieving his phone and fighting the urge to do it again.

As HE SAT in the backseat of Deputy Reed's cruiser—Reed had been waiting outside the hospital to give them a ride to Saddlestring Airport to meet the governor's plane—Joe said to Pope, "How's your neck?"

Pope was in the front seat, next to Reed. He kept hacking and rubbing his throat. "I just hope there isn't permanent damage," Pope said, his voice huskier than usual.

"Go ahead and press charges," Joe said. "Have me arrested. Take me officially off this case and then try to explain that to the governor."

"Don't tempt me," Pope croaked. "If it was up to me—"

"But it is up to you," Joe said, thinking if Pope fired

him again he'd have the freedom to pursue the killer on his own, without official sanction. He had a promise to keep, and being relieved of the bureaucracy might unleash him to keep it.

Pope turned stiffly in the seat, glaring at Joe. "The governor wants to see both of us. He's not happy. It would only be a little too convenient for you if you didn't show up, now wouldn't it?"

Joe shook his head. "The thought hadn't occurred to me."

"I'll bet."

Joe shrugged.

"Look," Pope said, baring his teeth, "if I had my way you would never have gotten your job back with my agency. You'd still be a ranch hand, or whatever the hell you were a year ago. We can't have cowboys like you out in the field anymore, not in this day and age. Just look at last night if you want evidence of what happens when you go off half-cocked. But I need you on this one, and I hate to say it. I *really* hate to say it. We need to find that shooter, and we need to do it fast. I need everybody I can get, even you. Especially you," Pope said with distaste, "since you know the area."

Joe looked away.

"But when this is all over," Pope said, "you're going to pay for what you did to me back there."

He turned around with a huff.

Joe and Deputy Reed exchanged glances in the rearview mirror, and Reed rolled his eyes, as if to say, *Bosses* . . .

REED HAD to slow his cruiser in front of the county building on Main Street because of the small demonstration taking place. Cable news satellite trucks partially blocked the street, and cameramen pushed through the crowd photographing the crowd.

As they skirted the gathering, Joe could see Klamath

Moore on the courthouse steps, his arms raised, leading the group of thirty-five to forty followers in a shouted hymn:

> *All things bright and beautiful,*
> *All creatures great and small,*
> *All things wise and wonderful,*
> *The Lord God made them all.*

"And to think," Reed said, "I used to like that song."

Pope snorted his disgust at the protest. "Look, there's nearly as many cameras as there are protesters. Where are the reporters covering murdered hunters? That's what I'd like to know."

Joe said nothing, but he surveyed the protesters as they passed by. Several he recognized from the airport. There was a group of four men who looked more like hunters than anti-hunters, Joe thought. The men were tall, burly, with cowboy hats and beards. Two of them—one angular with haunting dark eyes and the other beefy with a scarred face and an eye patch—glared back at him with hostility.

Off to the side of Klamath Moore, up on the steps, was the Native woman and her baby he had noted at the airport.

Many of the men looked hard, their faces contorted with grim passion as they sang. They were the faces of true believers, of the obsessed. He turned in the backseat to look at them out the rear window.

He wondered which of them was the shooter.

I sing,

> *The rich man in his castle,*
> *The poor man at his gate,*
> *God made them, high or lowly,*
> *And order'd their estate.*

And the words and melody, as always, seem to fill my sails, fill my soul, bringing me both relief and validation. But God, I am exhausted. I need rest. I can't remember ever going so long without sleep. There are hallucinations at the edge of my vision: blood pouring from the hole in Wally Conway's chest, the simpering sounds made by the other man, the one I didn't know. I hear he was the county prosecutor. He shouldn't have been there. It's not my fault he was. But his death haunts me, will always haunt me, but what's done is done.

I see the police car on the street, three men inside. I recognize two of them, the game warden named Joe in the back, Randy Pope in the front. Seeing them in the daylight, their faces pressed to the window as they pass, makes my blood boil. My reserve of will astounds even me. The sight of them fills me with renewed strength.

I wonder where they're going. One thing I'm sure of, though, is that they'll be back.

I sing,

All things bright and beautiful,
All creatures great and small,
All things wise and wonderful,
The Lord God made them all.

15

THE STATE-OWNED Mitsubishi MU-2 whined and shook
as the twin props gummed their way through the thin
mountain air and achingly pulled the airplane from the
runway into the sky. Joe kept his eyes closed and his hands
gripped tightly on the headrest of the seat in front of him
as the ground shot by, and he wondered if they'd reach
cruising altitude before the plane shook apart. For the longest time, he forgot to breathe. The aircraft was the oldest
one in the state's three-plane fleet, and Joe had heard it
described as "the Death Plane" because it was the same
make and model that had crashed years before and killed
the popular governor of South Dakota. Joe wondered if his
governor was sending them a message by ordering the old
death trap out of mothballs in the Cheyenne hangar and
sending it north to pick them up. Inside, the seats were
threadbare and a detached curl of plastic bulkhead covering vibrated so violently in the turbulence that it looked
like a white apparition. There were six seats in the plane,
three rows of two. Randy Pope sat in the first row and had
put his briefcase on the seat next to him so Joe couldn't use

it. Not that Joe wanted to. Instead, he took a seat in the third row so he could grip the headrest in front of him and, if necessary, pray and vomit unobserved.

Eventually, as the craft leveled out and stopped shaking, he relaxed his grip, took a breath, chanced looking out the cloudy window. It helped, somewhat, to get his bearings. The Bighorns rose in the west looking hunched, dark, and vast like a sleeping dinosaur, and the town of Buffalo slipped beneath them. He noted how the North Fork and Middle Fork of the Powder River, Crazy Woman Creek, and the South Fork flowed west to east, one after the other, like grid lines on a football field. Joe envisioned each from ground level where he was much more comfortable. It calmed him to put himself mentally on the ground on the banks of the rivers, either in his pickup or on horseback where he could look up and see the silver airplane like a fleck of tinsel in a blue carpet. He sat back, closed his eyes, and tried to slow his heart down.

JOE AWOKE with a start as the plane bucked through an air pocket that left his stomach suspended in the air a hundred feet above and behind him. He was surprised he'd actually fallen asleep. Joe gathered himself and looked outside and saw the rims and buttes of Chugwater Creek and the creek itself. It wouldn't be long before they touched down in Cheyenne. His feet were freezing from what he guessed was a leak in the fuselage, and he lamented that he'd not had time to change out of his bloody clothes before leaving for Cheyenne to see Rulon. He rubbed his face and shook the sleep from his head, saw that Pope, two rows up, was staring ahead at the drawn curtains of the cockpit. Not reading, not talking on his cell phone. Just staring, deep in thought.

Joe unbuckled his belt and moved up a row until he was behind and to the left of his boss. "Why did you bring Wally Conway?"

The question startled Pope, who flinched as if slapped.

"I didn't know you were there," Pope said. "Quit sneaking up on me."

"Why did you bring Wally Conway?"

Pope looked at Joe, his eyes furtive. "I told you. I wanted a friend with me. Someone I could trust."

"Then why did you leave your friend?"

"He wanted to help. What, did you want to leave Robey up there all by himself while you and Buck Lothar went on your little walkabout?"

"So why did *you* leave?"

"I told you," Pope said, his eyes settling on Joe's forehead. Despite the cold inside the cabin of the plane, tiny beads of sweat had broken out across Pope's upper lip. "I've got an agency to run. I can't run it and communicate with the governor while I'm out running around in the woods."

"Something's not making sense to me here," Joe said.

Pope squirmed in his seat and his face flushed red. "Wally Conway was one of my oldest and best friends." Pope's eyes misted. "I don't have that many friends anymore."

The admission startled Joe. Pope had never confided anything personal to him before.

"There's something I want you to see," Pope said, digging into the pocket of his coat and producing a small digital camera. He turned it on and an image appeared on the screen. He handed the camera to Joe with a hand that shook. "That's Frank Urman's head spiked to the wall of my room."

Joe cringed and looked away.

"Look at this one," Pope said, advancing the photo. "You can see the head of the spike he used to pound it into the wood. And here's a close-up . . ."

Joe couldn't bring himself to look.

"Disturbing, isn't it?" Pope said. "I'm finding it real hard to get that image out of my mind. It's hard to concentrate and think on my feet. I keep seeing that head on the wall."

"We're beginning our descent into Cheyenne," the pilot drawled over the speaker. "Make sure you're buckled up."

Joe returned to his seat chastened. In the last few hours he'd accused his boss of getting two men killed and also tried to strangle him. Maybe, Joe conceded, what Pope said about him was true.

As the plane eased out of the sky and the landing gear clanked and moaned and locked into place, Joe closed his eyes and once again gripped the headrest in front of him as if the harder he squeezed it, the safer he would be.

But he still wondered why Randy Pope had brought Wally Conway into the mountains and left him to die.

CHEYENNE WAS cool and windy and Joe clamped his hat on his head as he followed Pope down the stairs of the plane to the tarmac. A white Yukon with state license plate number one was parked behind the gate next to the general aviation building and he could see two forms inside the smoked glass. Joe recalled that the last white Yukon he'd been assigned from the state ended up a smoking wreck in Yellowstone Park. He doubted they would want him to drive this one.

Whoever was at the wheel of the Yukon blinked the lights on and off to signal them. Joe followed Pope, who walked briskly as if to signal to the people in the car he wasn't actually *with* his subordinate, but simply traveling in the same plane with him.

A highway patrol officer, likely assigned to the governor's detail, got out and opened the two back doors while a state aeronautics commission staffer unlocked the gate. Joe took a deep breath of the high-plains air. It was thin at 6,200 feet, and flavored with sagebrush and fumes from the refinery at the edge of the city. As he glanced to the south, the golden capitol dome winked in the sun over the top of a thick bank of cottonwood trees turning yellow and red with fall colors.

As they approached the gate, Pope said, "Try to keep your comments to a minimum when we talk to the governor."

Joe said, "I work for him."

"You work for *me*."

Joe shrugged. He climbed into the backseat of the Escalade next to Pope and the doors shut, instantly killing the howl of cold wind.

She turned around in the front seat, said, "Hi, Joe."

"Hello, Stella."

Stella Ennis was ivory pale, with piercing dark eyes and full dark lipsticked lips. She wore a charcoal skirt suit over a white top with a strand of sensible business pearls. Her hair seemed richer and even more auburn than Joe remembered, and he guessed she was coloring it to hide the strands of gray. She looked at him coolly, assessing him in one long take that seemed to last for minutes although it really didn't, and he couldn't read what she concluded.

"I'm Randy Pope," Joe's boss said to her.

"I know who you are," she said, not looking at him.

Joe saw Pope and the trooper exchange glances. Joe nervously fingered the wedding ring on his hand, something he'd done without realizing it the first time he met Stella in Jackson.

Stella said, "The governor wants to see you two immediately. As you can guess, there's going to be an investigation by DCI to determine what happened up there, and no doubt there will be questions by the media and some members of the legislature. Governor Rulon wants to make sure we're all on the same page before the shit hits the fan. There may be charges brought, so be prepared."

"Charges?" Pope blanched.

"One never knows," she said. "When three people are killed in an operation, there are always those who insist on some kind of accountability, someone to blame. Not that we want any scapegoats. But we think we can head off anything like that happening if we can get out in front of it."

"We'll work with you however we can," Pope said, trying to get her eye. She finally broke her gaze with Joe and her eyes swept over Pope as if he were out-of-place furniture as she turned back around.

"Let's go, Bob," she said to the officer.

Stella said, "Word about what happened last night is tearing across the state like wildfire. We are very, very lucky the legislature isn't in session, or it would be a sensation on the floor. This is the first time in the state's history a governor has closed down state lands to hunting. And our understanding from the Feds is that they will follow suit this afternoon. We're already getting e-mails and constituent phone calls saying Governor Rulon is a dictator and much, much worse."

"I can imagine," Pope said, but the words just hung there when she chose not to respond to him.

Stella said, "We called a press conference for three-thirty. The governor plans to let everyone know what's happened and what measures he's taken. It's important that we have our story straight and our plan in place."

Joe checked his watch. An hour and a half before the press conference.

As they traveled down Central to downtown, toward the gold dome, Joe looked out the window at the stately houses on the avenues.

Stella Ennis was still attractive and sensual and familiar. But she was also still a murderer, and only Stella and Joe knew it. This time, unlike the first time he'd met her, there was no *zing*.

For which he was grateful.

16

"PARDON MY FRENCH," Governor Spencer Rulon said after Joe detailed the events of the day and night before, "but it sounds like a classic clusterfuck."

"It was," Pope sighed, leaning away from Joe as if to distance himself both literally and figuratively.

Rulon asked Pope, "Did you come to that conclusion from the comfort of your hotel room after you cut and ran like a rabbit?"

They were crammed into Rulon's small private office in the capitol building on Twenty-fourth Street, as opposed to the public office and conference room where Rulon could generally be observed by constituents and visitors touring the building. Rulon's private office was dark and windowless with a high ceiling and shelves crammed with books, unopened gifts, and what looked to Joe like the governor's eccentric collection of fossils, arrowheads, and bits of bone. Also in the room, in addition to Pope, who sat next to Joe facing Rulon across his desk, and Stella, who sat at Rulon's right hand but managed to defer to him with such professional determination that she became an extension of him rather than his chief of staff, were Richard Brewer, director of the state Department of Criminal Investigation, and Special Agent Tony Portenson of the FBI. Joe and Portenson had exchanged scowls, and Rulon cautioned them, saying, "Now, boys . . ." They went back six years. Portenson was dark, pinched, and had close-set eyes and a scar that hitched up his upper lip so that it looked like he was sneering. The last time Joe had seen Portenson was in Yellowstone Park, as the FBI agent set up a scenario to betray Joe and lead Joe's friend Nate Romanowski away in cuffs.

Everyone was so tightly packed around Rulon's desk that it was both intimate and uncomfortable in equal measures, and Joe guessed that was exactly the atmosphere Rulon wanted to create. The governor was the only one with room, with the ability to wave his arms or pounce across the desk like a big cat to make a point. To Joe, Stella's silence and stillness only seemed to make her more conspicuous. Or at least it did to him.

Pope was obviously flustered by Rulon's question, and he once again withdrew his digital camera from his coat, turned it on, and handed it across the desk to the governor.

"This was in my room," Pope said gravely.

Rulon leaned forward, saw the image of Frank Urman's head, and winced.

Pope handed the camera to Brewer, who turned white when he saw it. Portenson looked at it and rolled his eyes and shook his head, as if to say, "You people out here are savages." When offered the camera, Stella shook her head quickly to refuse.

"The shooter knew I was up there," Pope said. "He wanted to send me a personal message."

"Looks like he did," Rulon said. "Has the press gotten ahold of this yet?"

Pope shrugged.

"They will," Rulon said, "and it will make a bad situation even worse."

"Expect to see it on the Internet," Brewer said. "Somebody will post it."

Rulon sighed.

Joe noted how skillfully Pope had steered the topic away from his leaving them on the mountain. He wanted to hear the answer. And he still wanted to know why Pope had brought Wally Conway.

"What happened to your neck?" Rulon asked Pope, fingering his own.

Joe thought, *Uh-oh.*

"Just an accident," Pope said quickly. "I walked into a branch up there in the mountains and nearly strangled myself."

Joe stared at Pope, wondering why he was protecting him.

"I feel really damned bad about Robey," Rulon said to Joe. "He was a good man. He was a buddy of yours, wasn't he, Joe? Please let me know about the funeral arrangements so I can be there, okay?"

Joe nodded.

Rulon said, "I've already alerted the AG to get ready for the civil suit from Buck Lothar's family, assuming he has one. Even though it sounds like the guy screwed up, according to Joe, it's gonna cost us millions, I'm sure."

"I'm sure," Brewer echoed, gesturing toward Joe. "The potential suit may hinge on my investigation of the incident, which I'm prepared to do immediately."

The governor waved him away, indicating there was no hurry.

"What about this other guy, Conway?" Rulon asked Pope. "Should we expect something from his family?"

Joe listened with anticipation.

"I wouldn't worry about that," Pope said, casually dismissing the notion out of hand. "That's the last thing I'm worried about. We've got a lot bigger trouble brewing."

"No shit," Rulon said.

Joe wondered what had just happened, what he'd missed.

"Do you boys remember the story of Eric Rudolph?" Governor Spencer Rulon asked in such a manner that it was clear he was going to tell the story no matter how Joe or Pope answered.

"Eric Rudolph," Brewer said, answering the governor's question. "North Carolina. Rudolph—"

Rulon proceeded as if Brewer had never spoken: "Eric Rudolph was and is a slimeball, a walking bucket of pond scum. But he may be relevant to our situation here. How? you ask. I'll tell you."

Joe settled back in his chair, wondering where this was going.

"Eric Rudolph was the miserable buckaroo who set off a bomb at the Atlanta Olympics in 1996 that killed two people and injured a hundred and eleven others. He also bombed an abortion clinic in Atlanta and a gay and lesbian nightclub in Birmingham, which killed a cop. Eric Rudolph was a true believer," Rulon said. "The problem was he was a true believer in a horseshit set of beliefs that included the Christian Identity Movement—whatever *that* is—and what he called global socialism. He said he was an anti-Semite who was against homosexuality, abortion, globalism, et cetera, et cetera. The only thing I agree with him about is he thought John Lennon's 'Imagine' was a despicable song."

Joe noted that Rulon's last comment brought a hint of a smile from Stella.

After a few beats, Randy Pope said, "Sir, I don't see what Eric Rudolph has to do with us."

Rulon made a pained face. "You don't?"

"No, sir."

"You don't see the similarities?" Rulon asked with incredulity.

"I'm afraid not."

Rulon heaved a sigh, leaned forward on his desk, and

lowered his voice. "Director Pope, Eric Rudolph was on the run for five and a half years before he got caught. Everybody knew who he was, knew what he looked like, knew all about him. Everyone knew he was in Appalachia, and most likely North Carolina, the whole time. But despite the best efforts of federal, state, and local law enforcement, he eluded them for five and a half years. Yes, *five and a half years.*

"Finally, in May of 2003, a rookie police officer in Murphy, North Carolina, caught Rudolph Dumpster-diving outside a Save-A-Lot store. Rudolph was unarmed and clean-shaven, wearing new clothes and new shoes. They found his little camp, which turned out to be a stone's throw from two strip malls and a high school. Apparently, the officers reported they could hear the highway traffic from where Rudolph's camp was—it was that close to civilization."

Rulon paused again. When Pope shook his head to indicate he still didn't get it, Rulon said, "For five and a half years, the top fugitive on the FBI's Ten Most Wanted list lived and prospered in the hills of North Carolina and was finally captured wearing new clothes and with a fresh shave, despite a one-million-dollar reward. Everyone was astonished when it happened, but they shouldn't have been. What those law-enforcement people should have been paying attention to was the fact that 'Run Rudolph Run' T-shirts and bumper stickers were damned hot sellers in the area, and that there were enough local sympathizers—true believers—to keep Rudolph fed, clothed, and well taken care of right under their noses. Despite a massive ground search and the best experts and high technology, this guy lived two hundred yards from a strip mall in a densely populated area."

Rulon slammed his desk with the heel of his hand. "The reason Eric Rudolph remained free was because of sympathizers who were true believers like him. Not the whole county, to be sure, but it doesn't take a whole county—just a few true believers. They'd rather take care of him and give him food, shelter, and clothes than collect on a million bucks. They believed in him and his cause.

"Right now," Rulon said, "Klamath Moore is up there in Saddlestring with a bunch of followers. Most of his people have come in from other states, but some, no doubt, are local. Joe, how many people in your county would you guess are pro-hunting?"

"It's hard to say, but I'd guess sixty percent," Joe said. "Maybe higher."

"What percentage just couldn't care less?"

Joe shrugged. "Twenty-five, thirty percent, I'd say."

"Which leaves us what—ten percent anti-hunters?"

Joe nodded.

"How many of them are true believers?"

"I have no idea," Joe said.

"Even if it's five or ten people," Rulon said, "that's enough to create a support network for the guy who is out there. And that's all he needs. Plus, he'll have a good percentage of the press and a lot of sympathetic elitists who despise hunting on his side. And make no mistake, there are more people in this country against hunting than for it. Right now, today, even in my own state, Klamath Moore is up there preaching to the converted and radicalizing maybe just a few more folks over to his cause. His aim is to build something that will last a long time. As hard as it is to believe, gentlemen, there are already people all across this country and the world who look to Klamath Moore and the killer as heroes. Some of the news coverage is already being spun that way—'Neanderthal hunters in Wyoming are finally getting their comeuppance.' The world is going mad, as we know, but all these years we've been isolated from that. Not anymore.

"I predict there will be T-shirts and bumper stickers printed within the week. That unless we find this killer real fast, we won't find him for years. And that for every week that passes, this murderer will grow in stature among the loonies until he's a legend. And so will Kla-math Moore."

Rulon turned his attention to Randy Pope. "Now do you see the connection? Do you follow?"

"Yes, sir," Pope said, unable to swallow. "My agency will be decimated by the lack of revenue from hunting licenses."

"Not to mention how it'll kill sales tax revenue," Rulon said. "But Director Brewer and *Special Agent* Tony Portenson have some information and a new theory," Rulon said, leaning back in his chair, using the words *Special Agent* as if they were curse words. "Much of this was unknown to me until about an hour ago, and I'd very much like you to hear it."

Portenson glared at the governor with naked hatred. Joe thought, *There's something going on here.*

"KLAMATH MOORE really wasn't on our radar screen until recently," Richard Brewer said, withdrawing a file from his briefcase and placing it on the governor's desk. "Not until Director Pope contacted us with his suspicions that the 'accidental' hunting deaths of John Garrett and Warren Tucker might be connected in some way. For that, we sincerely thank you, Randy, for your prescience in this matter."

Pope sat up and nodded to Brewer, obviously thankful for the compliment.

"Most of what we know about Mr. Moore comes from his website," Brewer said. "I put three of our best investigators on it. They've produced this report"—Brewer tapped the file he'd produced—"which is, frankly, very disturbing."

Brewer spoke formally with a deep, melodious voice. He sat ramrod straight in his chair. He had dark hair, a prominent jaw, and heavy eyebrows that conveyed his "I am a serious man" persona.

Joe could hear shuffling and murmuring coming from the conference room next door where the press conference would be held. He checked his watch—ten minutes until the governor was scheduled to address the media.

Brewer continued, "On his website, Moore stokes the fires of the extreme animal-rights movement. He makes no bones about the fact that he finds hunting abhorrent and hunters demented. He advocates interfering with hunters in the field, and sabotaging hunting seasons across the country and the world. He's clever in how he does it, though, always couching his advocacy in phrases like 'We're not asking you to break the law, but . . .' or 'We don't advocate violence or criminality in any shape or form, but . . .' types of caveats. Obviously, he's been advised by lawyers so that his words are clear but he covers himself so he can't be held accountable for what happens.

"The most interesting thing we found on his website is called 'The Forum,'" Brewer continued, opening the file and pulling out a thick stack of printouts. "It's where his followers can post messages and have discussions. Sometimes, Mr. Moore joins in. And in doing so, he is often not as careful about his words and meaning as he is in his more formal statements on the website.

"For example, there was a post three weeks ago from a person who calls himself Wolverine. Rather than read it, I'll let you," Brewer said, handing copies to Joe and Pope.

Joe glanced at the pages, recognized the comment format of a blog.

I Had A Dream.

Last night, I had a dream. In my dream, a brainless American hunter was struck down and his body mutilated in the same way he had been mutilating innocent animals all his life. When he was found, people were horrified at what had been done to him. And then they began to realize this is what millions of Mighty Men do all the time. And it made them think about the pathetically sad and disgusting people in their midst who derive pleasure from killing creatures who have just as much right to be on this earth as they do.

I know, dreams are just dreams. But I'm a gambler. I like the odds that turning hunters into prey will make a difference and change some minds.

It was a good dream.

by Wolverine on Mon Sept 05 08:37:26 AM PST.

Wolverine Dreams.

I think it was a good dream, too. Sometimes it takes a shock to the system to make folks sit up and say, "There's something wrong going on here."

I'm just talking out loud, but this might be the thing that would actually make a difference if one were brave, committed, and a warrior.

by Klamath on Tues Sept 06 08:53:22 AM PST.

Re: I Had A Dream.

Especially if it happened slowly, over time. First an incident that made them scratch their heads while recoiling in horror at the same time, followed by another incident worse than the first. And another. And another. Until there was no doubt the hunters were being hunted and that none of them were safe. Until they began to realize the terror they feel is what they put animals through every time they go out to get their jollies.

There are warriors among us.

by Wolverine on Wed Sept 07 01:37:26 AM PST.

Re: Wolverine Dreams.

In your dream, where would the campaign begin? That's important to know, because it would be important for the enlightened to be there and offer support and encouragement. There is no news unless the trees falling in the forest are pointed out in loud voices to a sympathetic press. And believe me, they *looooove* me.

by Klamath on Wed Sept 07 02:02:12 AM PST.

Re: Re: I Had A Dream.

In my dream, it would definitely take place in the reddest of the Red States, both in terms of politics and the color of blood. Hit 'em where they live, is what I think.

by Wolverine on Wed Sept 07 03:37:26 AM PST.

Re: Re: Wolverine Dreams.

Although IT'S ONLY A DREAM, I am absolutely charged up by the pure boldness of the vision. While none of us advocate violence or criminal acts in any way, WE CAN DREAM, TOO.

Please contact me off-line, Wolverine. MAYBE I CAN TALK YOU DOWN.

by Klamath on Wed Sept 07 03:55:12 AM PST.

BREWER SAID, "This exchange took place two weeks prior to John Garrett's death near Lander. Obviously, Klamath came to his senses at the end there and tried to cover his enthusiasm for the concept. And by the next day, the entire thread had been pulled from the Forum page. Luckily, my tech guys had somehow automatically archived it during the night so we have it. Did you note the reference to gambling? Gamblers use poker chips."

Joe was suddenly wide awake, his mind spinning.

"Obviously," Brewer said, "we don't have enough to make any charges or even a serious accusation at this point. But when we saw this we wanted to trace the IP address of Wolverine and see if we could find him. That was beyond our expertise, so we turned to our brothers in law enforcement who are proficient in this kind of thing," he said, gesturing to Portenson, who was now smoldering.

"I'll take it from here," Rulon said, "since it is now three-twenty-five and my friends in the press are clamoring to take a chunk out of me just outside the door."

The governor pushed his face across the desk as if it were a balled fist, aiming it at Portenson. As he spoke, his voice didn't rise so much as get harder-edged, until he was biting off his words and spitting them out, flecking the top of his desk and Brewer's file with moisture.

"So my DCI takes the information to the FBI just down the street, where we get absolutely stonewalled. In the meantime, another innocent man, Frank Urman, gets butchered, which leads to three more deaths last night in a clusterfuck and a severed head mounted on a wall. Finally, we get our entire congressional delegation on the same line this morning and pressure is applied by them on Homeland Security to such a degree that Mr. Portenson and his pals *have* to talk to us. And when they do, we find out they've been monitoring Mr. Klamath Moore and his followers for months because they're considered to be potential domestic terrorists, and they even have a man on the inside! And while we won't accuse the FBI of being an accessory to murder since they didn't know all we knew—"

"Oh, come on!" Portenson shouted. "We were doing our jobs! We couldn't blow our undercover investigation for an office that leaks like a sieve!"

"We can say to the press out there," Rulon continued,

"without equivocation, that if the FBI had cooperated with us when we first asked for cooperation we might not be here today."

"That's ridiculous," Portenson seethed. "We had no idea this Wolverine person was going to start killing people—and we still don't know it was him. We have no idea who Wolverine is. We don't even know if he's in this country. The IP address he used was from one of those Internet kiosks in the Atlanta airport, so we can't trace him. You're speculating and trying to point the finger at us."

Rulon nodded his agreement.

"Who do you have on the inside?" Joe asked Portenson.

"Oh," the agent replied, deflated, "some guy. I can't give you his name. But we asked him a couple of weeks ago to see if he could figure out who Wolverine is. He's working on it, but he doesn't know yet."

"We need his name," Joe said. "I need to talk with him."

"Not a chance," Portenson said. "We're in the middle of breaking this thing. This is what we do now—domestic counterterrorism. We can't blow his cover and put him in danger."

"A name," Joe said, thinking of the promise he'd made to Nancy Hersig.

"Stella," Rulon said calmly, "please go tell the press I'll be out in a moment with a very big announcement."

Stella nodded dutifully and stood up.

Rulon said, "Let them know we've learned that Special Agent Tony Portenson of the FBI withheld information that resulted in the deaths of six people and the shutdown of state and federal lands across Wyoming."

"You can't do that!" Portenson shouted. "You're out of your mind!"

Rulon arched his eyebrows. "This isn't the first time someone has said that."

"I'm this far," Portenson said, pinching his index finger and thumb together, "from breaking this Klamath Moore thing and getting my transfer out of this hellhole. I should have been moved up a year ago, but it didn't happen. This will absolutely kill me! This might get me sent to Butte, Montana!"

"What's wrong with Butte?" Joe said. "I *like* Butte."

"It's where bad FBI agents are sent to die," Portenson whined.

"That's your choice," Rulon said, nodding to Stella to go.

"No!" Portenson said.

She hesitated at the door.

"What do you want?" Portenson pleaded with Rulon.

"Access to all your files on the Wolverine investigation and the name of your snitch so Joe can question him," Rulon said.

"Okay," Portenson said as if in physical pain. "You've got it."

"What's my role?" asked Randy Pope, the forgotten man.

"You stay here," Rulon said. "I want you in your office leading your agency and deflecting the outrage we're already getting from constituents about the state lands closure. Plus, I don't want you in a dicey situation where you might run like a rabbit again. That kind of behavior makes me want to puke."

"You don't understand," Pope said, pleading. "The head was in my room . . . this is personal. I *have* to be involved."

"No," Rulon said bluntly.

Pope dropped his head into his hands. Joe was put off and embarrassed by the reaction.

"Okay, then," Rulon said, gesturing to Stella to open the door.

Joe sat up. "That's not all."

Portenson and the governor both looked at him. Stella hesitated, with her manicured hand poised above the door handle.

"No," Portenson said, his face flushing red. "I know what you're going to ask, and the answer is: absolutely not. Don't even ask."

Joe turned to the governor. "Nate Romanowski knows the area and he has contacts with extremist groups all across the West. I don't condone it, but he does. He's got special insight into somebody like Wolverine because, frankly, Wolverine reminds me more than a little bit of Nate. If you want me to continue this investigation, I need his help."

Portenson continued to shake his head.

"If he was released into your custody," Rulon said, "do you give me your word you'll bring him back for his trial when and if this investigation is over?"

Joe swallowed hard. "I'll do what's right."

Portenson hissed, "We can't release a federal prisoner on Joe Pickett's word! We can't release him, period!"

Pope surprised Joe by saying, "I concur. We need all the help we can get."

Joe said to Portenson, "You charged him with flimsy evidence that hasn't gotten any better. You're just hoping something falls into your lap between now and the trial or you know you're going to lose."

"We're building our case!"

"Just like you were building the case against Klamath Moore and Wolverine?" Joe asked.

Rulon stood up. "Stella, tell them I'm coming out with *explosive news*."

"No!" Portenson shouted again, his voice cracking. Then: "Okay, okay!" He pointed his finger at Joe. "But if he doesn't live up to this agreement, I'm going to throw both of them in jail."

"Agreed," Rulon said breezily.

Joe wanted to tell the governor he'd perhaps spoken too soon. Although he had some influence over Nate and Nate had promised years before to assist Joe and protect his family, he didn't *own* the outlaw falconer. Nate had always gone his own way, used his own methods, lived under his own code.

"Governor . . ." Joe said, as Rulon turned and Stella preceded him out the door. His words were drowned out by Rulon booming, "Men and women of the press, we've got a break in the case! Due to an unprecedented partnership between the state of Wyoming and the Federal Bureau of Investigation, I can tell you today that we're closing in on the vicious killer who . . ."

As he went on, Joe slumped back in his chair, as did Portenson.

Joe listened to Rulon assure the media that the end of the investigation was now in sight, that leads were being vigorously pursued, that the forests and high-country plains of Wyoming would once again be reopened for hunting, fishing, and recreation.

"I can't believe I just agreed to release Nate Romanowski," Portenson said sourly to Joe.

I can't believe it either, Joe thought.

"That governor of yours," Portenson said, jabbing a finger toward the conference room. "He fucked us both."

"And that's why we love him," Stella said, overhearing Portenson and leaning in the door, flashing her biggest smile at Joe.

17

STELLA DROVE the Escalade with Joe in the passenger seat to meet Tony Portenson at the Federal Building before it closed at five. Joe knew the layout of Cheyenne well enough to know she was taking an unnecessarily circuitous route via Lincolnway and Depot Square downtown. When she stopped at a red light under the galloping plywood horse and rider of a massive western wear store, she said, "I'm really sorry for the families of the dead hunters, but I can't help but think that maybe some good can come of this in the long run. I never knew that's what hunters did to animals. I guess I never thought about it before. It repulses me. I told the governor that."

"And what did he say?" Joe asked.

"He just shook his head. He's a hunter."

Joe said nothing. She had the radio on a news station, and the reporter was excerpting portions of Rulon's press conference, saying the authorities were following every lead and closing in on the killer.

"Well spun," she said, nodding at the radio with professional admiration.

"I wish I agreed with it," Joe said.

She laughed. "If the governor says we're closing in on the killer, we're closing in on the killer. Come on, get with the program."

"I'll never get used to this," Joe grumbled.

"Back to where we were," she said, turning the radio off. "So you're a game warden. How can you stand to be around the kind of killing and mutilation that happens out there? You have daughters—how can you stand to see Bambi murdered?"

He eyed her closely to see if she was baiting him. She was, but there was a grain of sincere incredulity as well.

"I've yet to see Bambi murdered," he said.

"You know what I mean."

"In a shallow and very superficial way, I do," he said. "But that isn't what this is about. It's about the murder of innocent men. This has nothing to do with *hunting*. That's just what the shooter and Klamath Moore want you to think."

"Struck a nerve, eh?" she said, a slight smile on her lips.

Joe sighed. "In order to process a game animal properly, the carcass needs to be field-dressed and the head and hide removed. Otherwise, the meat can be ruined. It's not a pretty thing, but it's necessary. And it's not the purpose of the hunt."

"What is?" she said. "To drink whiskey and grunt and run around in the hills with a rifle?"

"I don't think we have the time for this," Joe said wearily, thinking he was sitting at the longest red light in the state of Wyoming. "I just hope you ask the same questions the next time you sit down to eat dinner. What events occurred behind the scenes and out of your view to deliver that food to you? Some eggs get broken to make your breakfast omelet, you know. Do you ever think of that?"

"That's different," she huffed. "The food producers didn't do it for pleasure. It is just a job to them."

"Most hunters don't kill for pleasure either," Joe said,

"and at least they're honest enough to get down and dirty and take part in the harvesting of the food they eat. They're honest enough not to use proxies to do their killing for them."

"*Honest* enough?" she said with some heat.

"Struck a nerve, eh?" Joe said, and smiled. "Hey, the light's green."

"SO ARE you surprised I'm here?" Stella asked as she swung into the parking garage of the Federal Building.

"Very," he said.

"Have you ever told anyone about what happened in Jackson?"

"I told Marybeth there was an attraction but nothing happened," Joe said. "She doesn't like you very much."

"Not that," she said, whacking him on the shoulder with the back of her hand. "I mean about my relationship with Will Jensen. Does anyone know but you?"

"No," he said.

"I helped him do what he was incapable of doing at the time."

"So you say," Joe said.

She pulled the big SUV into a dark parking space and turned off the motor and handed him the keys. "The governor is assigning this to you until you get your truck back," she said. "Despite your reputation for destroying government property."

"What about the state plane?" Joe asked. "I thought it was flying me back."

"He said he wouldn't send his worst enemy on that death trap."

"But . . ."

"Don't even ask, Joe. That's what I've learned."

He took the keys from her.

"I really like my new life here," she said. "I like working for the governor. I'm damned good at my job. This is my second chance in life, and I'd like to leave my past behind me. You're one of the few who know anything about it."

"Okay."

"What I'm asking you is if you'll let it all go, what happened."

"I already have," Joe said.

She let a beat go by. "Do you ever think of me?"

"Only in the past tense," Joe said.

Her eyes misted, and she wiped at them angrily. "I *hate* it when I do that. I don't even mean to," she said. "There is nothing about you to make me react this way. You are no Will Jensen, that's for sure."

Joe nodded. "Agreed. And you're no Marybeth. Now let's go see Portenson and get Nate before they close the building on us."

As they walked to the elevator, she briefly locked his arm in hers, said, "I can be your best friend or your worst enemy, you know."

As the elevator doors opened, Joe turned to her. "Likewise."

THE FBI'S MAN on the inside of Klamath Moore's movement was named Bill Gordon, according to the file handed over to Joe by a reluctant special agent. Gordon was from Lexington, Kentucky. There were three photos of him in the file. The informant was tall and lean with a ponytail, a long nose, and soulful eyes. Joe thought he recognized him from the gathering in front of the county building that morning.

Joe skimmed the documents behind the photo, learning that Gordon had encountered Klamath Moore and a few of his followers on a tract of heavily wooded and undeveloped land outside Lexington two years before when Moore was searching for a good place to set up a camp and hold a rally. Gordon was a solitary, bookish outdoorsman who knew of Moore and his beliefs but didn't tell Klamath he vehemently disagreed with him. Instead, he shared tales of the Kentucky woods and helped Moore set up a campsite on the shore of a lake. Keeping his inclinations to himself, he stayed around for a small firelight rally where Moore spoke. Once Gordon felt he'd gained Moore's trust, he visited the FBI office in Lexington and offered to become their informant in exchange for travel expenses and enough compensation to buy a small cabin he had his eye on next to a fine trout stream. The FBI, flush with Homeland Security cash and a new emphasis on domestic counterterrorism, thought it was a good deal all around.

The file contained Gordon's reports from rallies across the United States and trips to Bath, England, and Tours, France. Joe closed the file, planning on reading later.

"Can you please let Bill Gordon know I'll be contacting him?" Joe asked the agent, who answered by looking over his shoulder toward the corner office where Portenson sat with his door closed and the blinds half-drawn, trying unsuccessfully to ignore Joe and Stella.

"I'll have to get permission to do that," the agent said.

"I'll need it before I can leave," Joe said.

The agent got up and approached Portenson's office and rapped on the door. Portenson signaled him in and Joe could overhear a sharp exchange.

When the agent came out, he looked chastened. "We'll do it, but we have to wait until Gordon checks in. We can't just call him on his cell phone in case he's in a meeting with Klamath Moore or something."

"How often does he call in?"

"Twice a week, Mondays and Thursdays. He calls during working hours."

"Did he call in today?"

"I didn't take the call, but he must have."

"So you won't hear from him for three days, until next Thursday?" Joe asked.

The agent nodded.

"I hate to wait that long," Joe said, mostly to himself.

The agent shrugged. "Nothing I can do."

"There's something else," the agent said. "Agent Portenson asked me to tell you they're bringing up the accused and the paperwork assigning him to your custody. He said Ms. Ennis needs to sign as well on behalf of the governor's office."

Joe and Stella exchanged glances.

"Don't screw this up, Joe," she said. "If my name's on the document you better make sure you bring him back."

Joe shrugged. "I'll do my best."

"I hope you'll do better than that."

Joe's phone burred in his pocket and he drew it out. It was Pope.

"You need to keep me apprised, Joe," Pope said, "every single step of the way. *Every. Single. Step.*"

"I don't work for you," Joe said.

"You don't understand," Pope said, his voice cracking. "This means everything to me. My agency, my career—"

Joe snapped his phone shut as the heavy doors opened and Nate Romanowski was led into the room in an orange jumpsuit, his cuffs and leg irons clanking.

But it wasn't the Nate he knew, Joe thought. The man who shuffled forward with the crew cut, sallow complexion, slumping shoulders, and haunted blue eyes just looked like the container that used to house Nate.

18

THEY DROVE NORTH on I-25 under a wide-open dusk sky striped with vermilion cloud slashes stacked on the western horizon. The lights of Cheyenne were an hour behind them. Mule deer and pronghorn antelope raised their heads as the Escalade passed by, the tires sizzling on the highway, acknowledging the fact that Joe Pickett and Nate Romanowski were reunited. Or at least to Joe it seemed like it was what they were doing.

Nate had a smell about him that hung in the closed space of the state Escalade. Sterile, institutional, vapid. A jail smell. He wore his orange prison jumpsuit and a pair of blue boat shoes without laces.

"Nice sunset," Nate said in a whisper so low Joe asked him to repeat it.

When he did, Joe said, "Yup."

"They've got nice sunsets down here on the high plains," Nate said. "I know this because I've watched three-hundred-and-five of 'em straight through a little gap in the window of my cell. This makes three-hundred-and-six."

NATE SEEMED to relax as they hurtled into the night, Joe thought, as if his friend were shedding bits of defensive armor that had formed on his body over the past year, leaving them to skitter across the highway behind them like chunks of ice from the undercarriage of a car. Nate said, "It's no fun to be in prison, I don't care what anyone says."

Joe grunted.

"Can you pull over here?" Nate said, gesturing to an exit off the highway that led to a ranch a mile away whose blue pole lights twinkled in the darkness.

Nate was out of the vehicle before Joe fully stopped it. Joe watched Nate stumble out and walk briskly into the brush, his broad back reflecting moonlight. Nate dropped to his knees and bent over forward, as if praying or in pain.

Joe called, "Are you all right?"

"Fine."

It took a moment for Joe to realize Nate was burrowing his face into the ground, breathing in the sweet dusky smell of sagebrush and grass, filling himself with fresh outdoor air as if fumigating his lungs of tainted, indoor oxygen.

While he waited for Nate, Joe called Marybeth on his cell phone.

"I've got him," he said.

"Nate? How's he doing?"

"I can't tell yet."

"Where is he now?"

"Outside the car smelling sagebrush."

She chuckled.

"How's Nancy?" he asked.

"Doing well, considering. I just left her at her house. She's got relatives on the way. I'm going to go home and bake her a casserole and bring it by tomorrow."

"How are the girls?"

"Fine. Joe, it's only been two days since you went up into the mountains."

"It seems longer than that."

"A lot has happened, hasn't it? You need to come home and get some sleep."

"I need *you.*"

"That's sweet, Joe. But you need sleep even more."

He shook his head, not thinking that she couldn't see him. "Did you hear the governor's press conference?"

She laughed drily. "Yes, it's good to know you're closing in on the bad guy."

"We aren't," Joe said with a sigh.

"I didn't think so. Maybe Nate can help you out."

Joe looked up to see Nate shedding his jumpsuit and rolling it into a ball, which he threw into the darkness like a football. Nate turned and walked back toward the Escalade in his laceless boat shoes, kicking off his baggy, dingy jail boxers. He left them draped in the branches of a mountain mahogany bush.

"You might not say that if you could see him now," Joe said.

"Tell him hello," she said. "Tell him we missed him."

"I'm going to tell him to put some clothes on," Joe said.

"What?"

"I'll explain later," Joe said.

"Call when you get close to town. Try to stay awake."

Nate climbed into the passenger seat, briskly rubbing his arms, chest, and thighs.

"It feels good to get that shit off," he said, closing the door.

Joe eased onto the highway and set his cruise control at two miles under the speed limit. He didn't want to risk being pulled over by a trooper while driving the governor's car and trying to explain why there was a naked man sitting next to him.

———

"Joe," Nate said as they got back on the highway, "I'm not going back."

"But—"

"I'm not going back."

"We'll discuss it later."

"There's nothing to discuss," Nate said with absolute finality.

To keep awake and try to make some sense out of the last two days, Joe detailed to Nate what had happened to the hunters and the investigation thus far. Nate listened silently, grunting and shaking his head.

At a convenience store near Casper, Joe filled the Escalade with gas and bought a set of extra-large Wyoming Cowboys sweats inside from a discount rack. He handed them to Nate, said, "Put these on."

"I was just starting to feel good again," Nate said sourly.

They were south of Kaycee when Nate finally said, "Amateurs."

"Who?"

"All of you. Everyone except the shooter. He's been playing with you people."

"Maybe I ought to take you back," Joe said.

Nate snorted. "Don't be so sensitive. When I think about what you've told me, there are some things that just don't fall into place like they should. When you lay it all out, there are some wrong notes in the narrative."

"What wrong notes?"

"I'm not sure yet," he said. "I've got to think about it more, let it settle and see what rises to the top or sinks to the bottom. But something just doesn't work right here. It all seems so neat while at the same time there's something wrong."

"I have no idea what you're saying," Joe said, taking the exit for Kaycee.

"Neither do I," Nate said. "But I get the feeling none of this has much to do with hunting."

"That's what *I* said."

"Great minds." Nate smiled. "Hey, I'm hungry. Pull over here."

AS THEY entered the town of Kaycee, Joe and Nate both raised imaginary glasses and clinked them, said, "To Chris," referring to the late, great singer, rodeo champion, and Wyoming icon Chris Ledoux, who died young and once lived there on a ranch outside the town limits. His family still did.

Nate and Joe pretended to toast and drink. It was something they did every time they drove by.

THE ONLY restaurant in Kaycee was closed, but Nate knew where the owner lived and directed Joe to a shambling log home in a bank of cottonwood trees outside the town limits. Nate got out and banged on the front door until a massive man threw open the door, ready to pound whoever was disturbing him. The fat, bearded man at the door was nearly seven feet tall and dressed in a wife-beater undershirt and thick leather gloves up to his elbows. Joe hung back while the man recognized Nate—a fellow falconer—and enthusiastically invited both of them into his home. The man pulled off the gloves he'd been wearing so his falcons could sit on his forearm while he groomed them, and started pan-frying two of the biggest steaks Joe had ever seen.

While they ate, Nate and the restaurant owner—he

introduced himself to Joe as Large Merle—talked falconry and hunting. Joe looked around the house, which was dark and close and messy. Merle obviously lived alone except for his falcons, four of them, all hooded and sleeping, perched on handcrafted stands in the living room. The place smelled of feathers, hawk excrement, and eighty years of fried grease and cigarette smoke.

"D'you get your elk this year?" Large Merle asked Nate.

"No," Nate said. "I was in jail."

"Poor bastard," Merle said. "And now you can't go, since Governor Nut closed the state down. Man, if I could get my hands on the guy who shot those hunters I would break him in two."

Large Merle eyed Joe for the first time. "You gonna find that guy?"

"We hope to," Joe said.

"You better," Merle said. "Or we're going to do it for you. That's why we live here. And it won't be pretty. How's your steak?"

"Huge."

Merle smiled and nodded. One of his prairie falcons dropped a plop of white excrement onto his ham-sized forearm like a dollop of toothpaste being squeezed from a tube.

"Borrow your phone, Merle?" Nate asked.

"You bet, buddy," Merle said, then turned back to Joe as Nate took the phone into the other room.

"I've heard of you," Merle said, looking at Joe's nameplate with narrowed eyes.

"Is that good or bad?" Joe asked.

"Mostly good," Merle said, not expounding. "Me and Nate go way back. He's the only guy I know who scares me. Whoever that knucklehead is killing hunters? He don't scare me. But Nate scares me."

Joe sat back and put his knife and fork to the side of his plate. He'd eaten half the steak and couldn't eat any more.

Merle leaned forward. "Did Nate ever tell you about

that time in Haiti? When the four drugged-out rebels jumped him?"

"No."

Merle shook his head and chuckled, the fat jiggling under his arms and his chin. "Quite a story," Merle said. "Especially the part about guts strung through the trees like Christmas lights. Ask him about that one sometime!"

Joe nodded.

"It's a hell of a story," Merle said, still chuckling.

BACK IN the Escalade, Joe said, "Don't ever tell me about Haiti."

"Okay."

"Because I don't want to know."

"Okay."

"It's gone pretty well so far over the years with you not telling me what you do for a living. I think that's best."

"Since you're in law enforcement, I'd agree."

"And let's not eat at Large Merle's again soon."

"I needed a big steak. Merle and I go way back."

"So I heard. So," Nate asked, "how's my girl?"

"Marybeth?" Joe asked, feeling the hairs on the back of his neck bristle.

"Sheridan," Nate said, rolling his eyes. "The falconer's apprentice."

Joe calmed. "She's sixteen. That's a tough age. She can't decide if her parents are idiots or what. All in all, though, considering what she's been through in her life, she's doing well, I'd say. I sort of miss her as a little girl, though."

"Don't," Nate said. "From her letters, she sounds smart and well adjusted. And she doesn't really think you're an idiot. In fact, I think she admires her parents very much."

Joe had forgotten about the letters. "So why did you ask? You know more about her than I do now."

Nate laughed but didn't disagree.

————

IT WAS nearly midnight as Joe crossed over into Twelve Sleep County. The full moon lit up pillowy cumulus clouds over the Bighorns as if they had blue pilot lights inside, and the stars were white and accusatory in the black sky.

"You can drop me here," Nate said, indicating an exit off the two-lane that led eventually to his stone house on the banks of the Twelve Sleep River. Joe slowed.

"You've got a ride?" Joe asked.

Nate nodded. "Alisha. I called her from Large Merle's. It's been a while."

Alisha Whiteplume was a Northern Arapaho who had grown up on the reservation and returned to teach third grade and coach girls' basketball at the high school. She was tall, dark, and beautiful, with long hair so black it shimmered blue in the sunshine. Nate and Alisha had gotten together the previous year, and Joe had never seen him so head over heels in love.

Joe stopped and got out with Nate. The night had cooled and Joe could see his breath. The air smelled of sage, drying leaves, pine, and emptiness.

"You don't have to wait," Nate said.

"I don't mind. I don't want to just leave you out here."

"It's okay," Nate said. "Really."

Joe looked at his watch—after midnight.

JOE FELT it before he actually saw it, a falcon in the night sky, silhouetted against a cloud. The falcon, Nate's peregrine, dropped from the cloud into the complete darkness beneath it and Joe lost track of it until it streaked through the air directly above their heads with a swift whistling sound.

"How could the bird know you're back?" Joe asked, as much to himself as to Nate.

"The bird just knows," Nate said.

The falcon turned gracefully before swooping against the wall of a butte and returned, landing in the darkness of the brush about a hundred feet from the truck with a percussive flap of its wings.

Nate turned to Joe. "You can go now. Let me get reacquainted with my bird."

"I'll be in touch tomorrow, then," Joe said. "Where will you be? Here or at Alisha's?"

Nate shrugged.

"Nate, I'm responsible . . ."

Nate waved him off. "Give me a couple of days. I need to get reoriented, get the lay of the land. I need to spend some time with Alisha and get my head back on straight."

Joe hesitated.

"Besides," Nate said, "you've gone the tracking-and-forensics route on this shooter, right? And you figured out exactly nothing. I need to try another angle."

"What other angle?" Joe asked.

"Go home, Joe," Nate said. "I'll be in touch."

Joe sighed.

"Don't worry. I'll be in touch. Get going—go home and see Marybeth."

AS NATE RECEDED in the rearview mirror, Joe had a niggling feeling about the brusque way Nate had said good-bye. While Joe had witnessed, in the past, Nate doing some horrendous things—like ripping the ears off suspects—he'd never known his friend to be *rude*.

After cresting a rise and dropping down over the top, Joe killed his lights and pulled off the highway and took a weeded-over two-track to the north. The old jeep trail serpentined through the breaklands and eventually culminated at the top of a rise. When he used to patrol the area, the rise had been one of his favored places to perch and glass the high meadows and deep-cut draws of the terrain. With his lights still out and using the glow of the moon and stars, Joe climbed the vehicle up the rise and carefully nosed it just short of the top, carefully keeping the mass of the hill between himself and where he'd left Nate on the highway. He was thankful there were binoculars in the utility box of the Escalade.

On his hands and knees, Joe scuttled across the powdery dirt, crying out when he kneed a cactus whose needles easily pierced through the fabric of his Wranglers.

He eased over the top of the rise, fighting back feelings of suspicion and guilt, trying to convince himself he was looking out for Nate, not spying on him.

He couldn't see Nate in the darkness, but he could see the black ribbon of highway where he'd left him. And from the direction of Nate's stone house, he could see a pair of headlights slowly picking their way across the breaklands toward Nate. Joe pulled the binoculars up and adjusted the lens wheel until the vehicle came into sharp focus. It was a light-colored Ford or Chevy SUV. He couldn't yet see the plates. He didn't know what Alisha Whiteplume drove these days so he didn't know if it was her car.

As the vehicle drew closer, Nate, with the peregrine on his fist, became illuminated in its headlights. He stood out, bathed in the halogen lights, darkness around him in all directions. Nate raised his arm with the falcon on it in greeting. The SUV stopped twenty feet from Nate. Dust from the tires lit up in a slow-motion swirl in the headlights. Joe swung the binoculars back to the car.

When the passenger door opened, the dome light inside the SUV lit up and Alisha Whiteplume, looking tall and thin and striking, hurled herself out into the brush and ran toward Nate with open arms. Joe started to follow her with the glasses when he realized there were others in the vehicle, something he hadn't expected.

Steadily, he moved the binoculars back. The dome light was still on because the passenger door was open. The man behind the wheel was Bill Gordon. In the backseat were Klamath Moore and his wife.

Joe's mouth went dry and his heart thumped in his chest. His hands went cold and slick and the binoculars slipped out of them into the dirt.

19

ON TUESDAY MORNING, Joe Pickett stood at the stove in an apron and made pancakes for his daughters whom, he hoped, would eventually wake up and want to eat them. When the pancakes were cooked he moved them to a large serving plate that he warmed in the oven so they'd be hot and ready. Bacon sizzled in his favorite cast-iron skillet and maple syrup warmed in a pan of water. The morning smells of breakfast cooking and brewed coffee were good smells, and he tried not to think of the roof that needed repair or the fence that needed fixing. It was nice to be home and doing something routine, although he didn't yet consider this house on this street to be home. He could see his neighbor Ed outside already in his perfectly appointed backyard, prowling the lawn while smoking his pipe, apparently targeting thin places in the turf where weeds might get a stonghold and grow when spring came. While Joe watched, Ed raised his head to look over the fence at the Pickett house, and Ed shook his head sadly, as if the mere sight of it made him want to weep.

For years, whether at the state-owned house on Bighorn

Road or the old homestead house they'd lived in on the Longbrake Ranch, there had been no neighbors except wildlife. When the bathroom was occupied, which was nearly full-time with a houseful of females, Joe was used to going outside to relieve himself, which felt normal and good because there was no one around. Sometimes, he would go outside and sit on a stump and smoke a cheap cigar and watch antelope or deer moving cautiously toward water. On the ranch it was cows. Sometimes he would just sit and think and dream, trying to figure out why things were, how they worked, what his role was in the scheme of life. He ended up short on answers. His only conclusion was that his purpose, his reason for being, was to be a good husband and father and not to shame either his wife or his daughters. Why he'd been chosen by the governor to be his point man in the field still baffled Joe. Rulon once said, "When I think of crime committed out of doors, I think of Joe Pickett. Simple as that." But it wasn't as simple as that, Joe thought.

In this house in town Joe felt contained, bottled up, tamped down. He longed to look out the window and see an antelope or a cow and not Ed. But he didn't have a choice at the moment other than to make more pancakes and try not to speculate that Nate Romanowski had betrayed him.

MARYBETH RETURNED from her morning walk with Maxine on a leash. She'd scarcely unclipped the leash before the Labrador collapsed in a heap and went immediately to sleep. "Poor old girl," she said, patting their old dog. "She still wants to go, but she sure doesn't have the energy she used to have."

Joe nodded. He didn't like contemplating Maxine's inevitable demise and tried not to think about it. Marybeth was much more practical about life-and-death matters and had said she would continue to take Maxine out until Maxine could no longer go. Then they'd have a decision to make.

"Breakfast smells good," she said. "I'll wake up the girls in a minute."

Joe handed her a mug of coffee.

"How are you doing?" she asked, taking it and sipping. "You tossed and turned all night long. Did you get any sleep?"

"Some."

They'd talked briefly the night before when he got home after one. He was still reeling from what he'd seen through the binoculars.

"Have you heard from him?" she asked.

"No."

She nodded. "On my walk I was thinking a lot about what you saw last night. I can't come up with a good explanation. What it all boils down to is you either trust him or you don't."

"He's never given me a reason not to trust him," Joe said.

"That's all you've got," she said, taking her coffee with her to wake up Sheridan and Lucy.

AFTER THE breakfast dishes were cleared away, Marybeth took Lucy to school and Joe read over the file he'd been given from the FBI. Bill Gordon was indeed deep inside Klamath Moore's organization, and one of the few of his followers to travel with Moore from rally to rally. The reports in the file were records of the calls Gordon had made to the FBI when he checked in on Mondays and Thursdays. They went back two years.

Six months before, an enterprising agent had summarized the reports up to that date.

The Klamath Moore Animal Rights Movement

KM is the self-appointed leader and spokesman of the movement.

The number of "members" is unknown and as far as BG knows there is no formal membership list. Based on the attendance at rallies, BG estimates the membership to be more than 200 and less than 500 hard-core followers. KM enjoys telling the media his sympathizers are "ten thousand strong," but there is no evidence to confirm this.

The movement has no formal name or charter. There are no officers or leadership structure. This is by design. BG describes the movement as "nonlinear," like al-Qaeda.

BG says KM has studied al-Qaeda and used the terrorist organization as a model for structure and purpose. KM says he can never mass enough followers to mount a legitimate, large-scale fight against hunting in the United States. But like AQ, he can—with a very small organization of loyal followers—strike surgically and create chaos far beyond their actual strength.

Communication with sympathizers is done exclusively via the Web. Access to the nonpublic URLs is password-protected and changed at random. It's unknown how many followers visit the nonpublic websites.

The financing of KM and his effort is murky. BG says KM always seems to have enough money to travel, self-publish pamphlets, and pay organization costs for staging rallies. The hat is passed around at rallies but BG says he's seen the results and the cash collected isn't substantial enough—amounting to a few hundred dollars, usually—to sustain such an effort. BG speculates that KM has a trust-fund inheritance and that he draws from it when he needs money. BG says only rich people never talk of money so he figures KM is rich. We have asked BG to investigate the funding angle further.

KM has close relationships with sympathetic reporters at two major television networks and one cable news network (names deleted). These reporters are rewarded for their sympathetic treatment of his cause by being tipped off ahead of time to the staging of events so they will have exclusives. KM will only talk to sympathetic reporters so portrayals of him in the media are generally positive.

KM claims to "own" two congressmen and one senator (names deleted).

KM's last known address is Boulder, CO, but he keeps constantly on the move. He lives like a fugitive, staying with sympathizers across the nation and around the world.

KM keeps in contact with like-minded organizations including PETA, the Animal Liberation Front, Earth First!, Animal Defense Alliance, and similar organizations around the world dedicated to animal rights and the anti-hunting movement (list attached).

JOE FLIPPED to the list and was shocked by the sheer number of animal rights organizations. He counted 248 groups in the United States and Canada alone, and thirty-six more in other countries. Most of the organizations stated that they were against "hunting, the fur trade, circuses, rodeos, and animal experimentation." The names were all unfamiliar to him, but varied from the Animal Crusaders in Tucson to Action for Animals in Oakland to SKUNKS, an acronym for the Palmdale, California, Society of Kind Understanding and Not Killing Skunks.

He shook his head and read on:

KM travels with a laptop computer from which he manages his public website and the nonpublic websites. BG says KM claims not to need more than three hours of sleep a night, and spends countless hours communicating with followers.

KM told BG a week prior to the trespass and arson at a Texas hunting ranch near Waco that "something big is about to happen," but KM could not be physically placed in Texas during the crime. BG didn't know KM's whereabouts during that week, but assumed he was involved.

KM was in nearby Wyoming when David Linsicomb, the most prominent of Idaho's domestic trophy elk breeders, was run off the road near Driggs and killed when his vehicle rolled over. On the night of the accident, BG could not verify KM's whereabouts.

KM's wife, Shannon, and his infant daughter frequently travel with him. BG gets along well with Shannon, who is Native American.

At rallies, KM traces his hatred of hunting and hunters to his boyhood in Oregon's Klamath Valley (hence the name he is known by, his actual name is Harold). KM's uncle used to take him deer hunting. KM says his uncle shot and wounded two deer but didn't pursue them because it was too much trouble. When he finally killed a large trophy near the road, his uncle stood by and watched the buck bleed out instead of putting it out of its misery. The instance so scarred KM that his life's mission was revealed to him at that moment, he claims. BG says KM hinted that his uncle eventually "got what was coming to him" but didn't elaborate. Bureau follow-up reveals that KM's uncle, one Everett Dysall of Klamath Falls, OR, died in 1997 from food poisoning. No foul play was suspected at the time. A bureau review of the autopsy and interview with the attending coroner corroborates the cause of death but provided no solid link to KM.

BG says KM seems excited about something about to happen, something BG thinks will be bigger than anything else thus far. Says KM hints that "something is in the works that will blow everybody away."

"GEE," JOE said aloud, "I wonder what he's referring to?"

He sat back and rubbed his chin. He was looking forward to talking with Bill Gordon. The hunting story concerning Moore's uncle made him angry. Nothing made him angrier than cruel acts by thoughtless hunters.

"If the story is true," Joe mumbled, "he deserved it."

"Who deserved what?" Sheridan asked as she entered the kitchen. She'd just showered and she wore a towel wrapped around her head.

"Hey, nice hat," Joe said.

She made a face at him because he'd made it a practice over the years to greet her that way when she was turbaned. Joe was surprised to see Sheridan.

"Why aren't you at school?"

"In-service training day for high school teachers. We've got the day off."

"Who deserved it?" she asked, sitting across from him at the table. "What are you reading?"

"Files on Klamath Moore," Joe said.

Her eyes narrowed. "I don't like him. He's a bully."

"You've *met* him?"

Joe was astounded by both the coincidence and the fact that a teacher had arranged for an in-school program by a man on the FBI's domestic terror watch list.

She told him the story from her class the day before.

"This was your teacher's idea?" Joe said, astounded.

"Mrs. Whaling's kind of, well, passionate about some things. I don't think she knew what kind of jerk he is. But I didn't call him a jerk. I called him an asshole."

Joe flinched.

"I liked his wife, though," she said. "She was kind to me."

"Shannon?"

"I didn't get her name. He didn't introduce her, which was just not cool. So," she said, tapping the file, "what does it say about him?"

"I really can't get into the specifics," Joe said. "Sorry."

"Do you think he has something to do with the murders?"

"I'm not sure," Joe said, "but he may know something about them. But please, keep this between us. I can't believe I'm even discussing this with you."

"I'm interested in this kind of stuff," Sheridan said, rolling her eyes. "I've been around it all my life, you know."

"I wish you hadn't," Joe said, stung.

She shrugged. "It is what it is."

"My, you're philosophical these days."

He could tell she had something on her mind, so he waited her out.

"What about what Klamath Moore says?" she asked. "I mean, he's a jerk and all, but . . ."

"But what?"

"Do people really need to hunt? I mean, there're easier ways to get food. Like go to the store."

"Do you really think that?" he asked.

She shrugged. "I'm not sure. On the one hand I do. But on the other . . ." She reached for a banana from a bowl of fruit on the table and began to peel it. "In order to eat this I need to literally pull the skin off. That's pretty gross if you think of it that way. And in order to get milk, some guy has to yank on the private parts of a poor old cow. I mean, yuck."

Joe smiled.

She took a bite of the banana. "It's too bad we can't figure out a way to live without making other creatures give up their lives, is what I'm saying. Or something like it."

"It's a dilemma," Joe said. "But let me ask you something. As people build more and more homes in places where wildlife lives, there are more and more encounters. Add to that the fact that the population of many species— deer, bears, mountain lions, elk—are increasing beyond carrying capacities. Is it better for that excess wildlife to starve to death, to be slaughtered by sharpshooters or hit by cars, or is it better for the animals to be harvested by hunters, who thank them for their meat and their lives? And you can't *not* choose one of them. People can't just say how much they love animals and turn their heads away and not have some kind of responsibility. My job as a game warden is to make that last choice—hunting—as efficient, biologically responsible, and sporting as possible."

Sheridan nodded slowly.

"I talked too much," Joe said, looking down.

"No, I appreciate what you said," Sheridan mused. "And there's another thing I think about. If I were given a choice to live in a world where some people still know how to hunt and survive in the wilderness or a world where it's all been forgotten, I want to live in that first world. I remember watching television after nine/eleven when all the news people started praising those police and firemen like they didn't even know those men were still around, like they'd sort of looked down on them for years and years. But all of a sudden, when people needed rescuing and somebody had to be physically brave, they were really glad those men were still around after all. It's sort of like that."

She said, "If something big happens and the electricity and Internet go out and we run out of gasoline and groceries, I'm not going to ask Ed Nedny next door or some computer game geek or Emo at school for help. I'm coming straight to you, Dad, because I know you know how to keep us alive."

Joe grinned, embarrassed but proud.

"One thing I do know, though," she said, chewing, "is that when somebody is as hateful as Klamath Moore is—

even if it is sort of for a good cause—I don't like them. It's too much."

Joe nodded. "You *are* philosophical. And maybe even wise."

She grinned at the compliment. "When people want to control other people . . . it's like those fascists, you know?"

Joe wasn't sure what to say. His daughter amazed him. Where had little Sheridan gone?

"Hey, nice hat," he said.

WHEN THE telephone rang Sheridan sprang out of her chair to answer it, assuming it was for her. She said, "Just a minute, I'll get him," and handed the handset to Joe.

"Your boss," she said, rolling her eyes. "Gotta go."

Joe sighed. "Yes?"

Randy Pope said, "Any progress?"

"None."

"None?"

"None."

"What's your plan of attack?"

"I don't have one," Joe said. "I'm reviewing the FBI files. I just got home at one in the morning."

Pope cursed. "So you're just *sitting* around? Do you not quite understand the significance of this case? Are you aware that your sheriff is assembling teams to go into the mountains and hunt the shooter down? That he is on the Associated Press saying, and I quote, 'Since the governor has thrown up his hands and gone to ground, we've got to take on this thing ourselves.'"

"I hadn't heard," Joe said. "But wouldn't it be good if the shooter was arrested? Isn't that what we want?"

Pope paused uncomfortably long. "Of course that's what we want."

Joe wondered, *Why the hesitation?*

"Is there something you're not telling me, Randy?"

Pope snorted. "Back to that again, eh? Why can't you

just do your job without constantly questioning me? If you spent half the time trying to find this killer that you do questioning my motives, we might actually have some progress. Have you thought of that?"

Nice dodge, Joe thought.

"I put my reputation on the line supporting your insistence on springing that Nate Romanowski," Pope said. "I hope you're in control of him. Is he there with you now?"

"No."

"No? Where is he?"

I don't have a clue, Joe thought, but said, "He's following some leads on his own." He hoped it didn't sound like the lie it possibly was.

Pope took an audible breath before shouting, "*On his own!* He's got federal charges against him and he was released to your custody! *On his own?* What are you thinking?"

Joe didn't respond.

"Are you out of your mind? If either the governor or the FBI finds out he's *on his own* you'll be toast. I'll be toast. And so will the governor! Jesus, what are you thinking?"

Joe swallowed. "Nate operates on different channels than we do. He works best with a loose rein."

"All I can say is you had better rein him in! Like right now." Pope moaned, and Joe could visualize the man pacing his office with his free hand flying around his head like a panicked bird. "I don't know why the governor even trusts you," Pope said.

Me either, Joe thought.

"I'm calling you tomorrow," Pope said, "and when I do, you had better be able to hand the phone over to your friend Nate Romanowski so I can talk to him. And if he isn't there . . . there will be hell to pay."

Joe raised his eyebrows.

"If he isn't there, I'm coming up there again to take over this investigation. Do you hear me?"

Joe punched off the phone.

———

HE DIDN'T like what Pope had told him about the sheriff, though. Not that the sheriff was disparaging the governor so much as McLanahan leading parties of armed men into the field was a recipe for disaster.

ATTACHED TO the summary of Bill Gordon's calls were several sheets of names Gordon had gathered from rallies around the country. Joe guessed it was the closest thing there was to a membership roster of Klamath Moore's movement. A caveat at the top of the first page, written by the agent who compiled the list, said the spelling of the names couldn't be verified.

Joe skimmed the list. A couple of names jumped out at him because they were Hollywood actors.

On the third page he saw it: Alisha Whiteplume.

He moaned and raked his fingers through his hair.

Joe recalled what Marybeth had said about Nate: "What it all boils down to is you either trust him or you don't."

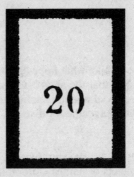

20

FOR THE REST OF Saturday and Sunday, Joe tried to reach Nate Romanowski while at the same time avoiding calls from Randy Pope. Joe tried Nate's home on the river and his cell (both long disconnected) as well as Alisha Whiteplume's home (no answer, but Joe left repeated messages) and her employer (Wind River Indian High School), who said she'd called in sick both Monday and Tuesday. As each hour went by with no contact from Nate, Joe knew he was digging himself deeper and deeper into a professional hole he may never be able to climb out of. He considered calling Bud Longbrake, Marybeth's stepfather, to see if the rancher could use a ranch foreman again, but decided to wait.

There were no more murders.

Joe's only progress, and it was minimal, was to learn via Deputy Mike Reed that Klamath Moore's followers were staying at the Blue Moon Motel, an ancient but clean twenty-room throwback to the 1950s at the edge of town. The motel was a favorite of budget-minded fishermen because it catered to weekly rentals and had kitchenettes. During hunting season, the owners allowed hunters to hang antelope and deer from a huge cottonwood in the courtyard. Joe wondered how Klamath's people would react to *that*—until he remembered that the state was all but shut down for hunting while the shooter remained free, so there would be no hunters.

He assumed that Bill Gordon would be at the Blue Moon Motel, and planned to contact the informant that evening after he'd checked in with the FBI and was notified of Joe's assignment.

Joe and Reed had agreed to meet for breakfast Wednesday morning at the Chuckwagon Diner to compare notes and catch each other up on new information or lack thereof. Maybe, Joe thought, Reed or someone in the sheriff's department had seen Nate.

JOE WAS downtown early to exchange the Yukon for his repaired pickup and to meet Reed for breakfast. As he drove to the Chuckwagon he happened on a spectacle taking place in front of the county building, something out of an old western movie, as the sheriff organized a posse to search for the shooter in the mountains. Each team consisted of at least four men, all heavily armed and recently deputized. Joe recognized many of the volunteers from out in the field or at high-school sporting events or simply around town. These were not the small-town elite, the city council types or the lawyers or cronies of the politicians or business leaders who met each morning at the Burg-O-Pardner to drink coffee and plot how to run the town. These men were the blue-collar guys, the ones who fixed cars and dug septic systems and stacked hay and kept Saddlestring operating. The men who worked hard so they could go hunting for two weeks out of the year, the men who asked, "Get your elk yet?" to one another by way of greeting. Joe knew them, liked them for the most part, respected them for both their work and their outdoor ethic, and wondered if the sheriff had any idea what he was doing.

The sheriff had assigned each team a sector and given them radios to check in with his dispatcher on the hour. McLanahan milled among them, slapping backs, shaking hands, asking if they wanted any of the coffee or doughnuts that had been donated to the cause by a bakery.

Joe pulled over to watch the assemblage and recognized Chris Urman lining up to be one of the volunteers. Leaving his truck running, he approached Urman and tried to keep out of McLanahan's view.

"How are you doing?" Joe asked. "Is your family okay?"

Urman shrugged. "My aunt is a mess, of course, but we're hanging in there."

"Be careful up there," Joe said. "It could be chaos."

Urman nodded toward the sheriff. "I get that impression. We're not exactly being organized here with military precision. But I've got to do somethimg to redeem myself."

"You are blameless for what happened."

"I wish I felt that way," Urman said. "I mean, I killed a man. It's the worst feeling in the world. I hope you never have to experience it."

Joe looked down at his boots. "I have and you're right."

"It changes you."

"Yup."

A SMALL GROUP of Klamath's followers stood to the side of the volunteers, jeering them. One of the protesters saw the same similarity to a western Joe had noted and started humming the theme to the old western television program *Bonanza*, and the rest eventually joined in . . .

Bum-duh-duh-Bum-duh-duh-Bum-du-duh-Bum BONANZA!
Bum-duh-duh-Bum-duh-duh-Bum-du-duh-Bum BONANZA!

. . . until the theme got stuck in Joe's head like musical peanut butter and he couldn't get rid of it the rest of the morning.

AT BREAKFAST, Reed shook his head and looked down at his uneaten eggs. "I felt real sad when those boys roared out of here all full of piss and vinegar. They'd love to find the shooter and bring him back so the moratorium will be lifted and they'll be a bunch of heroes. But I don't see it happening."

Joe said to Reed, "I don't think our shooter is just roaming around up there waiting to be caught. I doubt he's still up there at all."

Reed looked over the top of his coffee cup at Joe.

Joe said, "I would speculate that the shooter was there on the street this morning singing the theme to *Bonanza.*"

Reed snorted.

"I didn't see Klamath Moore or his wife in that assembly this morning," Joe said. "Did you?" *Or Bill Gordon or Alisha Whiteplume or Nate Romanowski,* Joe thought.

"Nope," Reed said.

"I wonder where he is."

Reed shrugged. "I hear the guy keeps on the move."

Joe hoped Gordon was still around.

Reed sat back and put his coffee cup down. He looked like a man with a pain in his stomach. "I just wish Klamath Moore and his ilk would go away," Reed said. "When they're around it's like I don't know this place anymore. Everything seems off-kilter, if you know what I mean. We've always been sort of insulated from all of that activist crap here in our nice little town."

Joe said, "Yup."

"Maybe this is the beginning of the end," Reed said. "Maybe all that stuff from the outside about animal rights and such has found us."

JOE PARKED his pickup at the side of Nate's house near the Twelve Sleep River and got out. It was high noon, still, cloudless, in the forties but dropping by the minute. He could hear the gossipy murmur of the river as he circled the house and the empty falcon mews. There was no point knocking on the door because there was obviously no one inside. And there were no birds in the sky.

What he noted, though, was a set of tire tracks coming in and going out. And the footprints—at least five sets—in the mud and dust near the front door. They'd been there, the whole carload of them, Joe thought. Nate, Alisha, Klamath Moore, Moore's wife, Bill Gordon. The footprints led to the threshold and came back out again.

So Nate, Mr. Neighborly, had invited them inside, Joe thought. Perhaps they'd all taken chairs around Nate's old dining table and sipped cocktails? Maybe Nate baked them a cake? Maybe they laughed and joked about how it had all come together as planned and Nate was now free to move about the country.

Just to make himself feel a little better, Joe kicked Nate's door with the toe of his boot before leaving.

Hard pellets of snow strafed the ground and bounced off the hood of his truck. He was glad he'd thrown his thick Carhartt jacket into his vehicle that morning because, *blink*, it was winter.

THE SNAP winter storm roared through the Bighorns throughout Wednesday and into Thursday. Sheriff McLanahan's search for the killer was postponed indefinitely Wednesday night when one of his volunteers—Joe and Marybeth's plumber—was mortally wounded by another volunteer who mistook him for someone suspicious and shot him in the chest in close to zero visibility conditions.

That night, Joe reread Bill Gordon's files and tried to watch television with Marybeth and Lucy but found himself wondering when, and if, Nate Romanowski would appear.

21

On Thursday, Joe cruised his pickup on the gravel roads of the Wind River Indian Reservation. Fallen leaves like tiny cupped hands skittered across the lawns to pile up against fences and brush. Wood smoke from the chimneys of small box houses refused to rise in the cold and hung close to the ground. Some houses had lawns, fences, trees, hedges. Some had pickup trucks mounted on blocks without engines or doors.

He had always been struck by the number of basketball backboards and hoops on the reservation. Nearly every house had one, and they were mounted on power poles and on the trunks of trees. In the fall, during hunting season, antelope and deer carcasses hung from them to cool and age. In the summer, they were used by the children. Joe counted six fat mule deer hanging in one block and realized the moratorium the governor had placed on state lands wouldn't apply to reservation lands, which were sovereign.

The reservation high school was a modern redbrick structure with well-kept lawns and nothing about to suggest the students were Northern Arapaho or Eastern Shoshone. The only student Joe saw outside was wearing a gray hoodie, smoking a cigarette, and listening to his iPod.

After checking the teachers' lot for Alisha Whiteplume's car (the SUV he'd seen through the binoculars), Joe parked and went in.

THE MAIN HALLWAY of the school was dark and empty. His boots echoed on the linoleum. Classes were in session, and he glanced through windows in the closed doors to see teachers teaching, students sprawled at their desks, a few catching his eye as he passed. The teachers' names were printed on construction paper outside each door, and he paused at the one reading MISS WHITEPLUME. Inside was obviously a substitute teacher—a man in his midtwenties with shoulder-length hair and round wire-rimmed glasses. He was explaining something to the students but their glassy-eyed response unveiled his ineffectiveness.

Student artwork decorated the walls, pen-and-ink the medium. Joe was struck by how similar the work was to what he saw in the hallways of Saddlestring High School in town; how little distinctively Indian was included in subject and theme. In fact, he thought, he'd seen more warriors and mystical American Indian scenes in town than he saw on the reservation. Plenty of typical teenage dark-minded fantasy stuff, though, as well as NBA, hip-hop, and NASCAR-themed scenarios. Farther down the hall, closer to the office, were framed photos of graduating classes dating back more than forty-five years, many of which had once been displayed in the old high school before this new one was built. The graduate displays slowed him, and his eyes looted through the cameo photos.

The faces that looked back at him from year to year reflected the styles and attitudes of the sixties, seventies, eighties, nineties, to the present. The number of graduates grew and receded from year to year, and he couldn't tell if there were many more students at present than there had been forty years ago. There were sullen faces, hopeful faces, fierce faces, doomed faces. Because of the high mortality rate on the reservation, he recognized some of the recent names as accident victims, overdose victims, shooting victims. Too many from the recent classes were already gone, he thought.

THE RECEPTIONIST looked up from behind the counter when he entered the school office. She was oval-faced and kindly-looking, a Native whose eyes showed she'd seen a lot over the years in that school. The name plaque on her desk read MRS. THUNDER. He liked that name and wished his name was "Joe Thunder."

Because he was wearing his uniform, Mrs. Thunder said, "Okay, who did what?"

"Nobody I'm aware of," he said.

"None of my boys shot a deer out of season or without a license?"

"Not this time," he said, placing her because of the way she said "my boys" as the heart and soul of the school, the Woman Who Knew Everybody And Everything. He always felt blessed when he met up with such women because they were generally the key to unlocking the secret doors to an institution.

"Ah," she said, "that's good to hear."

"I was going to ask to see the principal if he's in, but you can probably help me."

Mrs. Thunder shook her head, an impish grin on her lips. "I could, but it's not protocol. You should see the principal and he's a she. And she's in. I'll see if she has a minute. May I ask what you need from her?"

Joe said, "I want to ask about a teacher here, Alisha Whiteplume."

Mrs. Thunder's eyes flashed and Joe couldn't interpret the reaction.

"I'll be back," Mrs. Thunder said.

Joe wondered what he'd just done.

In a few moments, Mrs. Thunder reappeared and said, "Principal Shoyo is waiting for you in there," gesturing to an open door at the back.

Mrs. Shoyo was surprisingly young, Joe thought. She was dressed in a white blouse and business suit and wore a gold medicine-wheel pendant. She stood as Joe entered and they shook hands. Mrs. Shoyo had black hair that was swept back and piercing brown eyes. She was Native. He noted the pin on her lapel, a horizontal piece with a red wild rose on one side and a flag with parallel red and black bars on a field of white on the other side. The pin represented the two nations on the reservation: the rose the symbol of the Eastern Shoshone and the Northern Arapaho flag.

"Joe Pickett," he said. "Thanks for taking a few minutes."

"My pleasure," she said, sitting back down.

He glanced at the wall behind her where she displayed photos of her family: three beautiful dark-haired, dark-eyed girls, a shot of her husband, he assumed, on a knee next to a dead bull elk he was very proud of; her diploma from the University of Wyoming; a certificate naming her one of the "Top 100 American Indian Women Leaders of 2001."

"Mrs. Thunder said you were asking about one of my teachers, Alisha Whiteplume."

"Yes," Joe said.

"What about her?" Shoyo asked, her eyebrows arching, "Did she commit some kind of *game* violation?"

Joe laughed. "Not at all. I wish I weren't wearing this uniform shirt right now. No, I'm here because she was last seen in the presence of a friend of mine I'm trying to track down. I was hoping she could help me find him."

Mrs. Shoyo narrowed her eyes as if to read him better.

"I hope that's all this is about because Alisha is one of my best, if not *the* best teacher I've got here. She left the reservation after graduating from here and went off and made a success of herself. Then she chose to come back, to help her people. She's such a role model because she's bright and attractive and her students always do the best on the aptitude tests. She's also one of my closest friends."

Joe now knew why Mrs. Thunder had flinched.

"Then you know of Nate Romanowski," Joe said.

Mrs. Shoyo smiled gently, but Joe could see that she had placed an invisible shield between them. "Everybody knows Mr. Romanowski," she said, which somewhat surprised Joe. "But my understanding is he's in Cheyenne in jail waiting for his trial."

"He's out," Joe said. "He's supposed to be in my custody."

"But he isn't," she said.

"But he isn't," he sighed.

"Are you saying you think Alisha is with him, wherever he is?"

"Possibly."

"And by finding her you might find him."

"That's the idea," he said.

She raised her hand and fit her chin into her fist, studying him across the desk, making a determination, he assumed, about how much she should tell him and what she should keep to herself.

"Is Alisha in trouble?" she asked.

"No."

"Why should I believe you?"

Joe shrugged. "Because I'm telling you the truth. I just want to find Nate."

Mrs. Shoyo nodded as if she'd come to a conclusion. She leaned forward on her desk and showed him her palms. "I'd like to know where Alisha is as well because I'm starting to worry about her. She called in yesterday morning so we could line up a substitute teacher. I didn't talk with her, Mrs. Thunder did. Alisha told her she might be out for a few days so to try and get a good replacement. I don't think we did, though. I think we hired a man who spends all his time telling the students how hip and sympathetic he is to them instead of teaching them math and science."

Joe recalled the man in Alisha Whiteplume's classroom: it fit.

Joe asked, "Did she say where she was calling from?"

"No, she didn't," Mrs. Thunder answered from just outside the doorway, where she'd been listening.

"You can come in, Alice," Mrs. Shoyo said, doing a quick eye roll for Joe's benefit. "Nothing goes on in this school that Alice isn't aware of."

"I understand," Joe said, looking over his shoulder at Mrs. Thunder, who came into the room.

"I don't think she was calling from her house, though," Mrs. Thunder said. "I could hear the wind in the background, like she was outside somewhere. I assumed she was calling from her cell phone. I didn't question her. It's her right to call in sick and she hardly ever has until this year. She's had trouble shaking cold after cold this year, and she's missed quite a few days the past few months."

"Outside," Joe said. "Could you hear anything else? Background talk? Highway noises?"

"No."

"And she didn't call again this morning?"

Mrs. Thunder shook her head.

Joe dug in his pocket for two business cards and handed one to Mrs. Shoyo and one to Mrs. Thunder. "If she shows up or calls in again, can you let me know? And if she calls, can you please try to find out where she is and when she'll be back? I'm not asking you to rat on her—she's not in trouble at all. I just want to make sure she's safe and knows what she's doing."

Both women took the cards and looked at them in the long, contemplative, and deliberate way Joe had noted before in many American Indians.

"Alisha is a smart woman," Mrs. Thunder said, finally. "I'm sure she wouldn't do something stupid."

"But she's with Nate Romanowski," Joe said, immediately regretting he'd put it that way.

"How can she be," Mrs. Shoyo said slyly, "if he's in your custody?"

"Not you too," Joe moaned, and both women laughed.

As JOE walked back down the long hallway toward the parking lot, the bell rang. The hall was suddenly filled with students pouring out of doors, gathering books, chattering, bound for their next class. Rather than swim against the tide, he stepped to the side and flattened himself against the wall. Due to his uniform and sidearm he got his share of inquiring looks. A pack of fifteen- or sixteen-year-old boys passed close by him talking loudly to one another in a staged exchange:

"Benny, are we still on to go poach some antelope after school today?"

"Absolutely, man. I got two guns and a bunch of bullets in my car! We can shoot a whole herd of 'em just like we did last night!"

"It's a good thing there ain't no smart game wardens around here, huh, Benny?"

"Yeah, that's a good thing. Otherwise, he'd know we were killin' and poachin' fools!"

"Ha-ha," said Joe, and the boys broke up into self-congratulatory laughter.

As THE halls thinned and cleared he found himself looking at the framed photos of the Class of 1991, which had graduated seventeen years before. There she was, Alisha Whiteplume. Her beauty was striking, and intelligence shone in her eyes. But there was another female student two rows up from Alisha who was familiar as well. This girl exuded brash self-confidence. Her eyes seemed to challenge the photographer to take the picture, and she had an inscrutable smile of self-satisfaction. Joe knew her now as Shannon Moore, Klamath's wife.

"THAT DIDN'T take long," Mrs. Thunder said when Joe returned to the office.

"I was hoping you could give me some background on another student I saw in one of the photos in the hallway," Joe said.

"I'll try," Mrs. Thunder said. "I've been around this place for thirty years. If it's before that I might not be able to help you."

"Class of 'ninety-one," Joe said.

"That"—Mrs.Thunder beamed—"was a very good year. That's when Alisha graduated."

Joe nodded. "And the other student I think I recognize. Her name is Shannon Moore now, but I don't know her name at the time she graduated."

Mrs. Thunder sat back, puzzled. "Shannon?"

Joe's heart sank for a moment. Had he screwed up and mistaken one face for another? Then: "Maybe I can point her out to you."

"Show me," Mrs. Thunder said, plucking the 1991 high-school yearbook off a shelf behind her and opening it on the counter.

Joe used his index finger to guide him through the photos of graduating seniors. It settled on the one he'd seen in the hallway. As he read her name, Mrs. Thunder said, "So she goes by Shannon now, huh?"

"It says here her name was Shenandoah Yellowcalf," Joe said. "Do you know her?"

Mrs. Thunder snorted. "Do I know her? She was only the best girls' basketball player we've ever had here. I'm surprised *you* don't know her."

Joe explained he'd only been in the valley for eight years.

"Here," Mrs. Thunder said, flipping through the year-book pages, "let me show you."

Joe looked at countless photos of Shenandoah Yellow-calf in the activities section of the yearbook. There were action photos of her on the court, at the foul line, and in the lane, another of her cutting down the net at the state championship.

"You've never seen a girl play like Shenandoah played," Mrs. Thunder said softly, caressing the photos with a stubby fingertip as if drawing memories from them. "She had a blinding crossover dribble as good as any great NBA point guard as she brought the ball down the court, and she left her opponents flailing at air in her wake. She made us gasp the way she played. There has never been a player here with so much determination. She was so *fierce*. Shenandoah led our team, the Wyoming Indian Lady Warriors, which was made up of only seven girls, to win the state championship game."

Joe read from the yearbook. "She scored fifty-two points in the championship game?" he said. "Good Lord!"

"Oh, she was good," Mrs. Thunder said, shaking her head. "Alisha was on that team too," and pointed her out in the team photo.

"Was Shannon—um, Shenandoah—recruited by colleges?" Joe asked.

Mrs. Thunder nodded enthusiastically. "She was offered full-ride scholarships to over twenty universities, including Duke and Tennessee, all the national powers. We were so proud of her."

"Where did she go to school?" Joe asked.

"She didn't," Mrs. Thunder said sadly.

Joe shook his head, confused.

"Shenandoah's grandmother got really sick, so she stayed on the reservation to take care of her. I think she was scared—there was so much pressure on her—and I told her that, but she said she would go to college and play basketball when her grandmother was better. Like all those schools would just wait for her."

She looked up at Joe, moisture in her eyes. "I get disappointed to this day when I think about the potential she had and the opportunity she missed."

Joe nodded, prodding her on.

Mrs. Thunder looked down, as if she didn't want Joe to see her eyes, didn't want to see how he reacted to an all-too-common story on the reservation. She said Shenandoah did, in fact, nurse her grandmother for a year, then two. Her devotion was extraordinary for a girl her age, she said, but didn't entirely mask the fact that part of the reason she stayed was because of her fear of leaving the cloistered reservation for the punishing high-profile world of big-time college sports—or at least that's what Mrs. Thunder surmised. Plus, there was the pressure from those she'd grown up with, her friends and family and coaches. Too many people lived vicariously through her, saw her triumphs as their triumphs. When she failed, they failed too.

"Kind of like me," Mrs. Thunder said. "I'm guilty of that as well. I think of a lot of these kids as my own, and I wanted her to do so well, to make us all be able to say, 'I knew her when.' "

"Where did she go?" Joe asked gently, knowing where she ended up but not how she got there.

"Nowhere, for way too long, I'm afraid," she said. "The time away from sports didn't do her any good. She gained a lot of weight the way kids do when they're used to playing sports all the time and they just stop. It was pretty obvious after a couple of years that it would be tough if not impossible for her to get a recruiter interested, even if they still remembered her. But that's me speaking . . . I don't even know if she tried."

Shenandoah started running with the wrong crowd, she said, a bad mixture of Indians and town kids. She got involved with alcohol and drugs, and was arrested for dealing crystal meth, the scourge of the reservation as well as small-town Wyoming. Her grandmother died and Shenandoah drifted back and forth from the res to town. Mrs. Thunder said she'd hear of Shenandoah from time to time, that she worked as a barmaid, a waitress, even as a rough-neck on a coal-bed methane crew. She hired out as a cook and a guide for elk camps as well, Mrs. Thunder said, rais-ing her eyebrows as she said it.

Joe grunted. While there certainly were legitimate cooks for elk camps, there were also "cooks"—mainly younger women—who provided other services for well-heeled, mainly out-of-state hunters. Joe had seen and met some of the camp cooks in the mountains, and it was obvious few knew anything about making breakfast. He felt the same irony and sadness Mrs. Thunder conveyed as he imagined the scenario and looked at Shenandoah Yellowcalf's bold face and eyes in the yearbook. Those hunters had no idea that the chubby twenty-year-old Northern Arapaho "camp cook" they'd hired was once one of the greatest basketball players in the state of Wyoming, he thought. He searched his memory; there was something familiar about the story. Something about a young female Indian camp cook. Some-thing he'd heard years before when he was a trainee work-ing under the former game warden Vern Dunnegan . . .

But he'd sort that out later.

He asked, "Do you know if Shenandoah and Alisha were friends?"

Mrs. Thunder smiled. "They were best friends. I think Alisha did everything she could to help Shenandoah."

"Did they keep in touch?"

She shrugged. "I don't know. I assume they did."

Joe said, "Hmmmm."

"What?"

"I'm not sure," he said. "But I can tell you that Shenan-doah is back and doing very well. I saw her recently. She looks good and she has a little baby. She's married to a guy named Klamath Moore."

It was obvious from Mrs. Thunder's expression that she was grateful to hear the news but didn't know who Klamath Moore was.

"I'm so happy to hear that," she said, growing misty again. "That's so good to hear. Please, if you see her again, tell her to come by the school. Tell her I'd love to see her again."

Joe smiled. "If I get the chance, I'll pass along the invite."

"Tell her that old Alice Thunder wants to give her a hug."

JOE WAS buoyed as he walked out into the parking lot. The best entree to Klamath Moore would no doubt be through his wife, Shannon . . . and Alisha. *Maybe* that was the angle Nate was working.

If his friend was working on anything at all.

HE SAT in the pickup without starting the motor. His mind raced. What was it Vern Dunnegan had once told him about the Indian camp cook?

Vern told a lot of stories. He talked nonstop. Joe had learned to tune him out because the chatter was incessant and many of Dunnegan's stories were mean-spirited. Joe had tried to forget everything Vern had told him once Vern showed himself to be a liar and a criminal eight years before; he'd done all he could to expunge Vern Dunnegan from his mind. But he tried to remember this particular story about the camp cook. He hoped he'd written it down in his notebook at the time, and he planned to locate his old notes to try to refresh his memory.

THERE WERE two messages on his cell phone and he punched in the access number to hear them.

The first was from Stella, saying Randy Pope was doing everything he could to meet with the governor to get his blessing to leave Cheyenne and take over supervision of the case. She was running interference, but she said she couldn't hold him off forever. What, Stella asked, was going on?

The second was from Portenson of the FBI, saying Bill Gordon was prepared to meet Joe that night in the little town of Winchester. He said Gordon wanted to talk and he had something to say. Portenson said Joe was to be at the park promptly at eight. No earlier, no later. If Joe wasn't there on time and alone, Gordon, Portenson promised, would flee. And if something bad happened—if Joe was late or Gordon smelled a trap—there would be no more meetings, because the informant couldn't risk them and, frankly, he had no idea if Joe could be trusted in the first place.

"You've got one shot at our man," Portenson said. "Don't fuck it up."

Joe was grateful Portenson didn't mention Nate, which meant he didn't yet know. But Joe assumed the FBI would know soon, one way or another—possibly even Pope would tell them in an effort to take over—and he wondered if he'd hear the explosion from 350 miles away.

IT WASN'T the new knowledge of Shenandoah Yellowcalf, or the calls from Stella or Portenson that suddenly unnerved Joe, caused the hairs on his forearms and the back of his neck to stand on end, his flesh to crawl. It wasn't something that had happened or what he'd learned as much as what he was feeling: there was something malevolent in the air.

He was being watched.

Over the years, he'd come to trust his instincts in this regard. When he had felt he was being watched he habitually discarded the notion, convinced himself he was imagining things, tried to move on, only later to learn that he had been correct in the first place.

He raised his eyes, surveyed the cars in the parking lot. No one. He scanned the school grounds, anticipating the sight of a student skulking in the shadows and alcoves, maybe sneaking a smoke, keeping his eyes on Joe. He scanned the windows of the school for a face. Maybe Mrs. Thunder and Mrs. Shoyo looking out at him, seeing him off. Maybe those boys who had been pretending to be "poaching fools" were having another laugh at his expense.

He scanned the sagebrush-covered hillsides that flowed like frozen swells toward the foothills and the mountains beyond. There were pockets of pine and aspen, plenty of vantage points to hide in.

Joe saw no one.

22

I watch the game warden through my binoculars as he leaves the school building. He is wearing his red uniform shirt. He clamps his Stetson on his head and climbs into his green pickup truck. He's doing something in front of him or on his lap, eyes down. Probably checking a PDA or his cell phone.

Following him wasn't a problem and I'm sure he never suspected I was there.

The stand of aspen is behind me, the dried leaves rattling in the wind. I've parked my vehicle on the side of the old road in back of the trees, so it's hidden from view. My rifle is beside me, pulled from its case. I estimate 250 yards at most across the flat. It is a clear, sunny day. The wind is so slight it wouldn't be a factor in aiming.

Two things, though: I don't like long shots, and killing the game warden now would hurt me more than help me.

Shots at this distance can be problematic. There is no guarantee. I like them much closer; close enough there is no doubt. Beyond the game warden's pickup is the school, and the windows of the classrooms are at the same height as the windshield of his truck. I've heard of occasions when bullets were deflected by glass. If I missed—not likely, but always possible—I could kill a teacher or a student. An innocent.

More important is that I have nothing against the game warden, although I fear in his clumsy way he's getting closer. I don't fear the sheriff, or the sheriff's men in the mountains right now. They're hunting a ghost. But this game warden has worried me since the first time I saw him. There is something earnest and relentless about him that scares me in a way I can't articulate. He reminds me of me.

But why would he be at the school, if not to ask about Alisha Whiteplume? Or question the staff about the person once known as Shenandoah? If he makes the connection, it is a big step toward finding out about me. I can only hope in this case I am mistaken. I'm not ready to be found out.

Not yet.

The game warden has frozen up in a way that I think he must know I'm here. I can see a certain stiffness to his movements, an attempt not to give away the fact that he's looking for me, trying to find the eyes that he feels on him. I wriggle backward on the hill, in case he uses his binoculars or spotting scope.

I wait until I hear him start his pickup and drive down the road. I hear the crunch of his tires on the gravel road.

I don't need to follow him. I know where he's going.

23

PORTENSON HAD said Bill Gordon would be waiting for Joe in the public park at 8 P.M. in the little town of Winchester, population 729, which was eighteen miles northwest of Saddlestring via the interstate north to Montana. Joe was familiar with the park because years before he'd taken Sheridan, Lucy, and Maxine to a local dog show there. Maxine didn't place in any of the events but was awarded a "Most Unusual Color" consolation certificate that his girls were very proud of and that still hung on the refrigerator with magnets. None of the judges had ever seen a Labrador that had once been scared completely white. Nobody had.

The park consisted of a few picnic tables, a shelter, some benches, and a jungle gym and slide erected and maintained by the Winchester Lions Club, according to a sign. The park was a perfectly square town block. It was sealed off on four sides by neat rows of ancient cottonwood trees, which made it a good place to meet because of its seclusion on a cold fall night and because of its location off the main street.

As instructed by Portenson, Joe wore street clothes—

Wranglers, boots, snap-button cowboy shirt, his worn Carhartt ranch coat—and drove the family van instead of his game and fish pickup. Any suggestion that he was official would blow the meeting, expose Gordon if someone saw them together. The interstate was clear of snow but black and wet in his headlights. His twelve-gauge Remington WingMaster shotgun rested against the passenger seat, muzzle down, and his .40 Glock was clipped to his belt and out of view under the coat. He was edgy, unsure, which is why he'd brought his weapons. But he wanted to talk to Gordon. Joe had the feeling—and it wasn't more than that at this point—that he was getting somewhere, that momentum was finally with him. Not that he was solving the murders or understanding what was going on, but that finally he was in motion toward an end.

Winchester was primarily a ranching and timber town, five hundred feet higher than Saddlestring, where the foothills paused for rest before beginning their climb to become the Bighorns. Winchester's lone public artwork, located on the front lawn of the branch bank, was an outsized and gruesome metal sculpture of a wounded grizzly bear straining at the end of a thick chain, its metal leg encased in a massive saw-toothed bear trap. Joe thought it was one of the most grotesque and disturbing pieces he had ever seen, while at the same time reflecting the rough sensibilities of the little town.

At 7:45, Joe took the Winchester exit. He was close enough to the town limits he could smell wood smoke from the two hundred or so homes already battened down and prepped for a long winter when the whoop of a siren came out of nowhere on the side of the road and his van was lit up by the flashing red-and-blue wigwag lights of a police car.

Joe looked at his speedometer—forty-five, the speed limit—before slowing down and pulling over onto the shoulder of the road. The cruiser eased in behind him.

"What?" Joe asked aloud. "Why now? Why me?" *A burned-out taillight? What?*

The thought that Portenson had set him up crossed his mind.

In his rearview mirror, Joe could see the inside lights go on in the police car. The lone Winchester town cop looked to be in his midtwenties, with a heavy shelf of brow, a buzz cut, and a slight mustache. He wore a neat blue police vest over a crisp blue shirt. The cop was calling in Joe's license plate for a vehicle check before getting out and approaching. The look on the officer's face was serious and zealous. Joe had seen that look on overeager cops before, and it was rarely a good thing.

Joe groaned, bit his lip, debated getting out first to head off what could quickly become ugly if the cop shone his flashlight inside the van and saw the shotgun or his sidearm. Joe's badge was pinned to his red shirt on the back of a chair in his bedroom at home. He ran through his options quickly: get out, hope the cop recognized him as the local game warden and let him go quickly so he could meet Gordon in ten minutes (at the risk of the cop becoming alarmed by the armed violator he'd just pulled over); wait for the cop to approach him and try to explain away why he was entering Winchester with a shotgun and no badge or official identification, and beg the officer to let him pass; lie— say he was hunting coyotes or taking the shotgun to a gunsmith in Winchester to fix something, hope the cop didn't check for concealed weapons. But he was no good at lying. Maybe he could hide the weapons under the seat where they may or may not be found, accept a ticket for whatever it was he was pulled over for, promise to buy a new bulb for the tailgate or whatever, hope the transaction would be done quickly enough so he would be at the park by eight; confess everything—*I'm working directly for the governor and I'm undercover in order to meet with a confidential informant for the FBI who may have information on the murders of those hunters so you have to let me go right now*—and hope the cop believed him even though Joe, in the cop's place, wouldn't buy it for a second. Or he could peel away when the cop got out of the cruiser and try to lose him on the two-lane highway before doubling back to meet Gordon in the park. . . .

Joe thought, *All bad options.*

He watched the cop nod as he got confirmation on the plate and hung up his mike, then opened his door. His approach was textbook—Maglite in his left hand, his arm bent so the barrel of it rested on his shoulder with the beam directed into Joe's van to illuminate the backseat, the floor, the side of Joe's face. The cop's right hand rested on his pistol grip. He walked close to the side of the van and Joe read his name badge backward in the mirror: NORYB.

Joe toggled the switch to open his window.

"Officer Byron," Joe said, "I'm not sure why you pulled me over—"

"Put both of your hands on the steering wheel where I can see 'em," the cop barked. He'd seen the shotgun.

"Look," Joe said, "my name is Joe Pickett. I'm a game warden in Saddlestring—"

The cop stepped back and squared into a shooter's stance, his pistol out and aimed at Joe along with the blinding beam from the flashlight. "Get out of the car!"

Joe briefly closed his eyes, took a deep breath.

"I said, *get out of the car, sir.* Now!"

"Okay, I'm getting out," Joe said. "But I need to tell you right now I'm a peace officer myself and I've got a concealed weapon."

Byron, eyes wide and mouth set, aimed down his semi-automatic. Joe kept his right hand aloft while he opened the door with his left and stepped out onto the cold wet pavement with his hands visible. He couldn't believe what was happening.

Byron said, "Turn around and put your hands on the roof of the car and spread your feet."

Joe hated to turn his back on the cop, but he did. He

said, "This is a mistake. I'm on duty myself if you'd just let me explain."

Byron kicked the inside of Joe's left ankle hard, nearly taking his legs out from under him. The pain shot through his body.

"I said, *spread 'em*," the cop yelled. "There. And lean forward. Put your weight on your hands."

Joe felt his coat being pulled back and the weight of the Glock suddenly wasn't there.

"And what do we have here?" Byron asked, playing the tough guy.

"I told you I had it," Joe said, looking over his shoulder. "Now would you listen to me for a minute?" Byron tossed Joe's weapon into the borrow pit where it landed with a soft thud. Joe said, "Now, why did you do *that*?"

"Shut up. How many more guns do you have with you?" Byron asked, pulling the shotgun through the open window butt-first and tossing it into the wet grass as well.

"I don't have any more guns," Joe said, his anger rising. "Come on, this is ridiculous. What is it you think I did?"

"You mean before I pulled you over and found the guns? Start with speeding—forty-five in a thirty."

"*Thirty?* What are you talking about?"

Byron shone his flashlight down the highway until the beam lit up a SPEED LIMIT 30 sign so new and white it sparkled. "See?"

"When did you change it?" Joe asked, hot.

"Doesn't matter. It's thirty now."

"It looks like you guys put that up this morning."

"It was last week," Byron said, "but it doesn't matter when we put it up. It's up, it's the law, and I clocked you at forty-five. That gives me probable cause to look inside the car."

A set of headlights appeared coming from the town of Winchester. The vehicle—a light-colored SUV like the one he'd seen in his binoculars picking up Nate—barely slowed as it neared the van and the police car and swung

wide in the road to avoid them. Joe tried to see if the driver
was Bill Gordon, but the driver looked straight ahead,
didn't look over, which was odd in itself. Wasn't the driver
curious as to what was going on? Joe got only a glimpse
of the profile behind the wheel as the SUV shot by, and he
thought how much it resembled Klamath Moore. The red
taillights receded on the highway.

"Hey," Joe said, wheeling around, "we need to stop that
car!"

"Turn back around!" Byron hollered, pointing his gun
in Joe's face, his trigger finger tightening. Joe could tell
from Byron's eyes that he was ready—and willing—to
fire.

"Okay," Joe said, trying to calm Byron, "but you just
made a big mistake."

Byron laughed harshly. "I'd say the only guy making
mistakes around here is you. And you just keep making
'em."

Joe tried to keep his voice reasonable. "I'm a game warden for the state of Wyoming. I've got ID in my wallet and
a badge at home to prove it."

"Oh, I know who you are," Byron said.

"You do?"

"Yeah. You're the guy who busted my uncle Pete and
me up on Hazelton Road six years ago. You said we forgot
to tag the elk we had in the back of the truck, and you gave
Uncle Pete a damned citation."

Joe looked over his shoulder at Officer Byron, who'd
probably been seventeen or eighteen at the time. His face
did look vaguely familiar, and he recalled how filled with
attitude the boy had been at the time. He'd told Joe, "I'm
gonna remember this."

"Your elk didn't have tags," Joe said. "I was doing my
job."

"And I'm doing mine," Byron said, grinning.

Joe sighed deeply, and turned his wrist a little so he
could see his watch. Eight on the nose.

"Look, just give me my speeding ticket," Joe said. "Let me get the hell out of here. Here's the situation: I'm working undercover for the state, for Governor Rulon. I'm here to meet a confidential FBI informant, right now, in Winchester. This is about the murder of those hunters and Robey Hersig. You knew Robey, right? This guy may know something. If I'm not there he'll bolt and I may not get a chance to talk to him. Take my weapons and wallet and anything else you want. As soon as I meet my guy, I'll come to the station and turn myself over to you and you can check it all out. I promise. I swear."

And Byron laughed. "That's a new one. You must think I'm an idiot."

Well, yes, Joe thought.

Byron said, "Just keep your mouth shut and don't move. I'm going to check your ID. And I'll need to see your registration and insurance card."

Joe moaned with frustration and anger. Had Marybeth even put the registration in the car? And if so, where? It was her car, and he normally had very little to do with it other than maintenance.

He imagined that Gordon would be checking his watch and probably walking toward his vehicle with his keys out.

And what was Klamath Moore doing in Winchester, if that was him?

Byron said, "Never mind getting your wallet, I'll get it," and Joe could feel the cop lift up the back of his coat again. Dropping his chin to his chest and looking back under his armpit, he could also see Byron lower his weapon to his side while he dug into Joe's pocket with his other hand.

Joe swung back as hard as he could with his right elbow and connected with Byron's nose, the impact making a muffled crunching sound like a twig snapping underfoot. Joe spun on his heel and grabbed the cop's gun with both hands and twisted, wrenching it free. Byron backpedaled clumsily to the center stripe in the highway, reaching up with both hands for his broken nose.

Joe pointed the gun at the cop while at the same time not believing he was doing it. Dark blood spouted through Byron's fingers.

"Get in the van," Joe said.

"What are you going to do?" Bryon asked with a mouthful of blood.

"We're going to the park."

"The park?"

JOE STEERED the van into Winchester with his left hand on the wheel and Byron's weapon, pointed at the cop in the passenger seat, in his right.

"Don't hurt me," Byron burbled.

"I'll try not to," Joe said.

As he turned from the main street toward the park, Joe said, "I had my gun taken from me once. It sucks, doesn't it?"

"Mmmff."

BILL GORDON was sitting partially in shadow on a park bench when Joe arrived. Gordon appeared to be looking him over as Joe parked and opened his door.

"What about me?" Byron asked.

"Stay here. I'll be back in a few minutes and we can get this all straightened out."

"You're gonna shoot me, aren't you?"

"Of course not," Joe scoffed, "and I'd probably miss if I tried. I'm a horrible pistol shot."

Byron's eyes did a "now you tell me" roll.

Joe hoped Gordon wouldn't get nervous and run when he saw the cop inside the van. He was relieved when he shut the door and saw that Gordon was still there.

"Bill?" Joe called, walking across the grass that was stiffening with cold. "It's Joe Pickett. I'm sorry I'm late. I got nailed in a speed trap coming into town."

Gordon didn't move, just sat there slightly slumped to the side, a wash of pale moonlight on the side of his face.

"Bill?"

Joe froze when he was ten feet away. He saw it all at once—the gun held loosely in Gordon's fist, the small hole in one temple and the larger exit hole in the other, bits of brain and bone flecked across the backrest of the bench.

Joe whispered, "Oh. No."

24

JOE SAT alone at a scarred table in Witness Room Number Two in the Twelve Sleep County Building at one in the morning, waiting for Sheriff McLanahan and Deputy Reed to return. They'd been gone over an hour. On the table was a mug of weak coffee that had gone cold.

The amoral eye of a camera mounted in a high corner of the room watched him. The mirrored plate of one-way glass in the wall reflected the image of a man who very much wished he was home in bed. Anywhere but where he was.

He groaned and sat back, staring at the blazing light fixture inset in the ceiling. He thought, *I've really done it this time.*

AFTER HE found Gordon's body and confirmed he was dead, Joe called county dispatch and asked Wendy, the dispatcher, to locate the sheriff and send him to Winchester right away. He told Wendy he'd stay at the crime scene until the sheriff and the coroner's team arrived.

"And please put out an APB for a light-colored SUV heading toward Saddlestring from Winchester on the highway. The subject inside I believe is Klamath Moore, and he may have information on the death of the victim here on the park bench."

"That Klamath Moore?" Wendy asked.

"That Klamath Moore," Joe said, punching off.

"Jesus, is that guy dead?" said Officer Byron. Joe hadn't heard Byron walk up to him.

"Yes."

"This is my first dead body," Byron said. "I mean, other than a car wreck or some old lady dying of a heart attack. It sure looks like he ate his own gun, don't it?"

"That's what it looks like." But Joe had his doubts.

"I want my gun back now."

"No," Joe said. "Go sit down until the sheriff gets here. Don't get any closer to the crime scene."

Byron turned from Gordon's body to Joe. "You are in *so* much trouble."

"I know."

Joe made two more calls before the sheriff's department arrived, the first to Marybeth advising her not to wait up for him because he'd discovered a dead body and assaulted a police officer. She was speechless.

"Don't worry," he said.

"You assaulted a cop?"

"Sort of, yes."

"And you say not to worry?"

"I'll be home soon," he said, wishing it were true.

The other call was to Special Agent Tony Portenson, telling him his confidential informant had just been found dead.

Portenson had predictably exploded, and Joe told him he'd get back to him with more details and closed his phone.

———

ANOTHER HOUR. Joe paced the witness room, tried to see if anyone was looking at him through the one-way mirror into the hallway. The repercussions of what he'd done, what had happened, crushed in on him from all sides. At one point, he had to hold himself up with one hand on the wall and breathe deeply, get his wits back. His heart raced and slowed, raced and slowed.

When the door opened he jumped.

It was Deputy Reed, looking furtive. "I really shouldn't be in here," he said.

"What's going on?"

Reed pulled out a hard-backed chair from the other side of the table, the legs scraping across the linoleum like fingernails on a blackboard. He sat down heavily.

"Klamath Moore is in the other witness room," Reed said. "We found him where he was staying here in town. At Shelly Cedron's place. You know Shelly? She runs the animal shelter and I guess she's a sympathizer to his cause. Who would have guessed that? Man, you think you know people but you don't know what's in their hearts, I guess."

Joe nodded, urging him on.

"There was a light-colored SUV outside her home that sort of matches your description. Shelly herself is out of town at a conference, so she wasn't even there. But do you know how many vehicles match that description? I mean, this ain't LA. It would be unusual if you'd seen a sedan, or a coupe. Everybody's got an SUV. Hell, I've got two, and a pickup. Anyway, we woke him up—"

"He was sleeping?"

Reed nodded. "Says he was, anyway. And claims he was there all night doing IM conversations with his followers and talking with his wife. She vouches for him."

"Do you believe her?"

Reed shrugged. "Without anything more than your 'It looked kind of like Klamath Moore' story, we have nothing else to go on. One thing, though, his hair was wet. I asked him about that and he said he took a shower before he went to bed."

"That would clean off any gunpowder residue on his skin," Joe said. "Did you find the clothes he was wearing?"

"He pointed at a pile of dirty laundry in the corner of the bedroom," Reed said. "I bagged it up. But Shelly Cedron has a woodstove, just like everybody else. It's one of those really good airtight ones that burns hot inside."

"Will your crime-scene guys search the SUV?"

Reed shrugged. "You mean search for hair and fiber from Gordon? Sure. But we both know Gordon has been in the car before. That wouldn't give us anything."

"What about Bill Gordon?" Joe asked. "Have the crime-scene people looked at him?"

"Doc Speer says—preliminarily, at least—it looks like a suicide. The gun was fired so close to his head it's a contact wound consistent with suicide. No short-range or mid-range powder burns or anything indicating it wasn't self-inflicted. The weapon was a .45ACP Sig Sauer P220. Nice gun. And the suicide theory looks completely clean except for one thing: there were two bullet wounds in his head."

"What?"

Reed pointed at his own head to show Joe. "One in his temple; that was the wound you could see. But there was another one a couple of inches up from that covered by hair."

"Who shoots himself *twice* in the side of the head?" Joe asked.

"Someone who wants to be dead," Reed said. "Hey— that was the first thing I thought too. But Doc Speer says it isn't inconceivable that a suicide victim shoots himself deliberately and that his death reflex makes him pull the trigger again before he's even dead. There's only a four-point-five-pound trigger pull on that gun. I could see it happening. The second shot would be fired as the first one kicked the gun up, so you've got that second hole higher up in his skull."

Joe shook his head. "But it makes no sense. Why agree to meet me at that park and take every precaution in the world and then kill yourself?"

"I don't know. Guilt? Maybe there was something else going on in his life. Maybe he saw you drive up with a bleeding cop in your car and thought the jig was up."

"I didn't hear a shot, much less two shots," Joe said. "It was quiet in Winchester. I would have heard a shot. He was sitting on that bench like that when I got there. He got shot before I ever showed up."

"Or shot himself. We bagged his hands. They're checking for residue on his hands to confirm he fired the gun himself."

Joe shook his head, not believing it. "Or Klamath Moore shot Gordon in the head at close range, then put the gun in Gordon's hand and shot again so there would be plenty of residue on the dead man's skin. Klamath left the weapon in Gordon's hand so it would look like a suicide. Then Klamath went home and burned his clothes and took a shower and waited for you guys to find him. Reed, you've got to question his wife again, see if you can catch her in an inconsistency."

"We can try."

"Maybe if you sweated her," Joe said.

Reed shook his head. "No chance without more to go on."

Joe looked up at the light fixture again, trying to think of a way to snare Klamath Moore, trying to come up with a way to show the man was involved. Nothing.

"There's another theory," Reed said.

"What?"

"That maybe our governor's got such a hard-on for Klamath Moore and wants him out of the state so bad that you're seeing him everywhere, even in the dark on a two-lane with no highway lights."

Joe was surprised by the theory and hadn't seen it coming. It was then he felt the presence of someone outside in the hall, watching him through the one-way mirror, assessing his reaction. He looked hard at Reed, who broke off his gaze. Reed had been sent in to see if Joe would admit something.

Joe took a step back, his chin in his hand, as if mulling things over. Suddenly, he lashed backward and hit the mirror with the flat of his hand.

"Christ!" McLanahan yelled from the hallway, his voice muffled by the glass.

"Reed . . ." Joe said. "I thought you were better than that."

Reed looked down, mumbling so low it couldn't be picked up outside. "He sent me in here to see how you'd react. No offense, Joe."

"None taken," Joe whispered back. Then, loud enough so the sheriff could hear him again: "I'm not accusing Klamath Moore of pulling the trigger, although it could have been him. Or one of his sympathizers. And I'm damned sorry Bill Gordon is dead, because I think he was one of the good guys. But I want it known that while I do work for the governor, I'm not a hack. I'm doing this job for Robey, and Nancy Hersig. Not for the governor."

Joe turned to the mirror, addressing McLanahan. "You might as well come in, Sheriff." Reed looked up from the table. "Just so you can be prepared, Randy Pope is on his way here. McLanahan called him at home tonight and told him what happened. He's not happy, from what the sheriff said."

"Great," Joe said. McLanahan opened the door and came into the witness room and sat on a corner of the table. "You like to scared me to death with that stunt," he drawled, nodding toward the mirror.

Joe shrugged.

"Do you know what night it is? What night it was?" he said, looking at his wristwatch.

Joe was confused.

"It's *American Idol* night. My daughter and my wife

and I pop some popcorn every week and sit down and watch it. But not tonight, because I get a call right after the first singer saying we've got a body in Winchester Park and a busted-up town cop. Now here it is, one in the morning, and I haven't been home and didn't get a chance to vote. You may have ruined the whole season for me."

"Sorry," Joe said, feeling for perhaps the first time in his life some sympathy for McLanahan. Not because he'd prevented the sheriff from voting, but because McLanahan was denied a night with his family.

"He's likely to press charges," McLanahan said, meaning Byron. "You may be facing some time."

"It was a speed trap but it was personal on his part," Joe said, not even convincing himself.

"You busted his nose and kidnapped a cop. Think about it."

"I have."

"I don't know who is going to get you out of this one. I don't think even the governor's gonna try."

Joe sighed. McLanahan was right.

"Plus, I went against my better judgment and listened to my deputy here," he said, putting a hand on Reed's shoulder. "He said if you saw Klamath Moore leaving the scene, you saw Klamath Moore leaving the scene. So we rousted an innocent man who turns out to have an alibi, and we look like idiots and could face a civil suit. Klamath Moore's claiming he's a political prisoner, that the only reason we rousted him is because of his anti-hunting agenda. He says he's got a shitload of high-powered attorneys working pro-bono and he'll unleash 'em on us. And I don't doubt that he does."

Reed looked away from both Joe and the sheriff. He looked like *he* could shoot imself, Joe thought.

"I saw what I saw," Joe said.

"I've got a question," McLanahan said. "Randy Pope asked me and I couldn't answer."

"Yes?"

"He claimed you're working with Nate Romanowski, that he's in your custody. He asked me if Romanowski was with you tonight. I had to tell him that not only was that son of a bitch not with you, he is nowhere to be found. So I learn from a state bureaucrat that the suspect in the murder of Sheriff Barnum was in my county but nobody bothered to let me know. So tell me where he is."

Joe swallowed. "I don't know."

"You're lying."

"I'm not. I don't know where he is."

"And do you see a problem with that?" McLanahan asked, his face flushing. He was *really* angry.

"Yes I do."

"You are in *so* much trouble."

"I think I already heard that tonight," Joe said gloomily.

"I've got to go release Klamath Moore now," the sheriff said. "I've got nothing to hold him on and an eyewitness saying he never went to Winchester tonight. Then I've got to go see that little pissant Byron at the clinic and see if he wants to press charges against you. *Then* I've got to see Doc Speer to see where in the hell we're going to put another body, since the morgue is full."

"I wish you wouldn't release Moore," Joe said. "I'd like to talk to him."

McLanahan laughed angrily. "Not a chance. We already know what happens when you want to talk to people." The sheriff made a pistol of his hand and pressed his index finger to his temple and worked his thumb twice.

Joe winced.

"I should hold *you* tonight," McLanahan said. "But I'm just too damned tired to file the paperwork. So get out of my building and stay the hell at home where I can find you tomorrow."

"Okay."

"I mean it. And make that son of a bitch Romanowski turn himself in."

"That I can't promise."

The sheriff glared, on the verge of going into a rage but too tired to do so.

"Don't go anywhere," he said, and stomped out of the room.

Reed turned before following McLanahan, and showed a "what can I do?" palms-up gesture, and left the door open behind him.

JOE WAITED miserably at the front desk for the duty officer to find the keys to his van so he could go home. He didn't know if he'd ever felt so dirty, so gritty, so incompetent.

Finally, after ten minutes, the old deputy returned to the desk and handed Joe the keys.

"I've also got a shotgun and a service weapon, a .40 Glock," Joe said.

"You've *got* to be kidding," the old man said. "Come back tomorrow and get an okay from the sheriff."

JOE WENT out into the night to find that a fine snow had started. It sifted through the cold dead air like powdered sugar, coating windshields with a film. He breathed in the cold air, tried to clear his head. He found the van at the side of the building where one of the deputies had left it.

As he reached for the door handle, a voice behind him, in the dark, said, "Out a little late for a family man, aren't you?"

Joe froze, turned slowly to see Klamath Moore leaning against a light-colored SUV, arms crossed. Inside, in the dark, was the profile of Shannon Moore, looking straight ahead through the windshield as if she didn't want to see what was happening outside.

Joe said, "Is that Shenandoah Yellowcalf in there? Isn't she getting cold? You don't even have your motor running."

"She's fine."

"She's a legend around here," Joe said. "I just found out about her today. She's the greatest athlete the reservation high school ever produced. They love her. How can you make her sit in there like that in the cold?"

"I don't see where that's any business of yours," Moore said, ice in his voice.

"I just think you should appreciate her a little more, is all."

"I appreciate her plenty."

Joe said, "She enhances your image, for sure. It looks good for you to be married to an Indian. Makes you seem authentic. But you need to remember to introduce her to people. That way folks will think you like her."

Moore worked his mouth, as if trying to suck something out from between his teeth. Joe saw it as a way not to say whatever it was he wanted to say in anger.

"That was you on the Winchester highway," Joe said.

"I was home all night. I've got a witness."

"Did you pull the trigger or did you talk Bill Gordon into doing it himself? That's what I don't know yet."

Moore raised his chin, laughed at the sky. Unconvincing, Joe thought. As much an admission of guilt as if he'd signed a confession. But nothing Joe could use.

"You're nuts," Moore said. "You're an embarrassment. Hell, you broke more laws than anyone in this county tonight, from what I understand. Assaulting a cop?"

"What do you want, Harold?"

"Why'd you call me that?"

"Isn't that your real name? And another question: didn't you do the same thing to Bill Gordon that you did to your uncle Everett? Make it look like an accident?"

"I have no idea what you're talking about," he said, his voice rising, clearly getting agitated.

"Where is Wolverine?"

Moore got suddenly quiet.

"Where is he?"

"Wolverine? I don't know what you're talking about."

"Who is Wolverine?" Joe asked. "Or are you one and the same?"

"You're unhinged."

"It won't be long before I get you," Joe said. "I owe Nancy Hersig this one."

Klamath Moore shifted on the balls of his feet and clenched his hands into fists. Joe wouldn't have been surprised if Klamath had attacked. In fact, he would have welcomed it. Moore had several inches and thirty pounds on him, but Joe thought he could do some damage before being overwhelmed. Plus, it would give Joe a reason to arrest Moore and haul him back inside the county building where he could keep him for the night. But as he watched, Moore seemed to cool down, seemed to channel his anger into calculation. The transformation sent a chill through Joe, made him realize what kind of man he was up against.

"I bet you think I despise all kinds of hunting, don't you?" said Moore.

"That's what I understand."

"Not all kinds."

"What are you talking about?"

"Some animals deserve to die," Moore said, letting his face go dead. "Like rats. I don't like rats."

25

IN THE SHED in back of my house I set up a stepladder against the far wall, where the shelves with old garden hoses, automotive parts, and sporting equipment have been for years. I don't turn on the light because I don't want to alert my neighbors I'm in here. Instead, I bite on a small Maglite flashlight and use the tiny beam to see. The shed smells of dust and long-dead grass.

As I climb, the beam of my flashlight illuminates the contents of the shelves—canning jars, paint cans, baskets, bags of fertilizer and grass seed, potting soil, containers of chemicals. A heavy coat of dust covers it all, and I take pains not to disturb anything.

On the top shelf, behind a barrier of ancient cans of deck stain, I grope for the handle of my duffel bag. I lift it over the cans and take it down to the shed floor. I unzip the long bag and inventory what's inside: dark clothes, boots that alter my footprints, cap, rifle, cartridges. And one last red poker chip.

Randy Pope is coming back.

Soon, it will be over.

26

JOE WAS surprised to see lights on in the kitchen and living room of his house when he pulled into the driveway at 2 A.M. and killed the motor. He was exhausted and his stomach roiled. For a moment he sat in the dark and looked at the front door and thought, *I don't like this house very much*. He knew it wouldn't be many more hours before Ed next door would be outside getting his morning paper, smoking his pipe, commenting on the dusting of snow and finding it wanting, surveying the Pickett house to see if the fence was fixed yet, calculating how much the value of his property had dropped during the night due to his negligent neighbors.

But it wasn't just his house that was bothering Joe. Klamath Moore had all but confessed to murder back in the parking lot and there was little he could do to nail the man on it. Joe didn't have his digital recorder with him at the time, and it would be his word against Klamath Moore's. With Joe's apparent obsession with Moore—at least according to the sheriff's office—this latest revelation would be greeted with the suspicion it probably deserved. Plus,

Moore's words about hunting rats could be taken different ways, although Joe knew what was meant.

While he ran it through his mind, the front door opened and Marybeth came outside in a sweatshirt and jeans. He was surprised she was dressed, and felt guilty for keeping her up so late waiting for him.

He hauled himself out of the van and trudged toward her.

"Sorry to keep you up," he said.

"No bother," she said. Her voice was light, airy, not what he'd expected given the circumstances. "There's someone here to see you."

"It's about time," Joe said, suddenly awake.

NATE ROMANOWSKI and Alisha Whiteplume sat at the kitchen table. They'd obviously been there for some time judging by the empty plates, glasses, and coffee mugs that were pushed to the side.

"Nate," said Joe, "where in the *hell* have you been?"

"Joe . . ." Marybeth cautioned.

"Around," Nate said.

"Around," Joe repeated. "Do you realize what kind of heat I've been getting from Randy Pope and everybody else? They all thought I'd lost you. You're supposed to be in my custody, remember?"

Nate shrugged. "I said I'd keep in touch."

"I can account for his whereabouts," Alisha said coolly.

"And those whereabouts are . . . where?" Joe asked.

"Mainly in bed with me," Alisha said evenly.

Nate had a smug look on his face, Joe thought.

"Would anyone like more coffee?" Marybeth asked in a mock-cheerful tone.

WHILE A pot of decaf dripped into the carafe, Joe filled the three of them in on what had happened over the past days. He noticed how Alisha stared at him with barely disguised hostility while he described his visit to the high school, and how Marybeth covered her face with her hands and moaned while he detailed his assault on Officer Byron. Nate looked on skeptically when he heard about Bill Gordon's wounds. Both Alisha and Marybeth gasped when Joe recounted what Klamath Moore had said about rats.

"So he did it," Marybeth said. "My God."

Joe talked mainly to Nate, but shot side glances at Marybeth and Alisha while he did so. He knew he'd have to explain himself further to his wife later on, and that she'd have questions. What he couldn't understand was the antagonism from Alisha. Was it simply because he was the reason Nate had to resurface? Or something else?

"So that's where we are," Joe said. "Bodies everywhere, and the same suspect we've had all along but no proof to nail him with."

"Meanwhile," Marybeth said sourly, "Randy Pope is on his way up here to take charge or fire you again. But can he do that? Aren't you working solely for the governor?"

Joe shrugged. "I don't know what's going on anymore."

Nate and Alisha exchanged a long look. Joe stared. He felt Marybeth's hand on his arm.

"Joe, do you have a minute? There's something I want to show you."

He looked at her, puzzled at what could be of such importance. She looked back wide-eyed, nodding, urging him on.

"Excuse me," he said, getting up, following her from the kitchen and up the stairs to their bedroom.

"What?" he asked.

"Joe, you can be so dense sometimes," she said, shaking her head. "Can't you see what's going on?"

"No, obviously."

"Those two are deeply in love."

"That I can see."

"It's not just that," she said, rolling her eyes. "Nate wants to tell you something but Alisha isn't sure she wants him to. She thinks he'd be breaking a confidence with her, and he's asking her permission to do that. Alisha can't decide if Nate's relationship with you is more important than his relationship with her."

Joe was flummoxed. "How can you possibly figure that out? Is that why she's so angry with me? And what relationship are you talking about with me? Sheesh."

She shrugged. "Trust me on this."

"How can I look at them and not see any of that?" Joe asked. "How is that possible?"

"This is why you need me," she said, smiling. "You can be as thick as a brick sometimes."

He agreed. "So what is it Nate wants to tell me?"

"I'm not sure. But it's about Alisha and Shannon—or Shenandoah Yellowcalf, and probably what Shenandoah has told Alisha about Klamath Moore. You know how it can be on the reservation—they don't like to openly air their dirty laundry, and I don't blame them. Alisha has let Nate inside, and he respects that. You should too."

"But we're talking about murders here," Joe said. "I don't care about reservation gossip."

She sighed.

"What?"

"You might need to prepare yourself for losing him," she said. "I hope you'll be okay with that."

Joe made a face. "Are we back to the relationship thing again? Come on, Marybeth, we just *work* together."

"He may choose her and her secrets, is all I'm saying."

"This is getting too complicated," he said.

"It is what it is," Marybeth said ruefully.

He turned and opened the closet and squatted down, shoving old boots and shoes aside and reaching for a cardboard box.

Marybeth asked, "What are you doing?"

"Looking for some old notes," he said, sliding the box out and taking the lid off. "I've kept all of my old patrol journals since I was a trainee. I'm looking for the one from when I worked under Vern Dunnegan."

"I despise that man." She shuddered.

"Me too," Joe said, digging through the thick spiral notebooks until he found the one from nine years before.

WHEN JOE and Marybeth returned to the kitchen, Nate was still at the table but Alisha was across the room, leaning against the counter. She was stoic, avoiding his eyes, and Joe could tell nothing about what had gone on in their absence.

Nate cleared his throat, said, "When you told me about the governor hiring that master tracker and Randy Pope personally overseeing the murder of the hunters, it struck me as all wrong."

Okay, Joe thought, *Nate and Alisha had come to an understanding.*

Joe said, "How so?"

"It was typical law-enforcement procedure. Get the experts in to look at the physical evidence, try to figure out what was going on scientifically. And when Klamath Moore showed up it established a motive and a philosophy for the murders. You all put yourself in that particular stream of thought and never got out of it. You're like trout sitting in a channel waiting for insects to come to you. When the insects stop coming, you don't move to another part of the river. You just sit there, finning in one place, wondering why you're getting hungry. You, Joe Pickett, are right there with the rest of 'em in that stream."

Joe nodded, said, *"Finning,"* with a hint of sarcasm. He was used to Nate's circular and obscure reasoning and had learned to let it play out, see where it led. Sometimes it wound up nowhere, in the ether.

"There's nothing wrong with hiring experts and gathering evidence and doing forensics tests and all of that," Nate said, "but without on-the-ground intelligence it's all just technical jerking off. It gives bureaucrats something to do. I learned a long time ago when I worked for the government myself that there is no substitute for intelligence, for talking to people where they live. By being sympathetic, actually listening to what they say and sometimes what they don't. By doing that, you might find a whole other way to look at what's going on."

Joe flashed back to what Marybeth had told him upstairs, how they had both looked at Alisha and Nate and seen different things.

"But without hard evidence we can't arrest or convict," Joe said.

Nate shrugged. "It's not about the how—it's about the why. And until you can figure out the why, the how doesn't matter. But when you determine the why, the how evidence you've gathered will support it and prop it up."

Joe shook his head, confused.

Nate turned toward Alisha and arched his eyebrows.

She said, "Shenandoah was—is—my best friend. We're not blood, but we're closer than that. We were in cribs next to each other in the nursery at Fremont County General, and we grew up together. She is closer to me than my sisters. Since she's been back we've had some long, intimate talks. What you're asking me to do now is betray her."

"I'm not asking that," Joe said.

"If I talk to you, that's what I'd be doing," she said sadly.

Joe looked from Nate to Marybeth and back to Alisha. She looked both beautiful and sad.

"My friend Shenandoah is finally happy in her life," Alisha said, almost whispering. "She's a mother and at long last she's happy and grounded. She loves her family but she has a blind spot when it comes to her husband. Many of us do when it comes to the men we love." As she said it, she gestured toward Nate, who smiled a tiny smile. She continued, "This may destroy her family. I'm her best friend, and I could destroy her when she's finally happy.

Do you understand? Do you understand what you're asking me to do?"

Joe grimaced, not sure what to say.

"I've only ever seen her this happy when we were playing basketball," Alisha said, looking at Joe but not really seeing him. "She was so willful and determined. She was *so* good, and it was not as natural to her as many people thought. She made herself what she was. I was in awe of her. She'd practice by herself on the hoop above her grandfather's garage until her hands bled from handling the ball. She'd shoot at night, in the snow and wind. She'd even practice when her grandfather and her uncle went hunting and hung antelope and deer from the hoop—she'd dribble around them and pretend the animal carcasses were opposing players. She gave herself confidence and it became grace, and I loved her for that because I learned from her. That's one thing I fault many of my people on; we don't give our children confidence. That's why I'm back, to try to do that for them and help them see. But it was Shenandoah—she showed me how it was done."

Alisha paused to angrily wipe a tear away, then continued.

"I'm sure you heard that she could have gone anywhere on scholarship, and she could have. And it wasn't that she was scared like so many people think. It's that her grandmother *really was* sick. Her grandmother raised her because Shannon's mother was a violent alcoholic and her father could have been any one of seven men. Shannon owed her grandmother everything, so she stayed to take care of her because no one else would. I thought it was stupid and wasteful at the time because I didn't have the right perspective. We all laugh about Indian time, but it can be a noble attribute in a circumstance like that. Shenandoah had only one grandmother and that grandmother had lung cancer. Shenandoah could go to college and leave her sick grandmother to die or she could stay and nurse her. She made the choice to stay because her grandmother had only a couple of years left but Shenandoah had many. Shenandoah put off her own reward to take care of the only woman who'd ever really loved her and encouraged her. What she did was noble, not stupid. How many high-school-age girls can make a sacrifice like that?"

Joe and Marybeth looked at each other. Their girls were upstairs sleeping in their beds. Would Sheridan or Lucy give up their dreams to stay home and take care of a parent? Joe hoped not. But in his heart of hearts, he also hoped *so*.

"So she stayed," Alisha said.

"That's what I'm curious about," Joe said gently. "How did we go from there to here? When did she meet Klamath Moore?"

Alisha nodded. "I lost track of her for a while. I have to admit that for five or six years after I graduated high school and went to college and then on to my career, I really didn't want to see her. I was ashamed of her. I heard she got fat and started bouncing from job to job, from man to man after her grandmother died. I am ashamed now that I felt so ashamed then. You know, this is tough for me," she said, her voice cracking.

Joe heard Marybeth sniff back her own tears.

Nate rose to cross the room to comfort Alisha, but she shook her head at him.

"I'm fine," she said. "Just let me get through this."

She turned back to Joe. "Shannon got a little wild for a while there. It happens very easily here, and I hate to say it but there are many people on and off the res who enable and encourage a fall from grace for American Indians. Bigots expect it and it suits the worldview of many liberals. Too many people, both Indians and whites, are more comfortable with an Indian girl who gets fat and fails than one who breaks out and does well. Shannon let herself fall, and she got mixed up with the wrong people for a while. I wasn't here to help her like I should have been. I was only too happy to use her as an example of victimhood because that served me at the time with my professors. It was only later that I realized the only person I knew who truly thought for herself and did the right thing was Shenandoah. She wasn't a victim, she was a warrior who did what was right. She used to call me and write me, and I was so wrapped up in myself I let myself lose touch with her. When I abandoned her, she took it hard."

Alisha paused to fight back another round of tears. Then:

"But she got right again, from what she told me recently. She decided to go to college on her own, even though no one was offering her any scholarships anymore. To make some money to pay tuition she started up a little business where she guided and cooked for hunting parties. She always liked being outdoors. She was really popular with hunters, and she made a lot of money. Guiding and outfitting is really hard work. I know because my father was an outfitter and I used to go with him. But something happened while she was working once, and it knocked her right off the wagon. She said she drifted and did drugs and drank for two years after that before finally getting right again and enrolling at CU in Boulder."

"Where she met Klamath Moore," Marybeth said.

Alisha nodded. "Klamath fell hard for her and she fell hard for him. Since they got married, she's lost a lot of weight and become the Shenandoah I used to know. Especially since she had her baby."

Joe rubbed his chin, asked, "What was it that happened at a hunting camp that sent her reeling for two years?"

Alisha shook her head. "I'm sorry, I've said too much already. I promised her I would keep that between us."

Joe looked at Nate for help. He didn't give it.

"Come on, Alisha," Joe said, "it might be relevant. Something might have happened that completely turned her off hunting and hunters. Maybe that's why she and Klamath Moore hit it off so well."

"I'm not saying any more, I told you," Alisha said. "Besides, this isn't about Shenandoah. It's about Klamath."

"Granted," Joe said, "but if you could give me some insight into their relationship—"

"No," Alisha said firmly.

"Joe," Marybeth said, reaching across the table and putting her hand on his arm again, "I think that's enough for now."

"Yup," Nate said.

"Okay," Joe said, raising his hands to her and smiling. "I'll stop."

She nodded her appreciation to him.

"One more question," Joe said.

Marybeth sighed. Alisha arched her eyebrows, as if saying, *What?*

"Would she protect him, no matter what he'd done?"

Alisha didn't hesitate. "For the sake of her daughter, yes."

JOE EXCUSED himself while Marybeth and Alisha cleaned up the glassware and dishes. He was tired, but he was also charged up, thinking at last he was on the verge of something. In the bathroom he shut the door and drew his old notebook out of his back pocket, flipping through the pages until he found what he was looking for.

JOE AND MARYBETH saw Nate and Alisha to the door. It was 4 A.M. and cold and still outside. Joe thanked Alisha and apologized for asking so many questions. Nate held out his hand to say good-bye, and Joe shook it.

"Nate," Joe said, "are you available in three hours for a trip to Rawlins and back?"

"Rawlins? Three hours?"

"I'm not supposed to go anywhere, but I think we can get there and back by midafternoon before Randy Pope gets here and McLanahan even knows I'm gone."

Nate looked at Alisha. She shrugged.

"Why Rawlins?" Marybeth asked.

"Because that's where the state penitentiary is," Joe said. "Home of Vern Dunnegan."

27

IT TOOK three and a half hours—pushing the speed lim-it—to get to Rawlins from Saddlestring via I-25 south to Casper, then paralleling the North Platte River to Alcova, past Independence Rock and Martin's Cove on the Oregon Trail, then taking US 287 south at Muddy Gap. Nate slept for most of it. Joe listened to Brian Scott on KTWO out of Casper taking calls about the hunting moratorium but he had trouble concentrating on either the radio or his driving because he was testing and discarding scenarios that had opened up since the night before and thinking Nate was right when he said the investigation had been too narrowly focused.

Nate awoke and stretched as Green Mountain loomed to the east. The landscape was vast and still, sagebrush dotted with herds of pronghorn antelope, hawks flying low, puffy cumulus clouds looking like cartoon thought balloons.

With Rawlins itself nearly in view, Joe spoke for the first time since they'd left.

"Nate, do you have any idea what we're about to find out?"

"Do you mean did Alisha tell me?"

"Yes."

"No, she didn't."

"One more question."

"Shoot."

"When I dropped you off, did you know you'd be picked up by Klamath and Shannon Moore as well as Alisha?"

"Yup. Alisha told me when I called her from Large Merle's."

"But you didn't tell me."

"Nope. I knew if I told you, you'd get all hot and bothered and you wouldn't let me do my work on my own schedule."

"You're probably right," Joe said sourly.

"Plus, you'd probably mention it to somebody—the governor or Randy Pope—and it could have gotten back to Klamath. He's got sympathizers everywhere who keep him informed. He's even got someone at the FBI who told him about your meeting Bill Gordon."

"Apparently."

"True believers," Nate said, shaking his head.

WHEN HE was close enough to Rawlins to pick up a cell phone signal, Joe called the Wyoming state pen. Like all the inmates, Vern Dunnegan would have to agree to talk to Joe and put him officially on his visit list. If Vern declined, Joe would need to go to the warden and try to force a meeting where Vern could show up with his counsel and refuse to talk. The receptionist said she'd check with security and call Joe back. For once, Joe was happy he worked for the governor and therefore had some clout in the state system.

As Joe punched off, Nate said, "There are many things about this case that baffle me, but one really stands out for an explanation."

"What's that?"

"Your boss, Randy Pope."

"What about him?"

"He hates you and me with a passion and a viciousness reserved for only the most cold-blooded of bureaucrats."

"That he does."

"So why did he become your champion?"

Joe shrugged. "I've wondered that myself. My only answer is that he's more pragmatic than I gave him credit for. He values his agency and his title more than he hates me. I took it as sort of a compliment that when the chips were down he put our problems aside and even argued for your release."

Nate said, *"Hmmmm."*

"Maybe we're about to find out," said Joe.

THEY PASSED through town and dropped off the butte and saw the prison sprawled out on the valley floor below them, coils of silver razor wire reflecting the high sun. Joe's phone chirped. It was the receptionist.

"Inmate Dunnegan has agreed to meet with you," she said.

"Good."

"In fact, he wanted me to relay something to you."

"Go ahead."

"He wanted me to ask why it took you so long."

Joe felt a trill of cognition.

"Tell him I was finning in the wrong channel," Joe said.

"Excuse me?"

NATE STAYED in Joe's pickup in the parking lot while Joe went in the visitors' entrance of the administration building and put all his possessions including his cell phone into a locker. He'd left his weapon and wallet in the truck, taking only his badge and state ID. He filled out the paperwork at the counter, passed through security, and sat alone in the minibus that took him the mile from the admin building past the heavily guarded Intensive Treatment Unit (ITU) and other gray, low-slung buildings to a checkpoint, where he was searched again and asked the nature of his visit.

"I'm here to see Vern Dunnegan," Joe said.

At the name, the guard grinned. "Ole Vern," he said. "Good guy."

Joe said, "Unless he's trying to get your family killed."

The guard's smile doused. "You've got history with him, then."

"Yup."

To the driver, the guard said, "Take him to A-Pod."

When they were under way, Joe asked, "A-Pod?"

The driver said, "A, B, and C pods are for the general population. A-Pod is the lowest security and it goes up from there all the way to E-Pod, which is Max and Death Row. You don't want to go there."

"No," Joe said, "I don't."

At a set of doors marked A, the driver stopped. "When you're done, tell the guard at the desk and he'll call me."

Joe nodded. "So this means Vern Dunnegan is considered low-risk, huh?"

"That's what it means."

Joe shook his head. "Man, he's got you guys fooled. I guess he hasn't changed."

THE VISITATION room was large, quiet, pale blue, and well lit. It was filled with plastic tables and chairs, the kind used on decks and in backyards. The feet of the chairs were bound with athletic tape so they wouldn't squeak when moved. There was a bank of vending machines against a wall and a television set hanging from the ceiling with ESPN on with no volume. One corner of the room was filled with neatly stacked children's toys and multicolored pieces for kids to climb on while wives or girlfriends visited. Joe had to sign in again with an officer behind a large desk in the southeast corner. The desk itself was empty except for a clipboard and a huge box of wet wipes and a smaller container of disposable latex gloves. On the sign-in sheet were listed categories for visits including "Friend/Relative," "Legal counsel," "Religious," "Kissing Only," and "Other." Joe checked "Other," and the guard gestured expansively, indicating Joe could sit wherever he wanted.

The only other occupants in the room were a couple at a table in the far corner and their child (he assumed), a toddler, playing quietly with plastic blocks. Although the couple was required to sit on opposite sides of the table (she'd checked "Kissing Only"), they strained forward across the tabletop to get closer. She was dark and Hispanic, her perfume so strong Joe could smell it from across the room. He wondered how she'd outmaneuvered the admin guards in regard to the posted "No skintight or revealing clothing" regulation. She wore jeans that looked spray-painted on and a tight white Lycra top that clung to her breasts like a film. He was lean, shaved bald, olive-skinned, and heavily tattooed. His arms were outstretched, his hands on her shoulders, pulling her toward him. She strained toward him, her own arms outstretched, her fingers furiously caressing the tips of the collar of his white jumpsuit with a kind of unrestrained animal lust that Joe found both riveting and revolting. The inmate looked as if he would explode at any second. He was red-faced, his eyes wide, his face inches from hers. Joe hoped the guard had his wet wipes at the ready.

"I think I'll take the other corner," Joe said.

"Good idea," the officer said, then, shouting to the couple, "Hey, dial it back a notch over there! It's kissing only— no fondling. You know the rules."

A GUNMETAL gray door opened on the wall opposite where Joe had signed in and Vern Dunnegan entered the room. At the sight of his old supervisor, Joe felt his stomach and rectum involuntarily clench and his breathing get short and shallow. He hadn't seen the man for eight years, but here he was.

Vern wore an orange jumpsuit with no pockets and blue rubber shoes. He was thicker than he used to be, his face more doughy and his limbs and belly turned to flab. His hair was thinner and grayer and pasted back on his large head, and he was clean-shaven, which revealed a reptilian demeanor that had always been there but was masked by the beard he used to wear. Despite the avuncular smile on his face when he saw Joe, Vern's eyes were obsidian black and without depth, as if blocked off from the inside. Joe remembered the whole package. Vern could smile at you while he stabbed you in the heart.

Vern Dunnegan had once been the Wyoming game warden for the Saddlestring District. Vern had considered Joe his protégé and Joe naively thought of Vern as his mentor. But Vern was one of the old-time wardens, the kind who bent the law to suit his needs and curry favor, a one-man cop, judge, and jury who used his badge and the autonomous nature of the job to manipulate the community and increase both his influence and his income. In those days, before the discovery of coal-bed methane, Twelve Sleep County was in an economic slump and those who lived there were scrambling to stay afloat. Vern and Joe, both state employees with salaries and vehicles and insurance and pensions, were the envy of most of the working people. Joe fought against the uncomfortable recollection of how it once was between them, when he was the green trainee and Vern the wily vet. Although Marybeth always distrusted the man, Joe refused to see it while he worked under him. It wasn't until Vern quit and came back as a landman representing a natural gas pipeline company that Joe found out what Vern's bitter worldview was all about, as his former boss set up a scenario that led to Marybeth's being shot and losing their baby—all so Vern could enrich himself. The last time Joe had seen Vern was when he testified against him in court.

"Long time," Vern said, nodding hello to the guard at the desk and sidling up to Joe's table. "And here I thought you'd forgotten all about me, like you didn't care anymore."

The last was said with a lilt of sarcasm and anger.

Vern settled down heavily in the chair opposite Joe. In Vern's face, Joe could see traces of green and purple bruising on his cheekbones and the side of his head, and when Vern spoke Joe saw missing teeth. The man had been beaten, which really didn't bother Joe in the least. In fact, now that Vern was just a few feet away from him, all the things he had done came rushing back. Joe had to tamp down his own urge to leap across the table and pummel the man.

"Do you have any idea what it's like to be a former peace officer in this place?" Vern asked softly, reaching up and touching the bruise on the left side of his face. "I have to be ready to defend my life every goddamned day, every goddamned minute. I never know when someone will take a whack at me just for the hell of it. I've been in H-Pod so many times I know all the nurses by name and they know me."

Joe assumed the "H" stood for hospital but didn't really want the conversation to be about Vern Dunnegan's perceived victimization and self-pity.

"You probably noticed the color," Vern said, patting himself on the breast of his orange jumpsuit. "Orange means I'm segregated from the general population for my own protection—supposedly. What it really means is I'm a walking target for these predators in here. You have no idea what it's like. Some asshole will be walking behind me and for no reason at all he'll elbow me in the neck and just keep going. Or he'll cut me with a shiv . . ." Vern shot his arm out so his sleeve retracted, revealing a spider's web of old scars. "Not enough to kill me, just enough for stitches.

"I'm all alone in here," Vern said. "Nobody visits any-more. I get along with most of the guards but almost none of the population. It's a living hell. At least if I were on Death Row I'd get the respect those guys get. As it is, I've got at least four more years of this. Bad food. Bad dreams. Eight head counts per twenty-four hours. This orange jump-suit. Having to live my life with deviants, reprobates, and human scum as my neighbors."

"Gee," Joe said, "it must be rough."

Vern did his trademark chuckle, the one that meant ex-actly the opposite of how it sounded. "You've changed," he said. "You've gotten harder."

Joe glared at him.

Vern said, "I've been following your career with great interest. I've got to say that you've impressed me with your exploits. I never thought you had it in you, to be honest. I always thought you were a little slow—too naive, too much of a Dudley Do-Right. But you've matured, Joe. You're as cold and calculating as I was."

Joe shook his head. "Wrong."

"I'm not so sure," Vern said, leaning back and apprais-ing Joe with his cold eyes, the pleasant grin frozen on his face.

"Then you must have left that wife of yours by now," Vern said. "I always saw her as an emasculator."

Joe took a deep breath. "Nope. We're still together with our two beautiful girls."

"I'm shocked," Vern said, not shocked at all, but enjoy-ing the game of getting Joe worked up. Just like he used to do.

"Enough," Joe said. "You apparently know why I'm here."

Vern nodded. "It took you long enough."

Joe looked at his wristwatch.

"I understand you're now buddies with the governor," Vern said evenly. "And that he's desperate to solve these murders so he can open the state back up. I can help him do that. But there are terms."

Joe looked up. "Terms?"

JOE ASKED the desk guard if he could use his phone, and he was able to get through to the governor's office. He asked the receptionist to transfer him to Rulon. Joe stood waiting near the guard's desk. The guard pretended he wasn't eavesdropping. Vern sat perfectly still at the table, his big hands on the tabletop, fingers interlaced, watching the silent television flicker. He looked completely in control, Joe thought.

"Stella Ennis," she said crisply.

"Stella, it's Joe."

A pause. "Hello, Mr. Pickett." Did Joe detect an inappropriate purr?

"I'm at the Wyoming state pen and I've got quite a situation here."

"From what I understand, you've got a situation back at home as well. What is it I heard about an agent of the governor assaulting a police officer?"

Joe shook his head, as if she could see him. "I'll explain all of that later. Right now I need you to put that aside and listen to me."

"My, my," she said, "aren't we the tough guy this morning."

"Look, I'm here seeing my old boss Vern Dunnegan. He's served eight years of a twelve-year sentence for conspiracy and being an accessory to murder. He claims that he knows where to find the Wolverine. He says he'll tell me everything in exchange for the governor commuting the rest of his prison time." Out of corner of his eye, Joe saw the guard spill coffee all over himself.

Stella said, "Do you believe him?"

"Yes."

"This is *very* unusual."

"I know it is, and I hate to even call you with this. Vern should spend the rest of his life in here; it's where he belongs. But I really do think he knows how we can catch who we're after."

"How would a man eight years in prison know that?" she asked.

"That's what we need to find out."

"Hold on. I'll ask Spencer."

Not "the governor" or "Governor Rulon," but *Spencer*, Joe thought.

Rulon came on the line so quickly Joe could only conclude that he had either been listening in on another line or Stella was so close to him physically that he heard what Joe had told her. Joe briefly closed his eyes, thought, *Uh-oh*.

The governor sounded annoyed. "Is he there?"

"Vern Dunnegan? Yes, he's here."

"Let me talk to the son of a bitch."

"Okay," Joe said, crossing the room and handing the handset to Vern. "It's Governor Rulon."

Vern's eyebrows shot up, and a self-satisfied smirk crept across his lips. He took the phone. "Hello, Governor Rulon."

Joe sat back down and listened to Vern's side of the conversation. Occasionally, he could hear Rulon shout or curse through the handset. Again, he thought of how close Rulon had to have been to Stella to hear Joe clearly. He rubbed his eyes and listened.

"That's right," Vern said. "I can help you close this case and then you can reopen the state for hunting."

Vern listened for a while, said, "Why didn't I come forward sooner? Well, I have to admit that it didn't really register when John Garrett was killed. I mean, I knew the name and I vaguely remembered him, and when I read about it in the paper nothing clicked. Then I read about Warren Tucker a couple of weeks later and it started to make some sense to me. I *almost* told the warden of my suspicions at that point, but that's all they were, suspicions. A man can't bargain with suspicions. . . ."

A few moments later, "Right. Frank Urman was the clincher. When I heard his name I knew how the victims were connected. Wally Conway just drove the nail in the coffin, so to speak."

Joe glanced angrily up at Vern, who chatted away with the governor.

"What? No. Not anymore. I'm a prisoner of the state, remember? I have no kind of obligation anymore," Vern said, rolling his eyes.

Joe shook his head.

"Yes, there will be at least one more murder as it stands right now," Vern said. "Maybe more. I can promise you that. But if we can make a deal, I can help you prevent it. And you can be the hero. I'll keep my mouth shut."

Fat chance, Joe thought, seething.

"No, I can't give away any more. Not until we've got an under-standing."

Joe could hear the governor going on in his best growl.

"Sure, I understand," Vern said into the phone. "If what I tell Joe here turns out to be wrong, I know the deal would be off. But I think we both know I've got very valuable information that I'm willing to share."

As they negotiated, Joe glanced over at the table where the couple sat. It appeared that the inmate was *chewing* on her collar. He could see the man's jaws working, and his eyes rolling back in his head in pleasure. Her gaze was focused above his head, and she looked detached. Joe couldn't help but think of the old joke where the wife, beneath her husband in bed, says, *"Beige. I think I'll paint the ceiling beige."*

Joe tore himself away as Vern Dunnegan said, "So we have a deal then."

Then: "Okay, I want it in writing. You can fax it to the prison. I won't say a word to Joe here until I read it over and see that it says exactly what we discussed."

Then: "Sure, I trust you. You're the governor, right? What is there not to trust? But nevertheless, I subscribe to the Ronald Reagan notion of 'trust, but verify.' So I need that paper and your signature. . . . Sure, I'll wait. But visiting hours will be over in ninety minutes. I need the agreement by then. You're a wordsmith and a former federal prosecutor—it shouldn't take long."

"Here," Vern said, beaming, thrusting the phone back across the table, "he wants to talk to you."

"Yes," Joe said.

"We made a deal," the governor said wearily.

"So I heard."

"What an asshole."

Joe looked up at Vern, said, "Yup."

"So you think it's legit, then?"

"Yes."

"Okay, we'll fax the paperwork over within a half hour. Then he better spill the beans. Call me when you've got something solid and we'll proceed from there."

"Yes, sir."

"And, Joe . . ."

"Yes?"

Hesitation. Joe frowned.

"Nothing," the governor said. "Forget it."

"Is it about Stella?" Joe asked.

Rulon barked a laugh. "She's something, isn't she?"

Joe cringed, and punched off the phone.

As THEY waited for the agreement to arrive, Joe and Vern sat at the table in silence, each pretending the other man wasn't in the room. Joe kept checking his wristwatch. He shot another glance at the couple in the corner, and looked away guiltily. Vern chuckled.

"Caught you," he said.

"It looks like he's eating her neck," Joe mumbled.

"It's a con trick," Vern said. "The female cooks meth

down into crystal and hangs it from her necklace chain like a pendant. She sits there while he sucks it and gets high. The guards haven't figured that one out yet. They'll do a full-body and cavity search, but they don't think about testing the jewelry."

"My God," Joe said.

"It's a different world in here," Vern said. "I'll be glad to be leaving it soon."

THE DESK GUARD got a call, spoke a few words, and motioned Joe over.

"There's a fax from the governor for Vern Dunnegan at admin. They're bringing it over."

Joe sighed.

The driver who had delivered Joe to A-Pod brought the fax. As Joe took it to Vern, he read it over. It was on official letterhead stationery and signed at the bottom:

> I, Governor Spencer H. Rulon, agree to commute the remaining years of prison time for inmate Vernon Dunnegan in exchange for information that results in the arrest and conviction of the so-called Wolverine who has been responsible for the deaths of several Wyoming resident hunters. If no arrest and/or conviction is/are obtained, this agreement is rendered null and void.

AFTER VERN had told his story, Joe shut his notebook and said, "So this is all your fault."

Vern shrugged. "I was never like you, Joe. I wasn't in it to save Bambi."

Joe shot his fist across the table and hit Vern Dunnegan flush in the face, snapping his head back.

"Hey!" the desk guard yelled, standing. "Do I need to call my boys in?"

Joe, still enraged, stood up quickly and walked away.

He knew if he looked for another second at Vern's self-satisfied face or heard his arrogant words that he wouldn't be able to stop swinging.

"I need to get out of here," Joe said through clenched teeth.

"Yes, you do," the guard said, picking up his handset to call the driver.

"See you on the outside," Vern called from the table, one hand at his face to stanch the flow of blood, the other waving and flittering his fingers in a *toodle-do*.

Joe turned, squared his feet, and stared Vern down. "If I do," Joe said, meaning it, "you're going to wish you were back in here."

28

NATE WASN'T outside in the parking lot and neither was Joe's pickup. Joe stood seething in the space where he'd parked, but his fury was not directed at Nate—yet. Vern's words, *I was never like you, Joe. I wasn't in it to save Bambi,* echoed in his ears, but what enraged him was Vern's attitude, his casual disregard for what he'd casually set in motion so many years before. Vern's action—or inaction, in this situation—had resulted in ruined lives and the deaths, so far, of seven men. And in the end, instead of accountability, Vern was able to use his malfeasance as a bargaining chip to walk away free from prison.

"This isn't over," Joe said aloud.

A thick bank of storm clouds pushed their way across the sun, halving it, then snuffing it out. In the distance he could hear the muted roar of semitrucks on I-80. The air smelled of dust, sage, and diesel fumes. In his ears he could hear a similar roar that stemmed from anger and betrayal. Joe called Marybeth, said, "It's going to be a long night."

"What's going on?" she asked. "Did you meet with Vern Dunnegan?"

"I did." Joe said tightly. "And everything has just gone nuclear."

"Oh, no. What did he say?"

"It all goes back to Vern," Joe said.

"What did he say?"

"Honey, you can't say a word about what I'm going to tell you to *anybody*."

"Joe, I won't. I never do."

"You're right," he said. "Sorry."

As Joe explained, he looked up and saw his truck a mile away, descending toward the valley floor and the prison complex. In a couple of minutes it would be here. He hurried, rushing his words until all he could say was, "Nate's here. I've got to go."

"Joe!" she said. "You can't do what I think you're going to do."

"I'll call later," he said, and snapped the phone shut as Nate pulled up in front of him and stopped the pickup.

Nate said, "I hope you don't mind I borrowed your vehicle." He got out and left the driver's-side door open and walked around the front of the truck to get back in as a passenger. "I had to go downtown and check out a couple of pawnshops."

Joe grunted and climbed in. The scoped five-shot .454 Casull revolver Nate had found at a pawnshop lay formidably on the seat cushion between them, along with a heavy box of ammunition. It was a massive weapon, the second most powerful handgun in the world, manufactured by Freedom Arms in Freedom, Wyoming. Joe knew that a .454 bullet was capable of punching a clean hole through a half inch of steel, penetrating the engine block of a car and stopping it cold, or knocking down a moose at a mile away. It was Nate's weapon of choice, and he was an expert with it.

"I somehow figured I'd be needing that later," Nate said

by way of explanation. "The FBI still has mine. This baby's a little beat up, but it's got a nice scope and I got it for a song—eighteen hundred."

Joe slipped the truck into gear and began to climb out of the valley.

"So," Joe asked, "how does a man under federal indictment walk into a pawnshop and buy a hand cannon without raising any red flags in a background check?"

Nate smiled, handed back the wallet Joe had left in the pickup. "I didn't," Nate said. "You did. And tell Marybeth not to worry—I used your state credit card, not a personal one."

Joe moaned.

"Did you find out anything?" Nate asked, gesturing toward the prison.

"You were right," Joe said. "We were thinking Wolverine was targeting hunters in general. It turns out, the killer was after five specific men who *happened* to be hunters."

Nate nodded slowly, waiting for more.

JOE SAID, "Vern was at coffee in the Burg-O-Pardner like he was every morning, even during hunting season, when Shenandoah Yellowcalf walked in the place. This was ten years ago. I wasn't in the picture then. The breakfast crowd consisted of the city fathers, or who thought they were. Vern, Judge Pennock, and Sheriff Bud Barnum."

When he said the name *Bud Barnum*, Joe glanced at Nate and paused. Nate looked untroubled.

"What?" Nate asked. "Do you expect remorse?"

"I don't know what I expected," Joe said.

"Go on," Nate said impatiently. It was clear to Joe that what bothered Nate was not Barnum's involvement but Shenandoah's.

Joe said, "This was when Shenandoah was operating her camp-cook-slash-guide service. She claimed she'd been hired by a party of five elk hunters who held her against her will and raped her. Vern said she said it in front of the whole table, and she demanded that Barnum and Vern go arrest the hunters. Vern thought the whole situation was uncomfortable because—according to him—it was pretty well known at the time that Shenandoah did a lot more for hunters than cook and guide."

"That asshole," Nate whispered.

"I don't know if there's anything to that charge," Joe said. "I tend to believe there might be some truth in it, from what I've heard over the years and from what Alisha said last night. She said Shenandoah was wild back then, so it's possible what Vern said is credible. That's what I've got in my old notebook, that an Indian girl was prostituting herself under the cover of serving as a camp cook. No names, though. So there's some corroboration. But if it is, there's no evidence she made a claim of rape either before or after that incident. So in this particular case, she might have been forced and she wanted the hunters arrested.

"Vern said he went up to the elk camp with Barnum to talk to the hunters. There were five, like she said. The hunters were Wyoming men of some prominence. Vern said he recognized a couple of their names at the time. They said Shenandoah had been willing, even enthusiastic about taking them all on. They told Vern they'd been playing poker in their tent the night before and she invited them to her tent one by one. All of them were embarrassed, and begged Vern and Barnum not to tell their wives or girlfriends. They said Shenandoah must be shaking them down for money or something, because otherwise it made no sense to them that she'd come into town and make an accusation like that. The hunters said that if Shenandoah went public, it would ruin them for no good reason."

Nate sat back in the seat, said, "I can see where this is headed."

Joe nodded. "It's even worse. What they ended up doing, Nate, was arresting her for public intoxication and putting her in the county jail until she realized her charge was going nowhere. That must have made her a very bitter woman."

"And I don't blame her," Nate said.

Joe said, "She went from being seen as a star athlete to an alcoholic loser in the space of just a few years. There was plenty of gossip—probably some of it true—about her camp cook activities. So when she makes an accusation in public against five resident hunters, *she* gets charged. Whatever dignity she had left at that point must have been flushed away."

Nate said, "I'm surprised she didn't take it any further than that, like the Feds or the media."

Joe agreed. "I asked Vern about that, and he said she didn't take it any further because she realized she had nothing but her word against theirs. You see, Barnum and Vern 'lost' her original complaint. They didn't order a rape kit done, or send her to the clinic for photos or an examination. By the time she realized all of that—when she was released on bail—any bruises she had were healed and there were at least three well-known city fathers lined up and ready to testify that she had shown up drunk and raving at breakfast. She had no case and an entire valley—whites who resented her for being Indian and Indians who resented her for doing too well—lined up against her."

They drove in silence for the fifty miles from Lamont to Devils Gate under an unforgiving leaden sky. Joe could tell from the skitterish behavior of the antelope herds that low pressure and moisture were on the way. His stomach roiled and his hands felt cold and damp on the steering wheel. He'd told Nate the story Vern had relayed to him but he hadn't told Nate everything.

"What were the names of our poker-playing hunters?" Nate asked, finally.

"I think you know," Joe said. "Except for the fifth one."

"But I can guess. Randy Pope."

Joe said, "Yup."

"Which is the reason he was all over this whole thing

from the beginning," Nate said. "It explains why he unleashed you and me. He thought we'd find and kill the Wolverine before the story got out and ruined his career and reputation. Or if you arrested the Wolverine, Pope would be on-site to shut him up. That's why Pope is in Saddlestring right now, waiting for us."

"Yup."

"It also explains the poker chips. Only the men involved would know the significance of the poker chips."

Joe nodded. "But that detail wasn't released to the public. Only Randy Pope knew he was being sent a message."

"But he wasn't positive," Nate said. "He was suspicious, but he wasn't positive. So he invited his old friend Wally Conway up to the Bighorns with him, to see what would happen. And Wally got whacked."

"Yup. Unfortunately, Robey was collateral damage."

Nate shook his head. "Was Wally Conway dense? Didn't he realize what had happened to his old hunting buddies?"

Joe shrugged. "He might have known. We don't know what he discussed with Robey that night."

Joe saw Nate's hand drop and rest on the .454. "I don't know who I hate worse," Nate said, "Vern Dunnegan or Randy Pope."

"You're forgetting someone," Joe said.

"Who?"

"The Wolverine. The killer."

Nate shrugged. "Him, I can live with."

"I can't," Joe said. His stomach churned. He remembered something Nate had said to him the first time they ever met, and he knew it was the core belief of Nate Romanowski. Nate had said he no longer believed in the legal system but he believed in justice.

It was a leap Joe couldn't make, although there had been several times he'd stood at the precipice and measured the jump.

"Shenandoah finally got herself straightened out," Nate said, looking out the window, speaking as much to himself as to Joe. "Like always, she did it on her own, without anyone's help. Eventually, she told her husband about what had happened. She named names. He hated hunters anyway, and now he knew the names of the hunters who had violated his very own wife, the way *he'd* been violated by his uncle but never told anyone but Shenandoah, who told Alisha, who told me. And Klamath made a plan."

Joe said nothing, letting Nate go with it, mildly shocked at what Nate had revealed about Moore's uncle. Finally, the burning flame behind Klamath's obsession was clear.

"So it's Klamath Moore after all," Nate said.

As they shot past Kaycee, Nate said, "To Chris," and they drank another imaginary good-bye toast.

South of Buffalo, Joe speed-dialed the governor's office. Again, Stella Ennis answered.

"Am I okay?" Joe asked.

"You're okay as long as you get the killer," she answered.

"I will, but the state may lose a game and fish director in the process. I'm going to use him as bait. Can the governor live with that?"

In his peripheral vision, Joe saw Nate turn his head and smile at him.

Rulon, who had been on the line all along, said, "Officially, you never made this call and I never got it. Unofficially, the answer is *hell yes*."

Joe said, "What, is she on your lap?"

Rulon said, "Hell yes."

Joe snapped the phone shut.

Nate said, "I like this plan so far, whatever it is."
Joe thought, *You won't later.*

"WHO ARE you calling now?" Nate asked, as Joe scrolled though the list of numbers on his cell phone while driving.

"The FBI in Cheyenne. I'm going to brief them on what's going on."

"Are you crazy? Klamath's got an informer in that office."

Joe said, "Exactly."

"Ooooh," Nate said.

JOE SLOWED and swerved the pickup into a designated scenic pullout that overlooked a sweep of ranchland meadows rising up the foothills of the Bighorns.

Joe jumped out of the truck and took several deep breaths with his hands on his hips, trying to fight off nausea. When the turmoil in his stomach and soul were under control, he wiped moisture from his eyes and looked up. White shafts of afternoon sunlight poked through the cloud cover in a dozen places, making the vista look as if it were behind jail bars.

"Are you okay?" Nate asked from the pickup.

"Fine," Joe said. "Something I ate." Thinking, *Something I'm about to do.*

29

RANDY POPE'S state Escalade was parked in the driveway of Joe's house and Joe pulled in behind it.

"Rude bastard," Nate said, "using your driveway like that."

Joe grunted, angry that Pope had the temerity to come to his home to wait. Joe hated to involve his family any more than they were already involved, and hoped Sheridan and Lucy had after-school activities that had kept them away.

"Back in a minute," Joe said, swinging out.

Randy Pope was sitting on the couch with a half-drunk cup of coffee and a plate of cookies in front of him. Marybeth was in the overstuffed chair in her work clothes, her knees tightly pressed together and her fingers interlaced on her lap. She was uncomfortable, and she turned to Joe as he entered with an expression on her face that seemed to say, "Help me!"

"I stopped home to grab some files and guess who was here waiting?" she said to Joe.

Pope stood up, brushing crumbs off his jeans. He looked pale, distressed, angry. But even Pope wouldn't start yelling at Joe in front of his wife.

"Gee, Joe," Pope said, "I was starting to wonder if you'd ever show up."

"Here I am."

"I've been very concerned. Mary said you called from the road, but my understanding was that you had to stay in town until they got that assault charge straightened out." He spoke evenly, without intonation.

"It's Mary*beth*," Joe said, "and I needed to follow a lead. I spent the morning talking with Vern Dunnegan." He paused. "Remember him?"

Pope's face froze into a wax mask.

"Can we step outside?" Joe said calmly. To Marybeth, "I hope you don't mind."

She shook her head, but her eyes stayed on him, cautioning Joe to stay cool.

"Are the girls here?" Joe asked.

"Sheridan's at practice, Lucy's at the Andersons' practicing a play."

Joe nodded. "Good."

Pope hadn't moved. The only thing that had changed about him were his pupils, which had dilated and looked like bullet holes.

"Randy?" Joe said, stepping aside.

Woodenly, Pope shuffled toward the front door with Joe following.

Over his shoulder, Joe said to Marybeth, "I'll call. Don't worry."

"Joe . . ."

The moment Pope opened the front door he broke to the left and slammed the door in Joe's face behind him. Joe threw the door open and fumbled for his weapon, shouted, "Randy!"

But Pope didn't get far. He stood in the middle of the

neighbor's lawn, backing up with the .454 muzzle pressed against his forehead. Nate cocked the revolver and the cylinder turned.

"Can I shoot him now?" Nate asked.

"Not yet," Joe said.

"I'd really like to."

"Later, maybe."

Over Nate's shoulder, Joe saw his neighbor Ed wander out onto his lawn from his open garage. Ed was smoking his pipe, inspecting the lawn for stray leaves. When Ed looked over and saw what was happening—*on his very own property*—his pipe dropped out of his mouth.

"Evening, Ed," Joe said, as Nate backed Pope into Joe's pickup. Joe climbed in the driver's side and Nate shoved Pope inside between them. Ed was still standing there, openmouthed, as Joe roared away, headed for the mountains.

"THIS IS kidnapping, assault, reckless endangerment . . ." Pope said, his voice trailing off.

"Insubordination," Nate said, "that too."

"Call the governor now," Pope said to Joe. "Let's get this thing straightened out."

"I've already talked to him," Joe said.

Pope mouthed something but no words came out.

"That's right," Joe said. "He's willing to trade you for Wolverine, if necessary."

"But we can work together," Pope said, pleading. "You don't have to do it this way. We can work something out now, and for the future."

Joe seemed to think it over, to Nate's consternation. Finally, Joe said, "Nope. I saw how you treat your friends."

THEY WERE past Joe's old house on Bighorn Road when Pope said, "It wasn't like what you think."

"What is it I think?" Joe said.

"That we gang-raped her. It wasn't like that at all."

"How was it, then?"

"She was more than willing. I didn't even want her, but, you know, peer pressure and all. She was drinking and sitting in on the poker game, and she started rubbing herself all over Frank. We were all a little lit up by then, and Frank threw down his cards and took her to her tent. After a while, they came back and she started rubbing on Wally."

"So it was all her, then?" Joe said woodenly.

"It really, really was."

"But you all went along with it."

Pope shrugged. "Yes, of course."

"Even though you really didn't want to."

"In my case, yeah. I wasn't all that attracted to her."

"But you did it anyway."

"Yeah, I did it too."

"So why'd she try to get all of you arrested?"

Pope said, "It was extortion, maybe. And it was because she was ashamed. Of herself. She was ashamed of what she'd done, and she didn't want anyone to find out. So she blamed us and cried rape. I mean, if she really was raped, as she claimed, do you think we all would have stayed up there in that camp and waited to be caught? When she got angry and left to go to town . . . we realized how it would look."

Joe and Nate exchanged glances. Nate obviously didn't believe Pope's version. Joe wasn't so sure.

"What we did know was what would happen if the story got out," Pope said. "Five white guys, two married at the time, accused of gang-raping an innocent Native American girl in an elk camp. No matter what the facts were, do you think for one second that any of us would have had a chance? We'd have been tarred for the rest of our lives. I mean, all five of us grew apart after that incident and went on to become pretty successful. Frank was a bigshot in his community, and Wally was a great guy, head of his United

Way campaign. *I'm the director of the game and fish department.* If she'd taken us to court, none of that would have happened, and for what good reason?"

Joe said, "So you made sure she'd be discredited and shamed. You contacted Vern Dunnegan and the sheriff and told them ahead of time she was off her rocker."

Pope shrugged, held out his hands in a "what else could we do" plea.

Joe didn't respond.

"What choice did we have?" Pope asked, heatedly. "And even if she sees things differently now than I do, how can anyone justify these murders? She obviously convinced someone—and I think we know who—the five of us were evil men."

Joe had never seen Pope so desperate, so scared. He could smell his fear in the cab of the truck.

"What bothers me," Joe said, "is how long you knew about the connection."

"I wasn't sure!"

"But you said nothing. You kept it to yourself. My guess is you thought about it for the first time after John Garrett was murdered. Especially when you heard about the poker chip. Am I right? That's why you shut me down so fast when I brought it up."

Pope said nothing. Joe took his silence as confirmation.

"And when Warren Tucker was killed, and again there was a poker chip, you *knew* there was a connection. Two of your old friends in a row. Each hunting at the time, each with a poker chip on them. You *knew.*"

Pope stared ahead as if Joe wasn't speaking.

"That's what hacks me off so much," Joe said. "Neither you or Vern Dunnegan did the right thing. You sat there while two men were murdered, leaving behind widows, children, and grandchildren, and you didn't do a thing because all you could think of was yourselves."

"I wasn't *sure,*" Pope said softly.

Joe shook his head. "You can say that now. But you knew. That's why you were all over this when Frank Urman was butchered. You were just waiting for it. So for the first time in your professional career, you were on the scene. You wanted to be in charge so if we caught the killer you could mitigate the damage to you. And you offered up your buddy Wally Conway to get *him* out of the way so he wouldn't start talking. You were appeasing the shooter, offering up Wally, hoping that would put a stop to it. But when you saw how Klamath could get to you, could put a severed head in your hotel room, well, you knew it wasn't over after all. You knew you'd be next no matter what. Am I right so far?"

Pope snorted, as if Joe were amusing him. It wasn't convincing.

"But more than anything, you were hoping we'd trail the shooter and take him out so nothing would ever get out. Right? That's why you were there to help spring Nate, right? Because whatever you think of him, you know he's lethal."

"Damned right," Nate said.

"You're insane," Pope said. But his shoulders slumped in defeat.

THE TREES closed in around them as they ascended. The sky was gray, the air almost still. Two hours until dark. Joe pulled his truck off a two-track and turned off the motor.

"Recognize this place?" Joe asked Pope.

"Of course," Pope said, annoyed. "It's where Frank Urman was found."

"And where Randy Pope *will* be found," Joe said.

Pope's red-rimmed eyes filled with tears.

30

THERE IS a very specific way to skin an animal so that a taxidermist can create a flawless shoulder mount. It's called caping. It works best if the animal to be caped is hung up by the back legs.

Caping requires a sharp skinning knife with a short, fat blade like the one in my sheath. A slit is made in the skin behind the shoulder at the midway point of the rib cage. Another is made around the legs just above the knees. Or the arms, in this case. A third precise cut is made to join the slits on the back of the leg (or arm). The skin is then peeled like a banana toward the jaw until the neck is exposed. Then the very delicate work begins: cutting the skin away from the ears, skull, nose, and mouth. The weight of the hide—skin is surprisingly heavy—helps because it pulls the skin-peel downward. The skin is sliced away from the flesh with extremely light knife strokes. If the procedure is done correctly, the skin will drop away into a wet pile in the grass, showing an inverted, inside-out face.

This is what will happen to Randy Pope. My only di-

lemma is whether I'll cape him when he's dead or still alive.

THE TERRAIN, *of course, is familiar. As I stride— careful to step on exposed rocks and to keep slightly to the side of established and muddy game trails—I weigh the advantage of knowing this mountain and the exact location of my prey against the possibility that I'm being led into a trap. Given the odds and what I know to be true—that the FBI informant has yet to give bad infor- mation and that an opportunity like this is too great to disregard—I proceed.*

The sky concerns me. Even a skiff of snow makes track- ing easy. I vow that if it starts to snow I'll turn back the moment it begins, despite the opportunity offered me. I study the clouds and conclude it will snow, but later in the evening. After I'm done and back.

My backpack is empty except for several thick-ply plas- tic garbage bags. The pack will be heavier when I return due to fifteen pounds of skin.

I CAN'T *shake the feeling I'm being followed. I've neither heard nor seen anything to confirm my impression. Sev- eral times I stop and stand still, compelling my senses to reach out beyond their capacities to tell me something. The only thing I can point at that supplements my suspi- cion is the utter quiet—except for a slight breeze in the treetops—that remains in my wake. I've learned that after I've passed though an area, after a respectful period, the birds and squirrels begin talking to one another again. But I hear no resumption of sounds. It's as if I've shut out all life by being in its presence.*

There are conceivable justifications for the quiet. Low pressure can do it.

Either I'm imagining things or whoever is behind me is as good as I am. I proceed.

FINALLY, I'M CLIMBING the last rise and the trees start to thin. This is where Frank Urman was taken, just below the ridge I now approach. I drop to all fours, cradling my rifle on my forearms, and crawl to the top and look over the other side.

A quarter of a mile away, in that stand of trees, is Randy Pope. He's just standing there, his back against a tree.

JOE FELT the presence of the shooter without actually seeing anyone. The hair on the back of his neck rose, and a shiver rolled up the length of his body from his boots to the top of his head.

He was behind the upturned root pan of an enormous fallen pine tree. He could see Pope's shoulder through an opening in a gnarl of thick roots. He could tell by the way Pope shook that the man was sobbing.

They'd handcuffed Randy Pope behind his back to the same tree Frank Urman had been hung from and made a show of leaving the area. But instead of driving away, Joe snuck back into the tree stand and Nate hiked through the timber to a high granite knob that overlooked the tree stand, the ridge where Urman had originally been killed, and the mountain vista behind it. Both had radios turned low. Joe was armed with his shotgun filled with double-ought buckshot and the .40 Glock on his hip that he had no intention of using. Nate had the scoped .454 Casull.

Joe was thankful for the high breeze, the water sound of the wind in the trees, because it enabled him to communicate in low tones with Nate and remain out of Pope's hearing range. Joe and Nate had agreed to check in with each other every ten minutes whether they saw anything or not. The procedure they'd agreed on was a click on the transmitter button, followed by a murmured check-in. Murmurs tended to meld with nature sounds better than whispers. Joe didn't want Pope to know he was there and start begging and crying louder.

Joe wished Pope would stop crying. It made Joe feel cruel and awful, and he tried to shut Pope's suffering out. But his effort was in vain. Despite the things Pope had done and not done to exacerbate the crimes committed, Joe couldn't help but have sympathy for the man he'd handcuffed and offered up to the killer. Even Pope was a human being, although a diabolical and deeply flawed example of one. He didn't know how long he could let this go on before he rose and dug in his pocket for the key to the cuffs.

But the feeling of the presence shoved his feelings aside. He raised his binoculars to his eyes and focused on the ridge across the meadow.

As he did, Nate clicked on the handheld.

Joe momentarily ignored the chirp and focused his binoculars on the top of the ridge and saw a slight movement. It was quick: the dull glint of a gun barrel behind a knuckle of rock.

Nate said, "I've got a visual."

Joe pulled up the handheld from where it hung around his neck on a lanyard, said softly, "Me too."

Nate said, "He just came out of the timber and he's walking across the side of a meadow headed in your direction. Looks like he's got a rifle. ETA is ten minutes."

Joe was confused, and leaned into the binoculars. He could see no further movement, and certainly no one walking toward him.

"Nate, where do you see him?"

"To the east, about a mile from you. It's Klamath Moore coming your way."

Joe felt his chest clutch. Then who was up there on the ridge?

———

SHERIFF MCLANAHAN was exhausted. He stopped every ten to fifteen minutes to rest, falling farther behind his team of volunteers who were on foot, spread through the timber up ahead of him, sweeping the mountainside. He decided that as of tomorrow he would either suspend the investigation or at least not participate in the physical part of it. He was getting too damned old and out of shape for this, he thought. Besides, despite the enthusiasm from his boys for camping out, hiking in the woods with guns, and the horseplay in the camp at night, they hadn't found a damned thing and the shooter was still at large. McLanahan doubted the shooter was even in the state anymore.

So when his radio crackled, he was in no hurry to reach for it.

"I just cut a fresh track," someone said. McLanahan recognized the voice of Chris Urman.

"Where are you at?" It was Deputy Reed.

"Right here. See me? I'm waving my arm."

"Oh, okay. On my way."

"Oh shit," Urman said. "I see somebody up ahead. On the game trail."

A pause. McLanahan felt a trill and reached down for his radio as Reed came on, his voice excited: "I see him! I see him!"

The sheriff said, "Stay calm, boys, I'm on my way. Don't lose sight of him."

McLanahan holstered the radio, took a deep breath, and began to jog up the hill, his gear slapping him as it bounced.

NATE ROMANOWSKI peered through the scope of the .454, surprised that Klamath Moore was in the open. Moore skirted a small meadow, a break in the timber, the wall of dark pine on his left. Nate could see him clearly. Yes, Klamath had a rifle slung over his back. He appeared to be tracking someone because his head was down, not up. As

Nate watched, Klamath unslung his rifle and held it in front of him at parade rest as he walked.

In Nate's peripheral vision there was a dull flash of clothing through the timber to the side of where Klamath was in the meadow. Nate quickly swung the .454 away from Klamath into the trees. Through branches and breaks in the timber, Nate saw the heads and shoulders of several men moving toward Klamath. Nate frowned and brought his radio up to his mouth when he recognized McLanahan's heavy-bodied gait and familiar battered cowboy hat.

Klamath Moore suddenly froze and turned toward the rushing group of men, and a beat later Nate heard a shout—the reason Klamath had wheeled.

Nate almost cried out as Klamath raised his weapon, pointing it at the men in the trees, when a crackling volley of shots punched through the air and Klamath collapsed in the grass.

Nate keyed the mike. "Jesus—they shot him. Klamath Moore is down! It's McLanahan and his guys."

Four men, led by Chris Urman, appeared in the meadow, cautiously circling Klamath Moore's body.

"Joe," Nate said, "they got him. He's down and he looks deader than hell from here."

Nate lowered his weapon. He could see McLanahan clearly now, wheezing his way across the meadow toward the body of Klamath Moore, who was surrounded by Chris Urman and other volunteers. Somebody whooped.

Nate said, "Joe? Did you hear me?"

He heard Joe's voice, tight and forced. "I heard you."

"Are you okay?"

"No."

"What's happening?"

"The shooter is coming down the hill toward Pope."

Nate looked at his radio for a second, then shook it. "Come again?"

"Oh my God," Joe Pickett said. *"No."*

THE SHOTS in the woods behind me sent a bolt of fear up my spine. So many shots, so quickly. I drop to a knee and thumb the safety off my rifle, anticipating more fire that doesn't come. Who was it—hunters? The number of shots reminds me of when a group of hunters come upon a herd of elk—that furious fire as the herd breaks and runs. Is it possible there are hunters up here despite the moratorium? And if so, why didn't I see their camp or cross their tracks?

I wonder if it had to do with my earlier sense of being followed. The sheriff has men up here, I know. But they're incompetent. Maybe they circled in on themselves. Maybe I just heard friendly fire.

Or maybe Klamath followed me and got caught. I briefly close my eyes. It makes sense. He's always been suspicious of me, and the way he looked at me today when I excused myself—yes, it's possible. But there is no way to know for sure until later.

No matter. This was never about Klamath, despite what he thinks. Because in his world, everything is about Klamath Moore. Not this, though. This is about bestowing dignity and righting wrongs. Klamath just happens to be breathing the same air.

I look up. Randy Pope is within a hundred feet but somehow he has not seen me yet. His head is down, chin on his chest, arms behind his back. What is he doing?

The shots and Randy Pope's demeanor and appearance unnerve me. I abandon my plans to cape him. Simply killing him—killing the last one and stopping this—will have to be enough. It will be enough.

I rise and walk toward him, striding quickly. I could easily take him from here but I want him to see me. I want to be the last person he ever sees and the last thought he ever has in his mind.

"OH MY God," Joe said. *"No."*

He watched Shenandoah Yellowcalf Moore approach Randy Pope down the length of his shotgun barrel. She wore cargo pants, gloves, a fleece sweater, and a daypack. Her expression was tight and willful, the same face he had seen in the yearbook photos as she drove to the basket past taller players. The breeze licked at her long black hair flowing out beneath a headband. As he looked at her his heart thumped, making his shotgun twitch; his hands were cold and wet and his stomach roiled.

And suddenly, things clicked into place:

She'd been at the airport to greet her husband, Klamath, meaning she'd been in the area prior to his arrival, when Frank Urman was killed.

While Klamath's movements throughout the hunting season had been accounted for—mostly—by Bill Gordon, there had been no mention of Shenandoah's travels.

She knew the state, the back roads and hunting areas from traveling with her team and later as a hunting guide.

She knew how to track, how to hunt, how to kill and process game.

She had a motive.

It fit, but he wanted no part of this. He'd been convinced the Wolverine was Klamath himself or one of his followers working under Klamath's direction.

"Nate," Joe said, speaking softly into the radio, "I need your help down here."

"It'll take me at least five minutes."

"Hurry."

At ten feet, she fit the stock of her rifle to her shoulder and raised it until the muzzle was level with the crown of Randy Pope's head.

She said, "Pope, look up."

Joe could see Pope squirm, try to shinny around the tree

away from her, but he could only go a quarter of the way because his cuff chain hung up on the bark. She took a few steps to her left in the grass so she was still in front of him.

I RECALL not the night it happened but the next morning, when I woke up feeling dirty, bruised, and sore. I was alone in my tent wearing only a T-shirt. They hadn't even covered me up. I was damaged and it hurt to stand up.

The sun warmed the walls of the tent and as it did I could smell not only me but them. All five of them. I dressed—my clothes were balled up in the corner—and unzipped the flap and stepped outside where it was surprisingly cold. The campfire was going, curls of fragrant wood smoke corkscrewing through the branches of the pine trees, a pot of coffee brewing on my black grate. Three of them sat on stumps around the fire, staring into it as if looking for an explanation. They were unshaven; their faces told me nothing. They were blank faces, hungover faces. Maybe they were ashamed. But when they looked up and saw me, none of them said anything.

No one asked me if I wanted coffee. They weren't going to talk about it. They were going to pretend nothing had happened.

That was the worst of all. That's when the rage began. I was nothing to them. It was all about them, not me. This was apparently what they had expected when they hired me. The problem was, I felt the same way at that moment. I thought of their wives, their daughters, assumed they were having the same thoughts.

Randy Pope was there. He looked at me and then back toward the fire with a dismissive nod, as if I disgusted him. "If you say anything about this to anyone," he said in words I can still hear clearly, "we'll destroy you. You'll end up as just another grease spot."

That's when I decided to find the sheriff and press charges.

AT THIS RANGE, Joe knew, a blast from his shotgun would practically cut her in half. But he couldn't conceive of it—he didn't want to fire. Hell, he *admired* her. He wanted her to turn or look behind her back up the hill so he could stand and shout at her to drop the rifle. As it was, with her finger tightening on the trigger, his sudden appearance could cause her to fire out of fear or reaction. And he thought, *Would that be so bad?*

"Please," Randy Pope cried, "please don't do this. You don't have to do this."

"Yes I do," she said.

"No. Please. You know what happened in that camp. None of us hurt you. Nobody forced you."

She said, "Actually, I don't remember very much about that night. It's still in a fog of alcohol to me. But I do remember how you wouldn't look at me, how you threatened me. And I remember going to jail. I remember what was said about me afterward."

"It was years ago," Pope said. "We're all different now."

She laughed bitterly. "I have one more poker chip. Then it will all be over. You know, I carried those five poker chips in my pocket for years as a reminder to me of what you did and what I was. But I'm not like that anymore, and killing you kills what I was back then. I want my dignity back, and you're the last man in my way. I have a daughter now, you know. I don't want her to know about me then, or about you. She deserves better than both of us."

Pope moaned a long moan, and Joe felt the pain of it.

"I've fought through self-loathing before," she said. "This is how I cut the head off that snake."

Before pulling the trigger, Shenandoah took a second to glance over her shoulder in the direction where the shots had been fired, to make sure no one was on the ridge.

Which gave Joe the opportunity to shout, "Drop the rifle, Shenandoah! *Drop it now!*"

He rose so she could see him behind the root pan. His shotgun was trained on her chest. She'd lowered the rifle when she turned and it stayed low.

"I don't want to hurt you," Joe said. "Just let the rifle fall out of your hands and step back."

She looked at Joe, surprised but not desperate. The look of single-minded determination was still on her face.

"This is over," he said. "Please. You don't want your daughter to be without her mother."

He didn't say, *or her father.*

Pope, for once, kept his mouth shut.

"I don't want to go to prison," she said softly.

"You may not have to," Joe lied. "Lord knows you've got your reasons. Yours is a sympathetic case. This man assaulted you and then destroyed your reputation. Randy Pope will get what he deserves."

She nodded as if acknowledging Joe's words but discounting their meaning.

He hated himself.

"Just relax your hands, let the rifle drop."

She did and it thumped onto the grass. Joe kept his shotgun on her as he walked around the root pan.

"Do you have any other weapons?" he asked.

She shook her head, then said, "I've got a skinning knife. I was going to cape him."

"Don't tell me that," Joe said. "Now, ease out of your backpack and toss the knife aside."

She slipped out of her pack and let it drop, then drew the knife from the sheath and tossed it a few feet away.

"Unlock me," Pope said out of the side of his mouth as Joe passed the tree.

"Shut up," Joe said. To Shenandoah, "Put your wrists together. You're under arrest. I've got to take you in so we can sort this all out."

He chose not to cuff her behind her back and humiliate her further. He slipped hard plastic Flex-Cuffs over her thin wrists and pulled them tight. She was small, almost delicate.

"I don't want anyone to see me like this," she said.

"Alisha doesn't know, does she?"

"No."

"You killed my friend Robey."

"For that I'm eternally sorry," she said, her eyes leaving Pope for a moment and softening. "That wasn't meant to happen. It was an accident, and I'm so sorry."

"Did Klamath kill Bill Gordon, or was that you?"

"It was Klamath. I'm very upset with my husband. I liked Bill very much."

"Are you the Wolverine?"

She shook her head. "No. I think Bill was Wolverine. At least I always suspected he was leading Klamath on. I read the e-mail exchange and it inspired me."

"Klamath is dead," Joe said. "Those were the shots you heard. I'm sorry."

She nodded, blinked. For a second the fire went out of her eyes.

"He was following you," Joe said. "He ran into the sheriff's men."

"He knew it was me," she said. "He never tried to stop me. I was accomplishing his goal while accomplishing mine."

Joe couldn't reply.

"I want Alisha to raise my daughter," Shenandoah said.

"You don't have to talk like that," Joe said, feeling as if she'd kicked him in the gut. Her eyes were again fixed on Randy Pope.

She said, "Where is Nate?"

Joe chinned toward the granite ridge.

"Unlock me!" Pope shouted to Joe. "Get me out of here."

Joe ignored him.

Shenandoah glared at Pope. "He was the worst of them all. He let his friends die. I need to finish this."

"You don't know what you're doing, Joe," Pope said. "This will ruin me if she talks, if she takes the stand. The girl was willing—more than willing. It happened years ago, the statute of limitations has passed. Why dredge it up again? Why let this woman bring it all back?"

It happened so quickly Joe could barely react. Like the point guard she once was, Shenandoah faked to her right, drawing Joe, then darted to her left under Joe's outstretched hand. She ducked and snatched the knife from the grass at her feet and lunged at Pope.

Joe shouldered the shotgun, yelled, "Shenandoah, *no! No!*" but she sliced the blade cleanly through Pope's throat at the same moment Joe fired, the buckshot hitting her full force in the neck and kicking her sideways. She landed in a heap like dropped wet laundry.

He was horrified by what he'd done.

JOE SAT on a downed log and watched Nate walk down the slope. He was numb. He didn't feel like he was all there. His hands sat in his lap like dead crabs. They were bloody from turning Shenandoah over, hoping against hope she would somehow pull through, even though he was the instrument of her death. He wished she wasn't gone because of his failed effort to save Randy Pope's worthless life.

Her body looked so small in the grass, maybe because the life in her had been so outsized. Joe thought, *Promise kept, Nancy.*

But it didn't make him feel any better.

AS NATE approached, Joe could see his friend take it all in—Pope's slumped body still cuffed to the tree, every pint of his blood spilled down his shirtfront and pants and pooling darkly around his feet. Shenandoah's broken body thrown to the side, the knife still in her hand.

Nate holstered the .454 as he got closer and dropped to

his knees in front of her body. He took her lifeless hands in his, closed his eyes.

"I saw it happen," Nate said. "There was nothing you could do."

"Nate, I'm so sorry," Joe said, his voice a croak.

"No words," Nate said.

Joe couldn't tell if Nate was asking him not to speak or if no words could express what he felt.

JOE STOOD up dully and changed the frequency on his radio to the mutual-aid channel, and as soon as he did he was awash in conversation from over the hill. He heard Sheriff McLanahan, Chris Urman, Deputy Reed, and others congratulating themselves over the shooting of Klamath Moore, the monster who'd killed the hunters. McLanahan was talking to dispatch, telling Wendy to contact the governor and tell him the state could be reopened for hunting.

"Sheriff," Joe said, breaking in, "this is Joe Pickett. I've got the bodies of a couple more victims over the ridge."

The chatter went silent.

"Come again?" McLanahan said.

NATE WALKED over to where Joe sat on the log and put his hand on his friend's shoulder.

"I feel so bad," Joe said. "I mean, a woman. And not just any woman. *Shenandoah.*" He looked up. "Did you know it was her?"

"Not until the end," Nate said, raising his eyebrows. "Justice was done—all around."

"Here." Joe handed Nate his keys.

Nate looked at him for an explanation.

"Take them and get out of here before the sheriff sees you."

"I can't."

Joe shrugged. "Go. You don't have that much time."

"What about you?"

"I said I'd do what was right. The governor assumed I meant I'd bring you back."

"Joe, I—"

"Git," Joe said.

31

"BUY YOU A DRINK?"

Vern Dunnegan laughed, pulled the large woman with fire-engine-red hair on the next stool closer to him, said, "You bet. We'll both have one." And to the bartender: "Set 'em up, buddy."

"Another Beam on the rocks?" the bartender said.

"*Double* Beam for me and my lady," Vern said, "thanks to my benefactor here."

His benefactor was tall, rawboned, with piercing, ice-blue eyes and short-cropped blond hair. He had not taken off his bulky parka. Snow from the late November storm outside had melted into drops on the fur trim of his hood. The drops reflected the neon beer signs at the windows. Outside the glass, thick flakes blew by horizontally, looking like sparks from a fire.

"You just get out?" the man asked, leaning on the bar with his hands clasped in front of him.

"Yes," Vern said. "About four hours ago, in fact. This is my first stop. I plan to drink until drunk, eat until sated, and maybe later"—he squeezed the overweight redhead hard around her waist, nearly toppling her from her stool—"some sweet romance."

"Romance," she scoffed, blowing a cloud of cigarette smoke toward the back bar. The smoke curled around the framed front page of the Casper *Star-Tribune* with the head-line KILLER OF HUNTERS SHOT DEAD and a photo of smil-ing anti-hunting activist Klamath Moore.

"That's in a lot of bars around the state," the man said.

"As it should be," Vern said. "Hunters are hunting again and the bad guy is dead. Or so I read."

"You don't believe it?"

Vern said, "Rumor is the story's more complicated. But that's just jailhouse talk. Why should I doubt the word of the governor who set me free even though he took his own sweet time doing it? He said it was Klamath Moore, so as far as I'm concerned, it was Klamath Moore."

"May that son of a bitch roast in hell," the redheaded woman said, toasting the photo with her fresh drink.

"Perhaps she'd excuse us for a minute?" the benefactor said.

"Why?" Vern asked.

"Why?" she echoed.

"Just a little business."

"Do I know you?" Vern asked.

"No."

"Honey," Vern said, patting her on the butt, "give me just a minute, please."

"Fine," she said, sliding unsteadily off her stool. "I need to pee, anyway."

"Your girlfriend?" the benefactor asked.

"Of course not, come on. But she'll do for a Tuesday night in Rawlins, Wyoming."

The man smiled. It was a cruel smile, Vern thought. Did he know this guy? Had he met him on the inside, or on the outside? Did he arrest him once for poaching, back in the day?

"So today is the first day of the rest of your life," the man said.

"In a way." Vern was starting to get a bad feeling about this. "Have we met?"

"I said no. But we have a mutual acquaintance."

"Who might that be?"

"His name is Joe Pickett."

The light went out of Vern's eyes. "Oh."

"He's my friend, and he's in a bad way right now. The world has fallen in on him. I'm confident he'll be able to pull out of it, though. He's got the support of his family. He's not so sure about his boss." The man paused until it became uncomfortable. "And someone who looks out for him."

Vern felt the blood drain from his face. "I better be going."

"Not yet."

Vern felt something long and heavy like a pipe laid across his thigh. He looked down at the barrel of the biggest pistol he'd ever seen, the gaping muzzle an inch from his crotch.

"I was kind of hoping my freedom might last more than one night," Vern said, swallowing bitterly.

Nate said, "A false hope, as it turns out. Here, hold out your hand."

"What's this? *A poker chip?*"

"Yup," Nate said. "The last one. I found it on Shenandoah's body. Hold onto it tight and think about it while we go outside for your last walk."

Acknowledgments

The author would like to acknowledge research material used in this novel, including *Tracking: Signs of Man, Signs of Hope,* by David Diaz with V. L. McCann, and *Wilderness Evasion,* by Michael Chesbro.

Thanks to Wyoming game warden Mark Nelson, who provided invaluable information regarding tracking and investigative procedure, to Laurie Box and Ann Rittenberg, for reading the first drafts and offering better ideas, and to Don Hajicek, for www.cjbox.net.

A special tip of the black Stetson goes to the team of enthusiastic pros at Putnam and Berkley, including Ivan Held, Rachel Kahan, Michael Barson, and Thomas Colgan.

Turn the page for a preview of the next
Joe Pickett novel by C. J. Box . . .

Below Zero

Available in paperback from Berkley Prime Crime!

Keystone, South Dakota

MARSHALL AND SYLVIA Hotle, who liked to list their places of residence as Cedar Rapids, Iowa, Quartzite, Arizona, and "the open road," were preparing dinner when they saw the dark SUV with Illinois plates drive by on the access road for the third time in less than an hour.

"There they are again," Sylvia said, narrowing her eyes. She was setting two places on the picnic table. Pork cutlets, green beans, dinner rolls, iceberg lettuce salad, and plenty of weak coffee, just like Marshall liked it.

"Gawkers," Marshall said, with a hint of a smile. "I'm getting used to it."

The evening was warm and still and perfumed with the smell of dust and pine pollen particular to the Black Hills of South Dakota. Within the next hour, the smell of hot dogs and hamburgers being cooked on dozens of campground grills would waft through the trees as well. By then the Hotle's would be done eating. They liked to eat early. It was a habit they'd developed on their farm.

The Hotles had parked their massive motor home for the night in a remote campsite within the Mount Rushmore

KOA complex near Palmer Gulch, only five miles away from the monument itself. Because it was late August and the roads teemed with tourists, they'd thought ahead and secured this choice site—one they'd occupied before on their semiannual cross-country trips—by calling and reserving it weeks before. Although there were scores of RVs and tents setting up within the complex below, this particular site was tucked high in the trees and seemed almost remote.

Marshall often said he preferred the Black Hills to the Rocky Mountains farther west. The Black Hills were green, rounded, gentle, with plenty of lots big enough to park The Unit. The highest mountain—Harney Peak—was 5,400 feet. The Black Hills, Marshall said, were *reasonable*. The Rockies were a different matter. As they ventured from South Dakota into Wyoming both the people and the landscape changed. Good solid midwestern stock gave way to mountain people, who were ragged on the edges, he thought. Farms gave way to ranches. The mountains became severe, twice the elevation of Harney Peak, which was just big enough. The weather became volatile. While the mountains could be seductive, they were also amoral. Little of use could be grown. There were creatures—grizzly bears, black bears, mountain lions—capable and willing to eat him. "Give me the Black Hills any old day," Marshall said as he drove, as the rounded dark humps appeared in his windshield as he drove west. "The Black Hills are plenty."

Sylvia was short, compact, and solid. She wore a sweatshirt covered with balloons and clouds she'd appliquéd on herself. Her iron-gray hair was molded into tight curls that looked spring-loaded. She had eight grandchildren, with the ninth due any day now. She'd spent the day knitting baby booties and a little stocking cap. She didn't have strong opinions on the Black Hills versus the Rocky Mountains, but . . .

"I don't like to be gawked at," she said, barely moving her mouth.

"I hate to tell you this, but it's not you they're looking at," Marshall said, sipping coffee. "They're admiring The Unit." Marshall's belly strained at the snap buttons of his Iowa Hawkeyes Windbreaker. His face was round and his cheeks were always red. He'd worn the same steel-framed glasses so long they were back in style, as was his John Deere cap. He chinned toward the motor home. "They probably want to come up here and take a look. Don't worry, though, we can have supper first."

"That's charitable of you," Sylvia said, shaking her head. "Don't you ever get tired of giving tours?"

"No."

"It's not just a motor home, you know. It's where we *live*. But with you giving tours all the time I feel like I've always got to keep it spotless."

"Ah," he said, sliding a cutlet from the platter onto his plate, "you'd do that anyway."

"Still," she said, "you never gave tours of the farmhouse."

He shrugged. "Nobody ever wanted to look at it. It's just a house, sweetie. Nothing special about a house."

Said Sylvia heatedly, "A house where we raised eight children."

"You know what I mean," he said. "Hey, good pork."

"Oh, dear," she said, "here they come again."

The dark SUV with the Illinois plates didn't proceed all the way up the drive to the campsite, but braked to a stop just off the access road. Sylvia could see two people in the vehicle, two men, it looked like. And maybe someone smaller in the back. A girl? She glared her most unwelcoming glare, she thought. It usually worked. This time, though, the motor shut off and the driver's door opened.

"At least they didn't drive in on top of us," she said.

"Good campground etiquette," Marshall said.

"But they could have waited until after our supper."

"You want me to tell them to come back later?"

"What," she said with sarcasm, "and not give them a tour?"

Marshall chuckled and reached out and patted Sylvia's hand. She shook her head.

Only the driver got out. He was older, about their age or maybe a few years younger, wearing a casual jacket and chinos. He was dark and barrel-chested, with a large head, slicked-back hair, and warm dark eyes. He had a thick mustache and heavy jowls, and he walked up the drive rocking side-to-side a little like a B-movie monster.

"He looks like somebody," Sylvia said. "Who am I thinking of?"

Marshall whispered, "How would I know who you're thinking of?"

"Like that dead writer. You know."

"Lots of dead writers," Marshall said. "That's the best kind, you ask me."

"Sorry to bother you," the man said affably, "I'm Dave Stenson. My friends in Chicago call me Stenko."

"Hemingway," Sylvia hissed without moving her lips. *"That's* who I mean."

"Sorry to bother you at dinnertime. Would it be better if I came back?" Stenson/Stenko said, pausing before getting too close.

Before Sylvia could say yes Marshall said, "I'm Marshall and this is Sylvia. What can we do for you?"

"That's the biggest darned motor home I've ever seen," Stenko said, stepping back so he could see it all from stem to stern, "I just wanted to look at it."

Marshall smiled and his eyes twinkled behind thick lenses. Sylvia sighed. All those years in the cab of a combine, all those years of corn, corn, corn. The last few years of ethanol mandates had been great! This was Marshall's reward.

"I'd be happy to give you a quick tour," her husband said.

"Please," Stenko said, holding up his hand palm out, "finish your dinner first."

Said Marshall, "I'm done," and pushed away from the picnic table, leaving the salad and green beans untouched.

Sylvia thought, *A life spent as a farmer but the man won't eat vegetables.*

Turning to her, Stenko asked, "I was hoping I could borrow a potato or two, I'd sure appreciate it."

She smiled, despite herself, and felt her cheeks get warm. He had good manners, this man, and those dark eyes . . .

SHE WAS cleaning up the dishes on the picnic table when Marshall and Stenko finally came out of the motor home. Marshall had done the tour of The Unit so many times, for so many people, that his speech was becoming smooth and well rehearsed. Fellow retired RV enthusiasts as well as people still moored to their jobs wanted to see what it looked like inside the behemoth vehicle: their 2009 45-foot diesel-powered Fleetwood American Heritage, which Marshall simply called "The Unit." She heard phrases she'd heard dozens of times, "Forty-six thousand, six hundred pounds gross vehicle weight . . . five hundred horses with a ten-point-eight liter diesel engine . . . satellite radio . . . three integrated cameras for backing up . . . GPS . . . bedroom with queen bed, satellite television . . . washer/dryer . . . wine rack and wet bar even though neither one of us drinks . . ."

Now Marshall was getting to the point in his tour where he said, "We traded a life of farming for life in The Unit. We do the circuit now."

"What's the circuit?" Stenko asked. She thought he sounded genuinely interested. Which meant he might not leave for a while.

Sylvia shot a glance toward the SUV. She wondered why the people inside didn't get out, didn't join Stenko for the tour or at least say hello. They weren't very friendly, she thought. Her sister in Wisconsin said people from Chicago were like that, as if they owned all the midwestern states and thought of Wisconsin as their own personal recreation playground and Iowa as a cornfield populated by hopeless rubes.

"It's *our* circuit," Marshall explained, "visiting our kids and grandkids in six different states, staying ahead of the snow, making sure we hit the big flea markets in Quartzite, going to a few Fleetwood rallies where we can look at the newest models and talk to our fellow owners. We're kind of a like a club, us Fleetwood people."

Stenko said, "It's the biggest and most luxurious thing I've ever been in. It's amazing. You must really get some looks on the road."

"Thank you," Marshall said. "We spent a lifetime farming just so we . . ."

"I've heard a vehicle like this can cost more than six-hundred K. Now, I'm not asking you what you paid, but am I in the ballpark?"

Marshall nodded, grinned.

"What kind of gas mileage does it get?" Stenko asked.

"Runs on diesel," Marshall said.

"Whatever," Stenko said, withdrawing a small spiral notebook from his jacket pocket and flipping it open.

What's he doing? Sylvia thought.

"We're getting eight-to-ten miles a gallon," Marshall said. "Depends on the conditions, though. The Black Hills are the first mountains we hit going west from Iowa, and the air's getting thinner. So the mileage gets worse. When we go through Wyoming and Montana—sheesh."

"Not good, eh?" Stenko said, scribbling.

Sylvia knew Marshall disliked talking about miles per gallon because it made him defensive.

"You can't look at it that way," Marshall said, "you can't look at it like it's a car or a truck. You've got to look at it as your house on wheels. You're moving your own house from place to place. Eight miles per gallon is a small price to pay for living in your own house. You save on motels and such like that."

Stenko licked his pencil and scribbled. He seemed excited. "So how many miles do you put on your . . . house . . . in a year?"

Marshall looked at Sylvia. She could tell he was ready for Stenko to leave.

"Sixty thousand on average," Marshall said. "Last year we did eighty."

Stenko whistled. "How many years have you been doing this circuit, as you call it?"

"Five," Marshall said. "But this is the first year in The Unit."

Stenko ignored Sylvia's stony glare. "How many more years do you figure you'll be doing this?"

"That's a crazy question," she said. "It's like you're asking us when we're going to die."

Stenko chuckled, shaking his head. "I'm sorry, I'm sorry, I didn't mean it like that."

She crossed her arms and gave Marshall a *Get Rid Of Him* look.

"You're what, sixty-five, sixty-six?" Stenko asked.

"Sixty-five," Marshall said. "Sylvia's . . ."

"Marshall!"

". . . approximately the same age," Stenko said, finishing Marshall's thought and making another note. "So it's not crazy to say you two might be able to keep this up for another ten or so years. Maybe even more."

"More," Marshall said, "I hope."

"I've got to clean up," Sylvia said, "if you'll excuse me." She was furious at Stenko for his personal questions and at Marshall for answering them.

"Oh," Stenko said, "about those potatoes."

She paused on the step into the motor home and didn't look at Stenko when she said, "I have a couple of bakers. Will they do?"

"Perfect," Stenko said.

She turned. "Why do you need *two* potatoes? Aren't there three of you? I see two more heads out there in your car."

"Sylvia," Marshall said, "would you please just get the man a couple of spuds?"

She stomped inside and returned with two and held them out like a ritual offering. Stenko chuckled as he took them.

"I really do thank you," he said, reaching inside his jacket. "I appreciate your time and information. Ten years on the road is a long time. I envy you in ways you'll never understand."

She was puzzled now. His voice was warm and something about his tone—so sad—touched her. And was that a tear in his eye?

INSIDE THE SUV, the fourteen-year-old girl asked the man in the passenger seat, "Like *what* is he doing up there?"

The man—she knew him as Robert—was in his midthirties. He was handsome and he knew it, with his blond hair with the expensive highlights and his ice-cold green eyes and his small, sharp little nose. But he was shrill for a man his age, she thought, and had yet to be very friendly to her. Not that he'd been cruel. It was obvious, though, that he'd rather have Stenko's undivided attention. Robert said, "He told you not to watch."

"But why is he taking, like, big potatoes from them?"

"Do you really want to know?"

"Yes."

Robert turned and pierced her with those eyes. "They'll act as silencers and muffle the shots."

"The shots?" She shifted in the backseat so she could see through the windshield better between the front seats. Up the hill, Stenko had turned his back to the old couple and was jamming a big potato on the end of a long-barreled pistol. Before she could speak Stenko wheeled and swung the weapon up and there were two coughs and the old man fell down. The potato had burst and the pieces had fallen, so Stenko jammed the second one on. There were two more coughs and the woman dropped out of sight behind the picnic table.

The girl screamed and balled her fists in her mouth.

"Shut up!" Robert said. "For God's sake, shut up." To himself, "I knew bringing a girl along was a bad idea. I swear to God I can't figure out what goes on in that brain of his."

She'd seen killing but she couldn't believe what had happened. Stenko was so *nice*. Did he know the old couple? Did they say or do something that he felt he had to defend himself? A choking sob broke through.

Robert said, "He should have left you in Chicago."

SHE COULDN'T stop crying and peeking even though Robert kept telling her to shut up and not to watch as Stenko dragged the two bodies up into the motor home. When the bodies were inside Stenko closed the door. He was in there a long time before tongues of flame licked the inside of the motor home windows and Stenko jogged down the path toward the SUV.

She smelled smoke and gasoline on his clothes when he climbed into the cab and started the motor.

"Man," he said, "I hated doing that."

Robert said, "Move out quick before the fire gets out of control and somebody notices us. Keep cool, drive the speed limit all the way out of here."

She noticed how panicked Robert's tone was, how high his voice was. For the first time she saw that his scalp through his hair was glistening with sweat. She'd never noticed how thin his hair was and how skillfully he'd disguised it.

Stenko said, "That old couple—they were kind of sweet."

"It had to be done," Robert said quickly.

"I wish I could believe you."

Robert leaned across the console, his eyes white and wild. "Trust me, Dad. Just trust me. Did they give you the numbers?"

Stenko reached into his breast pocket and flipped the spiral notebook toward Robert. "It's all there," he said. The girl thought Stenko was angry.

Robert flipped through the pad, then drew his laptop out of the computer case near his feet. He talked as he tapped the keys. "Sixty to eighty thousand miles a year at eight-to-ten miles per gallon. Wow. They've been at it for five years and planned to keep it up until they couldn't. They're both sixty-five, so we could expect them to keep driving that thing for at least ten to fifteen years, maybe more." *Tap-tap-tap.*

"They were farmers from Iowa," Stenko said sadly. "Salt of the earth."

"Salt of the earth?" Robert said. "You mean plagues on the earth! Christ, Dad, did you see that thing they were driving?"

"They called it The Unit," Stenko said.

"Wait until I get this all calculated," Robert said. "You just took a sizeable chunk out of the balance."

"I hope so," Stenko said.

"Any cash?"

"Of course. All farmers have cash on hand."

"How much?"

"Thirty-seven hundred I found in the cupboard. I have a feeling there was more, but I couldn't take the time. I could have used your help in there."

"That's not what I do."

Stenko snorted. "I *know.*"

"Thirty-seven hundred isn't very much."

"It'll keep us on the road."

"There's that," Robert said, but he didn't sound very impressed.

As they cleared the campground, the girl turned around in her seat. She could see the wink of orange flames in the alcove of pines now. Soon, the fire would engulf the motor home and one of the people in the campground would see it and call the fire department. But it would be too late to save the motor home, just as it was too late to save that poor old couple. As she stared at the motor home on fire, things from deep in her memory came rushing back and her mouth dropped open.

"I said," Stenko pressed, looking at her in the rearview mirror, "you didn't watch, did you? You promised me you wouldn't watch."

"She lied," Robert said. "You should have left her in Chicago."

"Damn, honey," Stenko said, "I didn't want you to watch."

But she barely heard him through the roaring in her ears. Back it came, from where it had been hiding and crouching like a night monster in a dark corner of her memory.

The burning trailer. Screams. Shots. Snow.

And a telephone number she'd memorized, but had remained buried in her mind, just like all of those people who were buried in the ground all these years . . .

She thought, I need to find a phone.

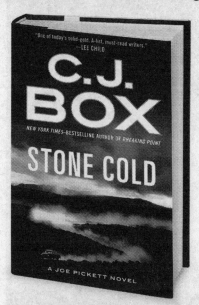

Joe Pickett thought he was saddling up for his last patrol. If only he'd known how true that might turn out to be...

NEW YORK TIMES BESTSELLING AUTHOR

C. J. BOX

NOWHERE TO RUN

A JOE PICKETT NOVEL

It's Joe's last week as a temporary game warden in the mountain town of Baggs, Wyoming, but his conscience won't let him leave without checking out the strange reports coming from the wilderness: camps looted, tents slashed, elk butchered. Not to mention the Olympic hopeful who'd been training in the region and then just...vanished. What awaits him is like something out of an old campfire tale, except this story is all too real—and all too deadly.

www.penguin.com
www.cjbox.net
facebook.com/AuthorCJBox

New York Times bestselling author

C. J. Box

The mystery series about Joe Pickett,
a Wyoming game warden trying to keep the wilderness—
and the family he loves—safe from danger.

OPEN SEASON
SAVAGE RUN
WINTERKILL
TROPHY HUNT
OUT OF RANGE
IN PLAIN SIGHT
FREE FIRE
BLOOD TRAIL
BELOW ZERO
NOWHERE TO RUN
COLD WIND
FORCE OF NATURE

THE JOE PICKETT NOVELS ARE:

"Muscular." —*The New York Times*

"Heartfelt." — *The Washington Post*

"Fascinating." —*USA Today*

"Suspenseful." —*New York Daily News*

www.cjbox.net
www.penguin.com

M25AS1112